FARIDA KARODIA was born and raised in a small town in South Africa, which was to provide the setting for her first novel, *Daughters of the Twilight*. She emigrated to Canada in 1969, having previously taught in Johannesburg and Zambia. In Canada she has worked in a variety of jobs, including teaching, and has written several radio dramas for C.B.C. She is now a full-time writer.

    Daughters of the Twilight was published in 1986 and was a runner-up in the Fawcett Prize. This was followed by *Coming Home and Other Stories* (Heinemann, 1988).

FARIDA KARODIA

A SHATTERING OF SILENCE

HEINEMANN

Heinemann Educational
A Division of Heinemann Publishers (Oxford) Ltd
Halley Court, Jordan Hill, Oxford OX2 8EJ

Heinemann: A Division of Reed Publishing (USA) Inc.
361 Hanover Street, Portsmouth, NH 03801–3912, USA

Heinemann Educational Books (Nigeria) Ltd
PMB 5205, Ibadan
Heinemann Educational Boleswa
PO Box 10103, Village Post Office, Gaborne, Botswana

FLORENCE   PRAGUE   PARIS   MADRID
ATHENS   MELBOURNE   JOHANNESBURG
AUCKLAND   SINGAPORE   TOKYO
CHICAGO   SAO PAULO

First published by Heinemann Educational in 1993

Series Editor: Adewale Maja-Pearce

British Library Cataloguing in Publication Data
A catalogue record for this book is available from the British Library.

ISBN 0435 905 93 7

Phototypeset by Cambridge Composing (UK) Limited, Cambridge
Printed and bound in Great Britain
by Cox & Wyman Ltd, Reading, Berkshire

93 94 95 96 97 10 9 8 7 6 5 4 3 2 1

To Mac
For the many years of friendship
and encouragement

Author's note

A Shattering of Silence is a work of fiction and does not
aspire to provide biographical or autobiographical
material, or historical, political or social analysis or
commentary about Mozambique, except as these issues
impact on the setting. The characters are fictitious and
merely representative of the reality of hundreds of
thousands of children, all over the world, who are
brutalised by war, hunger and political corruption. To
my knowledge none of the characters bears any
resemblance to any persons living or dead. The various
settings have been created out of my mind and memory,
and have been altered for dramatic effect in such a way
that they may or may not resemble existing places. This
story was motivated by the outrage I felt at the accounts
of the Tete massacres in Mozambique, which took place
in several villages prior to independence.

Prologue

It was hot in the plane. Sue, the young American woman who sat in the seat next to me, was nodding off to sleep. She had told me that this was her first trip to Africa and that she was going to Mozambique to work with an aid agency. My attention returned to the landscape below, searching for familiar scenes.

I was returning to Mozambique twenty years after having fled the country with the Portuguese government forces in pursuit. If it hadn't been for the guerrillas assisting us, we might never have made it. I thought about how complicated issues were in Africa, and how easily the tables could be turned if conditions were right. Compounding the conflict between different factions within the country, for the past seventeen years, since independence, the country had been systematically destabilised by outside forces. And now there was talk of peace.

Had it not been for a small item in the paper that I had seen purely by chance, I might not have come back at this time. Sometimes unpredictable things happen and events gain a momentum of their own.

It was one of those drab, wet October days in London. I was in the cluttered kitchen of my small central London flat, watching as the sun valiantly struggled through the cloud. My table was littered with reading material. I am a voracious reader and I had kept up with my writing by doing articles for various literary and professional journals.

I had, of course, recorded my own experiences. On my kitchen table were five notebooks which more or less represented my life in Mozambique. The books were written a few years ago while I was going through extensive psychiatric and medical rehabilitation.

The writing had been a form of therapy which helped immensely with the recovery of my memory. The small neat handwriting represented my story, in effect, my voice. In it my voice sometimes rang out clearly, sometimes it was warm and evocative, and at other times it was muffled and child-like. The last entry about my life in Mozambique had been completed about five years ago when my therapy ended. The entry detailed my escape on November 14th 1972, a date which I had symbolically underlined in red.

I shoved aside the clutter, set my teacup down and reached for the newspaper. The item was buried in the third page, hardly noticeable except for the by-line 'Mozambique', which immediately caught my attention.

The report was about a woman, who, paralysed from the waist down, had died recently after escaping from a prison camp run by the Mozambican rebels. Stunned, I slowly read the article again, the name Lodiya Chidekunde . . . Dear God! Lodiya!

Years ago we had heard from Nino that Lodiya had been captured and since our enquiries had yielded nothing, I had assumed that she had died either in conflict or in captivity. I sat in the stillness of my kitchen, harbouring the hope that this might be some other Lodiya Chidekunde, not the one from my childhood. But I knew that they were one and the same person.

I thought of Rita and wondered whether she might still be alive, too. I had tried to locate her through the convent, but without success. Suddenly I had so many regrets. Regrets about Lodiya, about Rita and the way I had lost touch with them.

In the first years after my escape I had worked like a demon to promote the cause of the children. At my first address to a United Nations sub-committee, I had insisted on using sign language and an interpreter to communicate to my audience. It was the only way I could make my point about the hundreds, if not thousands of children, who had had similar, or worse experiences than I. Then, after the initial two years of frantic activity, I suffered a breakdown.

My reflections about the past were interrupted by the announcement to fasten our seat-belts. Sue sat up and sleepily leaned forward to glance out of the window.

From the air the city appeared to be laid out in an orderly fashion, blocks of buildings neatly separated by streets. From this distance, there was no inkling of the ruin that lay concealed beneath the greenery of the tree-lined boulevards.

'Well, we're almost there,' Sue said, leaning forward to look through the window. 'Is someone meeting you?'

'I've sent friends a telegram,' I said.

The plane banked and then turned in a wide circle for its approach to the airport. On the hills overlooking the city lay the area which had once been home to the elite Portuguese families.

I gazed down at the emerald-green ribbon of shallow coastal water which scalloped the edge of the land mass. Further out, small fishing boats bobbed on the surface of the deeper waters.

'It looks very pretty from up here, but it must be hell down there,' Sue said. 'By the way, I have a car and driver meeting me, so if there's no one to meet you I'll give you a ride.'

'Thanks.'

We turned and descended towards the airport; there were fewer trees and one could get a sense of the miserable conditions which existed for the tens of thousands of refugees who had migrated from the countryside to the city. Shanties, wrapped in pieces of green and black plastic had sprung up everywhere.

The stories about the devastation wreaked by decades of war and famine obviously had not been exaggerated. Independence had not fulfilled the dreams and aspirations of the Mozambican people.

I thought about David, an old friend of mine, who had once observed that Africa would always be vulnerable to the vagaries of political ambition. He had predicted that once weakened by poverty and disease, Africa would eventually be recolonised by new masters.

The ground around the runway lay dry and cracked. An occasional stunted bush dotted the landscape, valiantly hanging on despite the harshness of its surroundings. Mozambique, like the rest of sub-Saharan Africa, had been ravaged by drought.

A torn sheet of tar-paper on the roof of the hangar flapped forlornly in the breeze, and except for a few people waiting on the upper level, the terminal seemed desolate and deserted. Our small plane with its prop engine, touched down with a screech of tyres. Once on the ground, the plane slowed, turned and lumbered towards the terminal.

Passengers eager to get out, started reaching for their luggage.

'If I miss you in there,' I said to Sue, 'I'll try to find you outside the terminal.'

We waited for the stairway to be pulled into position and when the doors opened we were assailed by a blast of hot, humid air. I

3

carefully descended the steps. With a sense of trepidation I stepped into the gloomy interior of the terminal building. The sight of the uniformed customs and immigration officials instantly created a knot of anxiety in my stomach.

As I searched for the appropriate queue, I wondered absently, which of the people I once knew might still be around. Albertina and Hugo da Silva were contacts I had made through my work with the United Nations agencies. They had promised to locate some of the names I had given them, but I hadn't heard whether they'd had any success. I knew that it was going to be difficult to find people. Many of them had been moved, displaced or were dead. I wondered who was left now to help me connect with my past.

I had worried throughout the journey that coming here at this time might be a mistake. But of course sooner or later I would have returned. Lodiya's death three months ago had just made it sooner.

In the airport terminal a noisy queue had already formed at the immigration desk. Sue pushed her way to the front of the line. There was a steady hum of voices and with a start I realised that they were speaking Portuguese – that I was actually here in Mozambique.

In the front of the other line a woman coming home from South Africa was involved in a loud altercation with an overzealous official who was subjecting her to some harassment. Other women had gathered around to support her, interjecting and adding their own opinions. Eventually the official backed down and the woman went on her way, grumbling loudly about his stupidity. There was a warmth and a crazy energy about that exchange which reminded me of those early days.

With the dispute resolved, the line inched foward again. It was hot in the building, the air stagnant and buzzing with flies. I shuffled forward, staring out with unseeing eyes. My return had brought a flood of memories which I could not hold at bay. Images flashed through my mind. I thought of Lodiya. I could actually see her face with the small butterfly scar on her cheek. There were other faces and images from my childhood, too. My parents, Mama Kirina, Mamaria, Rita, Doña Maria, Rhonica . . .

Some of the images had altered quite dramatically during the years I had struggled to recapture the past. In a way I hoped that by coming back, I'd be able to gain some new understanding about

4

my life here. I had been told that the fundamental problems for the Mozambicans had not changed. The only difference was in the scope of the devastation and their suffering.

It was my turn. The immigration officer scribbled a notation on my passport, peered into my face and compared it with the photograph. He turned to make some comment to the fellow in the next booth which I couldn't hear, and then, with a last glance at me, stamped my passport and waved me through. As passengers left the terminal they were accosted by the noisy clamour of beggars and young boys jostling to carry luggage. I saw a young woman holding aloft a placard which had my name on it. I guessed that this was Albertina da Silva and that the man beside her was her husband, Hugo. I waved at them and they hurried forward to greet me. Albertina was a young woman in her mid-twenties; her husband Hugo, an artist, was about fifteen years older. Hugo took my luggage and they ushered me out of the building. Albertina and I waited at the main door while Hugo went to fetch his car. In the chaos I missed Sue, but I had her name and address and I had promised to meet her as soon as I could.

Outside the airport terminal building, the children crowded around, some of them in rags, begging for something to eat. There were so many of them, all reaching out. Albertina smiled indulgently.

'You can go mad,' she said, 'trying to feed all of them. It's very difficult even for us, so I can imagine how difficult this will be for you.'

Hugo arrived, grinning apologetically for the condition of the car. He undid the door which was tied shut with a rope.

'No spare parts,' he said ruefully.

'There weren't any during my time here either,' I said.

Hugo loaded my bag into the car and we drove off. I gazed around.

'It's not so much the shortages and the hardships,' Albertina said. 'It's the total collapse of social order.'

'How long have you lived in Maputu?' I asked.

'All our lives. We've never been away,' Albertina said.

We lapsed into silence as I glanced around, shaking my head at what I saw. 'Things look bad,' I commented.

'It's getting better slowly. But we can see the difference,' Hugo

5

said as he turned into a side street, scarcely avoiding an enormous pot-hole in the road.

'I've located someone who knows your friend Rita. She is in Beira. I've sent a message,' Albertina said.

I reached out and touched her shoulder. 'Thank you so much. I can't tell you how much I appreciate your help.'

Albertina nodded and smiled, exchanging glances with Hugo.

A while later we arrived at their flat which was in a once picturesque cobbled street. It was on the top floor of a run-down building which was sorely in need of paint and repair. For the da Silvas' it was home, their own space, a place of refuge from an increasingly violent environment.

Hugo unlocked the wrought iron gate and then worked on the two locks of their door. Theirs was a small flat, sparsely furnished with heavy burglar-proof bars on all the windows. Despite the fortification, the flat had a warm feeling. It reminded me of the flat I used to have here years ago.

Albertina showed me to the small spare room. They had managed to squeeze in a narrow bed and a chest of drawers and Albertina had brightened it up with a colourful bedspread. I was truly appreciative of what they had done.

Albertina gave me a spare key to the flat, and warned me of the dangers in the street. She advised me not to go out after dark and to make sure that I walked only along the busier streets. There were no buses or taxis, and cars were rented at exorbitant rates, usually for foreign exchange. Yet, despite the danger from street gangs, everyone walked, and life continued as best it could under the circumstances.

That evening, over a meal of fish and rice, we sat talking. Hugo showed me some of his paintings; they were remarkable pieces and I had nothing but admiration for the two of them who had managed to survive so well with limited resources at their disposal. They both worked with various agencies, Albertina with a women's organisation and Hugo with the Department of Information; both of them were very aware of their good fortune. I sensed some guilt about the fact that they had a little more than others.

The next day I tried to find my bearings and went for a walk, keeping in mind my hosts' warnings to be cautious. I walked along the main avenue and was able to recognise some of the old buildings around the park. Although the wrought-iron gates were still there at the entrance of the park, there was little else that was unrecognisable. The botanical gardens, now lay in ruins, another victim of drought and neglect.

As I walked through the city, I could see that life had returned to the city streets despite the destruction and devastation of years of cruel war. This had gone on for such a long time – it was obvious that everyone was exhausted by the fighting. They needed time and the opportunity to rebuild their lives and their country. But how?

I sat under a huge old tree. It had already been old long before I was born and even though it could well endure beyond my lifetime, this old tree could so easily be destroyed by a single blow from an axe.

It was as though an axe had been wielded against the branches of society and all that slow-growing complexity had been destroyed. It was gone and could never be restored. A sense of despair crept over me and under that old tree I wept as I hadn't wept in years.

Painful memories welled up in me of a day which had started out so peacefully forty years ago, in a remote village in northern Mozambique, and ended in tragedy: robbing me of my voice, my history, and much of my life.

BOOK ONE

Chapter One

The events of that day forty years ago, are astonishingly clear even now. I was eight years old and on that particular morning I was standing on the verandah gazing out over the familiar panorama as the mist rolled off the forest canopy. Classes had been cancelled for the day and my father was doing repairs in the schoolroom, an open-sided mud and thatch structure, built on ground which fell away towards the valley.

I was still in my nightgown, risking a scolding from my mother who, despite our isolation, strictly observed certain conventions. According to her it was important that we appeared in public properly attired at all times, our behaviour and decorum above reproach.

My parents were Protestant missionaries from Canada who had arrived in this remote village in northern Mozambique three years prior to my birth. Here, cut off from civilisation by mountains and forests, we had carved out a niche for ourselves. Except for the occasional trek to the city two or three times a year to pick up supplies and mail, we had little contact with Europeans.

Ours was a simple existence and, except for a few of my mother's personal touches, our home was spartan. Unlike the other village huts, ours consisted of a single mud structure which incorporated the areas for cooking and sleeping, with a small clinic and dispensary added on at the rear. It was larger than the other dwellings and my mother often referred to it as a 'cottage', evoking notions of greater comfort and grandeur. Mama had often talked about adding on a room for me, but we had never got around to it.

The front of the house was part of the original structure built by our predecessor some fifteen years before. The windows were openings in the wall, covered by jute matting which my mother had ingeniously rigged so that they could be raised or lowered like

9

blinds. In this way we managed to keep the interior dark and cool in summer. In my parents' bedroom, sheets of mosquito netting, suspended from a bamboo hoop tied to the ceiling, fell around the bed like puffy white clouds. I used to love crawling into bed with them. It was like being ensconced in a cocoon of cotton wool.

But all of this dreamy luxury came to an abrupt halt one day around the time of my sixth birthday, when Mama decided that it was no longer appropriate for me to share a bed with her and Papa. Without prior warning, and much to my dismay, I was transferred to the 'sitting room' where I had to sleep on a pallet.

I used all my childish wiles to get back into their favour, but my mother was adamant. All my pleading and cajoling was to no avail. Even my father seemed unaffected by my fate and so I had no alternative but to accept my exile from their bed. I eventually found, however, that there was more than enough in the other room to stimulate my childish imagination. I particularly liked the framed canvasses which my mother had painted several years before. Two of the smaller paintings were of exotic birds with brightly coloured feathers. The larger canvas was a pastel portrait of a young girl with wide amber eyes and straw coloured hair. I was five years old when my mother painted the portrait. I remember what an impossible subject I was, squirming and whining about having to sit so still.

On the opposite wall, above rows of shelves lined with books were several Maconde carvings. One of these figures, carved out of a single piece of teak, was done by Papa. The demon-like figure, dubbed *Salazar*, occupied a prominent place on the shelf.

At night, when all was silent, I could hear the gurgling of the stream which ran along the fringe of the forest about four hundred yards behind us. Here at the top of the hill near the stream a wide swath of forest had been cleared for cultivation. On moonlit nights I could see the silvery fronds of the tall, slender trees standing guard against a forest waiting to reclaim its domain.

Those early years of growing up in the village provided me with wonderful experiences. I was fortunate to have enjoyed the freedom and innocence of such a carefree childhood. I can look back now on those few years when I was protected and loved by my extended family of villagers. There was a special bond between the women and children – it was a bond steeped in warm camaraderie which brought everyone together as a family.

The men were often away labouring on distant estates, so

responsibility for cultivating the small plots of land usually fell to the women and children, including myself. We were a noisy bunch, chattering happily in one of the dialects of the region, preferred over Portuguese, the official language of the country. Since Portuguese was also the meduim of instruction in schools, I was fluent in several languages, including a smattering of English picked up from my parents.

My mother, who ran the clinic and dispensary, never had the time to participate in village life to the same extent as my father and I. In the small clinic, no bigger than our kitchen, my mother weighed babies, examined women, mended broken limbs and even performed emergency surgery. To assist her with the routine work, she had trained two of the village women. Relieved of the more mundane tasks, she had more time to document some of her unusual cases, and to do the much needed follow-up work.

Sometimes one could see her frustration when dealing with patients who had come to her when it was too late. At times she raged about the problems created by rituals which resulted in complications of blood poisoning, tetanus and gangrene. I remember one day a woman came to her after receiving an 'injection' which consisted of an incision in the arm and the insertion of a black powder. It was the first time ever that I had seen my mother so angry – I can't imagine what bodily harm she might have done to the poor woman, had my father not interceded. The powder, inserted in the pregnant woman's arm to help with childbirth, had caused blood poisoning.

'I'm *not* against traditional medicine!' she cried when my father tried to pacify her. 'Am I not the one who's been documenting the remarkable cures effected by some of those forest plants? Haven't I been gathering and collecting plants with which to treat the villagers. For heaven's sake, Alex, what I can't abide is when they use unsterile devices to cut into their bodies for the sake of nonsensical rituals. I've told them time and time again how dangerous it is . . .'

Throughout this tirade, the poor woman had sat quietly, stunned by my mother's outburst.

Although my father agreed with her to some extent, he more often than not stuck to his belief that indigenous people ought not to be pushed to develop too rapidly. According to him nature, as in

11

everything else, had to take its course. It was mainly on this point that their opinions differed.

Years later I realised how naive we had been. We had intervened in so many ways, never once suspecting that we were jeopardising not only ourselves, but the villagers as well. It was almost as though we somehow believed that being different had made us immortal and infallible.

I remember as I stood on the verandah that morning that there was a peculiar stillness in the air. Not a breath of wind, not a breeze stirred the leaves or the trees. The air was so still, in fact, that I could pick up snatches of conversation from a group of women at the far end of the compound. I could also hear the early morning chorus of birds and the staccato bark of a lone forest animal carried from a long distance.

In this peaceful setting amidst the mountains and forests, there was no hint of the apocalyptic events which were to follow. I was too young to interpret the significance of the troubled glances exchanged by my parents. I had no idea either, why some of the men had gone off with Joseph, and others had stayed behind to guard the village.

Joseph Coelho, one of the few labour organisers who had managed to elude capture, had arrived in the village a few days before, accompanied by five men, two of whom had been wounded in an exchange of gunfire with pursuing government agents.

With the arrival of Joseph and his men, we saw very little of my father. Most of his time was spent in their company. Occasionally I glimpsed him in the classroom, poring over notes, or distractedly cleaning his eye-glasses which had lenses like the bottoms of glass bottles. He always seemed to be engaged in earnest conversation as he ambled alongside the shorter village men, head thrust forward as though to reduce his height to theirs.

Beneath that quiet, self-effacing manner, my father was a determined man. He made many changes when he first arrived in the village to run the school. One of these was to dispense with the practice of having students memorise the names of early Portuguese explorers like Vasco da Gama, Bartholomew Diaz and Prince Henry the Navigator. He believed that none of the early colonial history, drummed into students by previous missionaries, had any relevance in this remote part of the world. At best, he claimed, it could only reinforce the sense of inferiority instilled by the colonialists. He

12

wanted to teach the children about their own history. To this end he documented many of the stories handed down in the oral tradition.

When the estate owners eventually got to know about my father, they were outraged. They had always controlled every aspect of village life, determining everything from what the villagers ate, to what they could grow and where they could sell their cash crops. Many of these estate owners were a law unto themselves, their actions either condoned or ignored by the colonial government.

The village men were *chibalos*: men without rights, used as forced labour. In this area most of them worked in the cotton fields and the cashew-nut plantations owned by Raul Morais, one of the largest landowners in the region. My father said that working conditions for the Mozambicans on these estates hadn't changed in a century.

In that part of the world, change if any, was slow to arrive and when it did, it was stamped out by those who abhorred change. We knew very little about what was happening elsewhere in the country. Most of the time the only news from the city filtered in by way of mail, or from the infrequent journey into town. Occasionally we were visited by Arab or Portuguese traders who passed through the village and brought some news from the capital.

More rare, however, were visits by political organisers, some of whom had managed to evade capture and were making their way north to Dar-es-Salaam and safety. Strangers wandering around the countryside were often picked up by estate owners and routinely shot or hanged. Joseph was one of the lucky ones who had eluded capture and had come to organise a strike against the estate owners. The impact of such a strike was expected to have far reaching consequences as thousands of acres of unpicked cotton would end up rotting in the fields. Everyone knew of the danger associated with such action, but were nonetheless determined to go ahead with their plans.

Some time before the arrival of Joseph, my father, appalled by the working conditions, had attempted to arbitrate on behalf of the workers, encouraging the election of a spokesman from amongst the elders. He thought this was a civilised way to deal with the situation, and had arranged to present a list of grievances to Senhor Raul Morais. One of the most contentious issues at that time was a system which taxed the villagers on everything, including their

13

dwellings built out of mud and thatch. Even the dugouts built from logs felled in the forest were taxed because the trees ostensibly belonged to the government.

As arranged the list of grievances was presented to Senhor Morais. A few days later the spokesman's body was found hanging from a tree near the village.

With all that had transpired in the past few months, there was no doubt in anyone's mind that Joseph was in grave danger. There was a long history of early political and labour organisers who had ended up like the elder spokesman, their bodies strung up in the forest as an example to others.

I was still on the verandah in my nightgown when I heard my mother's voice. Instead of rushing indoors, I lazily observed sixteen-year-old Lodiya as she bustled about in the lean-to outside their hut. I dallied a while longer then went indoors to dress.

By the time I had changed into my pinafore and had gone outside again, it seemed as though the temperature had been pushed up another notch. Lodiya, who was still busy in the lean-to, saw me. She waved and crooked her arm to dab at the beads of perspiration on her brow. The heat had already induced an overwhelming lethargy and I sank on to a step in the shade of the verandah.

In the grove of trees, Lodiya's mother and the other village women had gathered to do their chores. Accompanied by the rhythmic pounding of the grain in the wooden vessels, they were singing and chanting. It was too hot out and I was thinking of returning indoors. In fact, I had got up off the step and was at the door when I heard the most frightful din. Startled, I glanced up, shielding my eyes against the bright sun.

My parents rushed out, my mother's hands clamped over her ears, my father's frantic gaze searching the sky. Suddenly the source of the commotion appeared, skimming over the forest canopy, heading straight at us. At the last moment it swerved and passed out of sight, whirling dust and debris in its wake.

'Good Lord, it's a helicopter!' my father cried, astonished.

'What is it doing here, Alex?'

'I don't know.' He watched it circle. Then abruptly, as though struck by a horrifying possibility, ushered us indoors.

But my mother and I were transfixed. In the compound pandemonium had broken out. Children, goats and chickens scattered in fright.

14

The sound, like the flapping of gargantuan wings, grew louder, engulfing the village until the very sky seemed to throb. For a brief instant the helicopter hung in the air before whirling down to the clearing.

'Senhor Morais' men have come! They have come!' Mama Kirina, Lodiya's great-grandmother shouted. 'Run, Lodiya! Take the children. Run!' she cried, pushing the children forward, urging them to flee. 'Go with Lodiya!' But instead the children bolted for the shelter of the flimsy huts.

Bewildered, Lodiya hesitated.

'Go,!' Mama Kirina cried, giving her a push.

Then almost as quickly as the helicopter had set down in the clearing, it rose again, veered slightly to the left and whirled away, the whopping sound replaced by gunfire.

'Get down, Rebecca!' Galvanised by the gunfire, my father dragged my mother down beside him. 'Faith!' he yelled at me.

Startled, I swung around. He grabbed hold of the hem of my pinafore and yanked me down so forcibly that my dress ripped. Pressing my head down low, he pushed me ahead of him.

Scuttling across the verandah on all fours like crabs, we headed for the safety of the brush beside the house. Rounds of fire landed close enough to throw dirt on to the roof. Chunks of petrified mud fell from the walls.

'Ma, Mama!' I screamed.

'It's all right, darling,' my mother said, gathering me in her arms. 'It's all right, I'm here.' Her frightened eyes sought my father's. 'Dear God . . . what's going on?' she whispered.

'Don't worry . . .' But the rest of my father's assurance was drowned in a loud burst of gunfire.

'They must be after Joseph! Alex, if they find out we provided refuge and treated their wounds . . .'

'I have to stop them,' said my father, starting to get up.

'No, Alex!' My mother shook her head. 'Wait . . .'

Lodiya, dodging bullets and chunks of flying debris, dashed over to where we were. 'They are killing everyone!' she said.

'Who are they Lodiya?' my mother asked.

'They are Senhor Morais' men! They will kill us all!'

Lodiya's terrified glance flitted between my parents, hoping for a solution from them.

'Alex! No! ' My mother cried as my father half-rose again. She put a restraining hand on his arm. 'No! You'll be killed too.'

'I have to do something. I can't just sit here.'

'Alex . . . *Please*.'

The anguish in her voice stopped him and he paused for an instant. Then abruptly he recovered. 'Quick! Head for the forest,' he shouted, gesturing towards the dense brush about five hundred yards behind the house.

None of us moved. One of the Portuguese, apparently the leader of this expedition, was heading towards us. Unlike the others who were in khaki uniform, he was wearing green and khaki fatigues and a maroon beret. His sleeves were rolled up to above the elbows and he was puffing on a cigarette as he strode over, his rifle loosely dangling from his shoulder strap. My father pushed us back, out of harm's way, and stepped forward to meet the man.

'Who are you?' Papa demanded, 'and what are you doing here?'

Smiling insolently, the man ignored his question.

'You've terrified the villagers,' my father continued. 'I warn you, I'm going to prepare a complete report of this incident . . .'

'Where is Joseph?' the man asked my father.

'Can't you see he's not here?'

The man's glance slid from one face to the other as we waited. I gazed back, defiantly at first, but then felt trapped by his glance like a rabbit in a beam of light. He lowered his arm and I noticed the tattoo of a scorpion with an enormous tail on his forearm.

He studied us for a moment longer, then without another word, strode off to join his companions in the compound. There were about twelve or fifteen men. All of them, with the exception of the man with the tattoo, were dressed in a nondescript khaki uniform. Roughly half were Portuguese, the other half were black Mozambican.

When the man had gone, my father turned to us with renewed urgency. 'Go! Go quickly,' he said.

We hesitated.

'Please, for God's sake, hurry!' he cried. In desperation he pushed my mother on. She staggered forward a few steps and then turned back to him. He took her arm. 'Take Faith . . .' he said to her. 'Go with them, Lodiya. Stay out of sight until I come for you,' he instructed.

'No!' my mother cried, wrenching her arm free.

'For God's sake, Rebecca . . .' he pleaded.

But my mother's expression was set.

'Look, they are coming!' Lodiya pointed in the direction of a group of men heading towards us.

The sound of gunfire sounded much closer now.

'Take Faith,' my mother said, putting my hand in Lodiya's.

Dazed, Lodiya appealed to my father.

I clung to my mother, but she pried my hands loose and with a quick kiss on the brow, pushed me away. 'Run!' she yelled.

'Rebecca!' my father cried, dismayed that she was not accompanying us.

Although Lodiya's grip on my hand was like a vice, I resisted, tugging and digging my heels into the ground. But she was determined to drag me away and headed for the safety of the trees.

I glanced back once and saw my mother standing with her head bowed, hands clasped, as if in prayer.

Lodiya did not pause to catch her breath until we had reached the banks of the small stream which ran along the periphery of the forest.

'I'll carry you. It'll be much faster,' she told me crouching down.

I climbed up on her back, my arms locked around her neck, legs around her waist. She tramped through the garden plots and waded across the shallow stream carrying me on her back. A few times she almost lost her balance on the slippery moss-covered stones. Eventually we reached the other side, scrambled up the bank and hurried towards the cover of the trees.

Alarmed by the sound of something crashing through the bush, I whispered nervously, 'I think someone is coming.'

'*Sim*, I heard it too,' she whispered back, gazing around frantically in search of a good hiding place. In her haste to find protective cover, she tripped over a root and pitched forward. I landed on the ground, slightly winded by the impact. Lodiya, bleeding from a gash in her knee, crawled on all fours, trying to get up on her feet, but she was weak and shaky and I had to help her. A forest deer dashed by us, and Lodiya and I gazed at one another in relief, taking the opportunity to get our breath.

'I'm frightened, Lodiya,' I whimpered.

'Me, too,' she admitted.

'I want my mother.'

'Not now. Come on,' she urged, pushing me ahead of her.

A few feet above the path, between two enormous boulders, was a small crevice wide enough in which to hide. When Lodiya was sure that we were not being followed, she gathered some of the dried underbrush and arranged it around the entrance to conceal it from view. We crept in behind the brush, the dried twigs scraping and gouging our legs. We were much closer to the compound than either of us had realised, and had a clear view of what was happening down below.

Lodiya's great-grandmother, Mama Kirina, was felled in the first volley of shots. We could see my parents waving their arms and gesturing at their attackers. I recognised the man with red beret and tattoo. I watched as he raised his rifle. There was a sickening knot in my stomach because, young as I was, I knew what was about to happen.

My parents went down with two shots. I might have run to them had Lodiya not dragged me back. I sank to the ground, hugging my knees, my back pressed against the wall of rock. I buried my face in my knees, sobbing bitterly.

We continued to watch helplessly as pandemonium broke out below with panicked villagers scattering, only to have their paths blocked by the attackers. Some, realising that they were trapped, tried to head for the bush, but it was too late. Their escape was cut off by another group of men at the rear and they were herded back into the clearing like stray cattle.

The attackers separated the men from the women and forced them to their knees. Those who resisted were clubbed into submission. The attackers then opened fire on the huddled men, most of whom were old men and boys.

The shooting lasted several minutes – minutes which seemed to drag on for an eternity. The women pleaded for mercy from the black men in the group, but they proved even more brutal than their Portuguese counterparts.

The inert air hung like a pall over the village, boxing us in. Then just when it had become unbearable, and one could feel the brittleness of it all around, as if it would again be shattered into a thousand fragments, a solitary voice rose from the midst of the huddled bodies, keening for the dead men. Soon other voices joined in. The sound, filled with such utter despair, seemed to hover,

18

struggling to push through the stillness. Freed, it rose and stirred the motionless air, rustling the leaves in the trees above us.

Mothers tried to hide their children under their loose garments, but the soldiers found them. Stunned and hollow-eyed with grief, grandmothers pressed infants to their withered breast to protect them.

One of the men pointed his rifle at the woman known as Firipa, who was wearing a bright yellow head-scarf. In her arms she held her six-month-old son, Xavier. She got to her feet and shuffled forward, her son perched on her hip. She stood before her executioner as he levelled his rifle. A single shot rang out and she fell at his feet. Her son disengaged himself from her lifeless arms and crawled close to her body, wailing loudly.

After the attackers had killed the children and infants, mercilessly smashing their skulls against the hard ground, they slit open the bellies of the three pregnant women, destroying the fetuses. Finally they corralled the young girls, brutally raping them in full view of the other women, before putting the women out of their misery.

When their guns were finally silenced, not a single figure stirred. The only sound in that eerie silence was the frenzied screeching and flapping, as hundreds of birds, startled by the gunfire, flew up into the air.

Dazed, I glanced up at the heavens. Against the blue sky the dark shape of a hawk glided like a kite carried on a current of air.

My attention wandered back to the compound as the other men returned with captives: three youths who had been discovered hiding in the bush. Prodding the frightened young men with the barrels of their rifles, they shoved them into a hut and set it alight.

'*Vamos! Vamos!*' Let's go! let's go! the leader called.

The sound of the returning helicopter mustered the men who scrambled aboard, randomly firing into the remaining structures. The roar of the helicopter's engine increased to an ear-splitting whine before lifting off. In a whirl of wind and dust it banked and clattered away.

I don't know for how long we stayed in that crevice. Time was irrelevant. The killers had long gone, and much of the day had passed before either of us stirred behind our barricade of under-brush. The sun was midway in the afternoon sky when, still in a state of shock, we crawled out of our hiding place and returned to the village.

Scattered about were the charred remains of human bodies and animal carcasses. A few clay pots lay shattered, the shards covered in dust. In the midst of all the carnage stood a large calabash riddled with holes. In the afternoon sun the leaking water glistened like teardrops.

A pall of smoke hung over the village. The air, thick with the stench of scorched flesh, was buzzing with flies. Lodiya held my hand as we searched for her mother and great-grandmother. We found them lying together, heads almost touching, bodies pulling away from each other. Her mother's eyes were wide open and encrusted with flies.

We found my parents. The bullet hole in my mother's forehead had turned black. Her head had ultimately come to rest on my father's chest, her hair spread like a sheaf of wheat. My father's one leg was curled under, his glasses broken, the frames askew.

Lodiya held me close, rocking me gently, patting my hair and mumbling soothing words of comfort. But I felt nothing. It was as if I had been emptied of all thought and emotion. I could barely move.

There was nothing more for us to do there. Lodiya told me that we would have to go to the mission at São Lucas which meant a long journey.

In the ruins of our home she found some food, clothes and a blanket. She tied whatever we needed into a bundle which she placed on top of her head. We then set off for the mission which was a full day-and-a-half's walk away.

When Father Fernando, who was in charge of the Catholic mission at São Lucas, heard about the massacre from Lodiya, he went immediately to see what could be done about burying the dead.

By the time he arrived, news of the massacre had already reached other remote areas and many of the villagers had come to view the extent of the carnage. With their assistance, he buried the remains of the slain villagers. Some of the bodies had already been partly devoured by wild animals.

On my parents' graves he placed a wooden cross on which he carved the names Rebecca and Alex Smith. A few days later, accompanied by another priest, he journeyed into the city to report the incident.

Government officials assured Father Fernando that there would be a full investigation. But fearing further reprisals if it became known that there had been eye-witnesses, Father Fernando told authorities that there had been no survivors.

The promised investigation was never conducted.

I had no memory of the massacre, only a dreadful sense that something horrendous had happened. I tried to remember the events, but the only vague recollections were of my father shouting at us to run, and of my mother standing with her hands clasped and her head bowed.

At first I half-expected my parents to come walking through the mission door to claim me. After a while though, a thread of reality took hold. With limited understanding I began to wrestle with the fact that they were dead and that I would never see them again. The significance of what it all meant began to sink in and with it came a gnawing dread and terror of the future. Mama and Papa, that indefatigable source of love and security, were no longer there to support me.

The enormous sense of loss and confusion about the events of the past few days paralysed me. I had lost everything: my parents, my home, my memory and my ability to speak. The shock left me numbed, unable to cry.

For days I lay curled up on my pallet, incapable of moving, limp with a listlessness brought on by my grief. In those first terrible days at the mission, Lodiya and I clung together, drawing comfort from one another.

Chapter Two

With the assistance of Sister Luisa, Father Fernando ran the mission church, the school, the clinic and the orphanage at São Lucas. The trading store was run by Ali, a thin, bony-faced Arab-Mozambican with dark, predatory eyes.

The store carried staple foodstuffs, some clothing, a supply of colourful beads, fabrics and plastic shoes. Since this was the only trading store in the district, business was always brisk. With the constant flow of people passing through, the mission station had an open-air bazaar atmosphere.

The dirt track leading there had been polished as smooth as a man's palm by generations of bare feet. In the shade of the gigantic baobab trees, villagers congregated to exchange gossip, to socialise and to trade their wares. It was to this particular spot that children came each morning, walking for miles, to attend classes in the open-sided thatched structure, where two Mozambican teachers vied for their exhausted attention.

Many of the villagers came to the mission for help in times of need. In exchange for this assistance they committed themselves to Christianity.

Some days the countryside rang with shouts of '*Mashala*', the Makonde greeting, or '*Jambo*', the Swahili greeting, as weary travellers from far and wide came to rest under the trees. The women, wrapped in *khangas*, the colourful lengths of cloth tied across their breasts, resembled beasts of burden. Balanced on their heads were enormous loads of goods brought to the mission to trade or barter. Some of them, finding a spot in the shade, settled down to sell peanuts, sugar cane and coconuts.

Newcomers arrived, wobbling under the weight of their load. Women carried their infants in slings of cloth suspended from their necks, the older children walking alongside. Glistening with sweat, the women seemed immune to the heat as they tended to the needs of the children who whimpered with thirst, hunger, and exhaustion.

Cattle, covered in a film of ochre dust, loped across the open savannah, driven by young boys in no better physical shape than the cattle. On this hot inhospitable plateau, as I watched young girls collecting cow-dung, I longed for the verdancy of our valley.

Father Fernando was a relative newcomer. Charged with the task of running the mission station, he had arrived at São Lucas ten years earlier to replace Father Martin. It was coincidental that he had arrived at the mission at about the same time my parents had arrived in the village. In one of her black moods, Lodiya hinted at the possibility that Father Fernando and my parents had competed for Catholic and Protestant converts.

The suggestion of such rivalry to convert people to Christianity, was offensive. I preferred to remember my parents as gentle and caring, a young couple full of altruistic ideals who had come to this inhospitable land to make it a better place.

There had always been a certain mystique about Europeans who ventured off into the backwaters of relatively unexplored countries. But even in those out-of-the-way places, with incidents of atrocities on the increase, much of the innocence had been lost. This new development, the killing of European missionaries, made Father Fernando aware of the mission's vulnerability.

Despite Lodiya's insistence that Senhor Raul Morais was responsible for the massacre, Father Fernando remained reluctant to lend credence to her story, for fear of reprisal.

'We will be safe here for a while,' Lodiya said, 'but this is not the place for me.'

I clapped my hands over my ears. I didn't want to hear any more. The thought of being here with Sister Luisa was frightening enough without having to deal with the added threat of being left on my own. I became so paranoid about losing Lodiya that I wouldn't let her out of my sight, even for a moment.

But when Sister Luisa saw how I clung to Lodiya, she told me to report for classes. I dreaded going to school because of my inability to speak. As I was different and was shunned by the other children, I seemed to gravitate more towards those who possessed physical or emotional handicaps like my own. Even in my limited experience, I realised that we had something in common. I had no choice but to comply with Sister Luisa's instruction to attend classes. If I didn't,

I knew that she'd devise some dreadful form of punishment for me. So each day I dragged myself off, panicking when I was unable to find Lodiya after classes. Lodiya knew how afraid I was of losing her and often waited near the school when we were dismissed. The sight of her was reassuring and sometimes we'd sneak off to find a quiet place out of sight of the mission station and particularly out of sight of Sister Luisa.

I was in a rather peculiar situation here at the mission. There were no documents to confirm my existence and yet the Catholic Church had become my unofficial guardian. Father Fernando's report had clearly stated that there had been no survivors. Lodiya and I had, to all intents and purposes, died in the massacre.

Lodiya was becoming increasingly restless about being at São Lucas. I guessed that she was staying only for my sake. She had no liking for the highly structured doctrinaire existence, or the way our day-to-day activities were supervised, beginning in the morning with prayers and ending at night with prayers.

'They offer us religion and their new ways,' she fumed, 'but all they do is kill our spirit. There's no life here! No life at all! It is as if the spirit of this place has been killed.'

She was as contemptuous as ever about the way the mission had altered the rhythm of the indigenous culture.

Although Father Fernando was officially in charge of the mission station, Sister Luisa was the driving force behind it, because he was away a great deal. The teachers and the assistants were mostly Mozambicans, converted to Catholicism. We heard that there were usually ten nuns working at the mission, but a week before our arrival, two of the five nuns had been transferred to Beira. Sister Luisa was furious about being short-staffed and even though everyone tried their level best to make up for the deficit, she remained hostile and disgruntled.

One of the Mozambican novices, Sister Domina, was taken from her assigned duties at the orphanage to work in the clinic. Although she had never worked in a clinic before, she was bright and adaptable. It wasn't long before she had mastered her duties, tackling them with remarkable skill and proficiency, all of which was lost on the ungrateful Sister Luisa. Despite the constant criticism from Sister Luisa, the young novice went about her work with characteristic cheerfulness.

Lodiya scornfully condemned the Mozambicans for allowing

24

themselves to be subjugated by religion. She didn't care in the least whether Sister Luisa overheard her comments or not. Sister Luisa, wary of Lodiya, concentrated her attention on saving other heathen souls, like mine.

Once I overheard her talking about Lodiya to Sister Consuela, the other Portuguese nun: 'I wish Father Fernando would see that girl for the trouble she is. I just pray she'll leave here, soon. She's a bad influence on that child. She's evil. I can feel it each time she comes near.'

I hated Sister Luisa as much as Lodiya did, perhaps even more. Sometimes the sheer effort of controlling the churning cauldron of emotions, was too much for me and I'd have to retreat to some quiet place to escape the turmoil. There were times when I wanted to shut my eyes and never open them again.

I attended school with the other children, but had very little interest in being there. The medium of instruction in the classroom was Portuguese and children were discouraged, on pain of punishment, from speaking any of the African languages. Those who came to São Lucas had to forsake their heathen beliefs and traditions. Children who wore ritual amulets or charms were punished severely. The only charm allowed on the premises was a crucifix.

Apart from basic reading and writing skills, students were taught that the Church was benevolent and, no matter what their sins, would take care of them. I paid little attention to what was said. My mind was sealed as tight as a drum. Nothing could get in or out.

Lodiya never talked to me about what had happened in the village, but I knew how worried she was about my inability to speak. She and Sister Domina were convinced that my loss of speech was temporary and would return in a matter of time.

'Soon, soon you'll speak,' Sister Domina assured me.

I waited in vain for the miracle that would restore my speech.

Apart from Sister Luisa, the rest of the staff were good to me. They believed that Europeans were not accustomed to suffering and were more affected by grief than Mozambicans. They urged me to play, pleaded with me to eat. Sister Domina who was only a few years older than Lodiya was very concerned about me.

'Faith, you must play with the other children,' she said to me one day. 'It isn't good for you to sit with a face *so* long and *so* sad. But you must eat first, to give you strength.'

As usual I had no appetite and toyed with the food. Sister Domina, frustrated by my lack of co-operation, took the fork from me and started to feed me. Lodiya, dressed in the enormous, shapeless garment given to her at the mission, looked like an avenging angel as she descended on us, snatching the plate from Sister Domina and throwing it to the ground.

'You want to die, eh? You want to die?' she demanded, seizing me by the shoulders and shaking me. 'You want to die?'

I was convinced that I survived only thanks to Sister Domina's timely intervention. Frightened and bewildered by Lodiya's outburst, I could only stare at her in mute astonishment.

But Lodiya had not yet vented all her anger. 'You think you are the only one here who has lost a mother and a father!' she cried, squeezing my face between her thumb and forefinger until it hurt, forcing me to look at the other children who watched curiously. 'Why do you think all these children are here? What about *them*? They have seen worse. They have seen much worse than you.'

Eventually she calmed down and her hands dropped limply to her sides. Anguished, she gazed at me with an expression of utter helplessness.

Hurt and confused I sat down under the tree, hugging my legs to my chest. I had known her all my life and yet I had never seen her behave like that before. Later when she tried to make up to me, my own hurt was still too fresh and I turned away from her.

In the meantime Father Fernando, who was concerned about my lack of progress, asked Sister Luisa to take me under her wing. I tried as much as possible to give her a wide berth, but nothing escaped her. Punishment was meted out indiscriminately. She was particularly harsh on those who did not speak Portuguese or who participated in African traditional dancing.

It was impossible to get away from Sister Luisa. No matter where I was, she always found me, pouncing unexpectedly, finding fault with my unkempt hair, or the fact that I might be unwashed, or that I hadn't finished my chores. As punishment for one of these imagined transgressions, she'd have me kneel for hours on the hard ground until my legs felt like rubber.

'I'll teach you humility, if it's the last thing I do,' she used to say. 'Father Fernando has spoilt you and that other one,' meaning Lodiya. 'You are here to stay. It's time you learnt to get along with the others.'

One day, about a month after our arrival at the mission, I suddenly took ill. I remember my stomach hurt terribly and I couldn't keep anything in. I didn't go to school that day and Lodiya stayed in the dormitory with me, pressing a wet compress to my head while I writhed in agony.

The dormitory was a dark, inhospitable barrack-like room which housed twenty of us. Lodiya didn't like the place, but I didn't mind it. In a perverse way, the gloomy interior provided me with sanctuary from Sister Luisa. Unfortunately that day she had found out that I was not at school and had come in search of me.

There was a big frown of disapproval on her face when she saw me curled up on my pallet. Lodiya ignored her and continued tending to me.

'There's nothing wrong with you!' Sister Luisa said. 'You're just a lazy girl.'

Lodiya who was sitting on the ground beside me, was about to protest, but the nun interrupted. 'Out!' she cried. 'Get out and go and help Sister Domina with the children. Right now!'

Lodiya hesitated and Sister Luisa scowled at her. Lodiya saw my fear and anxiety, but she had no choice. She got up and went reluctantly. As soon as she left the room Sister Luisa removed the leather strap from the wall and gazing at me, her face ruddy with suppressed rage, she approached, lightly swinging it.

I was feeling much too miserable to offer any resistance as she hauled me to my feet and gave me several lashes. I just stood there slightly stunned and wide-eyed, unable to cope. It was as though I had been anaesthetised.

'So, you won't cry, eh? I'll make you cry!' she snarled, the strap snapping and curling around my legs. I gazed up into her face with almost weary resignation and in a horrifying moment saw that her expression was the same as the ones carved into demon masks.

The strap descended again and again. But no matter how hard she tried, she could not wring the desired response out of me.

'You have been sent by the devil to try me!' she cried, eventually releasing my arm.

I staggered backwards almost losing my balance, but stubbornly I remained on my feet, a dull ache in my chest. My eyes stinging with unshed tears, drawing blood from my lip as I forced them back. I wasn't going to give her the satisfaction of seeing me cry. I shuffled back to my pallet and more agonising than the lashing was the pain I felt inside me. It was an ache like nothing I had ever experienced before. I curled up on my pallet in a pool of urine, yearning for the sound of my parents' voices, their laughter, the soft silky texture of my mother's long hair, the sky blue of her eyes and the scent of flowers which lingered long after she had left the room.

'What have you done to her?' Lodiya cried when she saw me lying there.

Sister Luisa remained silent, gazing directly ahead of her. It was as if the effort of punishing me had drained her. Her face and hands were mottled and swollen from a condition brought on by the heat and exertion. The cumbersome habit increased the puffiness in her face, the knife edges of the white wimple squashing the loose folds of skin forward until her face resembled a piece of dough.

'Get her some water,' she ordered as she got up out of her chair and came over to where I was lying.

But Lodiya was not going to leave me alone with Sister Luisa again. The nun crouched down beside me, placing an arm under my head in order to raise me into a sitting position. I shrank from her touch and that sudden movement was catastrophic. With an uncontrollable motion I heaved, and vomited right into her lap.

With a yelp of disgust, she leaped to her feet, staring in disbelief at the mess. 'You little miserable . . . filthy . . .!'

I remember how, almost with a sense of detachment, I watched the cream-coloured mass slide down her habit leaving a shiny-silvery trail on the inky blackness of the fabric.

'How dare you! How dare you!' she shouted, her voice edged with hysteria.

Transfixed, Lodiya and I stared at her. Then with one quick movement, Lodiya pulled me to my feet and backed me out of Sister Luisa's reach. 'Leave her alone. She's ill,' she cried.

'Get out!' Sister Luisa screamed. 'Get out!'

'No! You get out!'

The vehemence in Lodiya's voice stopped Sister Luisa in her tracks. She fell silent and for a moment watched as Lodiya comforted me. Then with a shudder, she clutched the crucifix hanging round her neck and left the dormitory.

Lodiya got me out of there, carrying me on her back into the open, to *our* tree, where she gently set me down in the shade. She drew my head down on her lap the way Mama Kirina used to

28

comfort her when she was younger. I felt the soothing stroke on my brow and shut my eyes.

Years later the memory returned of Mama Kirina's ample lap, and how we all used to take turns sitting in it as she held us and rocked us. The older children used to sit at her feet in a semicircle as she told her stories. Some related to battles between good and evil spirits lurking in the forests, others were about her ancestor, the Mwena Mutapa, a rich and powerful king who ruled this land long before the arrival of the Portuguese.

Through her stories we learnt about the great stone structures erected by the Mwena, in the *dzimbabwe* empire, which still stood five hundred years later in a country they called Rhodesia; about the vast gold deposits and how the Mwena had created a rich and progressive empire with trading links to the Arabs.

I used to lie in her lap too, tracing the tribal scar on her cheek with my finger. My imagination ran riot as she told us how, once a year, all the fires throughout the Mwena's empire would be extinguished and his vassals would dispatch servants to the Mwena's residence to bring back a torch lighted from the royal flame. They were wonderful days, surrounded by loved ones.

'We have to get away, Faith,' Lodiya said as I opened my eyes. 'But where will we go? How far can I get with you? What if Senhor Morais comes after us?' she asked.

Sister Domina, who had heard about the incident, came over to find us. Lodiya told her what had happened and she sat in silence, listening. Eventually she remarked, 'Sister Luisa should never have come out here. I don't think she likes it.'

Sister Luisa was one of those people who, try as they might, would never have adapted to the harsh life. For her there was no romantic appeal about the heat, the dust and the disease. One could only surmise that she felt anger and betrayal about being sent here to a place that she hated.

'She prays a lot,' Sister Domina told us. 'I have seen her doing penance. Sometimes her knees are grazed and bleeding. But it's no use. I think it's not how much penance you do, it's what is here inside you,' she said, tapping her chest.

29

'She should be sent away,' Lodiya said sharply.

Sister Domina shrugged. 'She thinks she is doing God's work. Perhaps one has to forgive her. God . . .'

'God!' Lodiya interjected. 'What God? There is no God! Look what happened to those who believed in him. Mama Kirina was a Christian. A good Christian. Now she's dead! Where was the Christian God when the men came into our village, eh? Why didn't he come to help us? Where was the Christian God then, eh?' she demanded, leaping to her feet. This was the first time that I had ever seen tears in her eyes.

Sister Domina bowed her head. She was too young and too inexperienced to deal with Lodiya's anger.

Lodiya hauled me to my feet. 'Look what your Sister Luisa did to her! How can you talk to me of God, when such things happen in his name?' she went on, flipping up the hem of my dress to reveal the welts on my legs and thighs.

Sister Domina kept her head bowed, refusing to look. It was as if she feared that by acknowledging the welts she would somehow be implicated because she was Christian.

I was ill for days after this incident, racked by malarial fever. Lodiya and Sister Domina nursed me through the illness. Eventually I regained my strength and inadvertently relaxed my vigilance, believing that Lodiya had abandoned plans to leave São Lucas.

Had it not been for Sister Luisa and the traumatic circumstances that had taken us there, São Lucas might have been as good a sanctuary as any for us to heal emotionally. It was an interesting place, to say the least. Sister Domina referred to it as the spiritual crossroads of Mozambique. I didn't know what this meant. Neither did she. Lodiya said she was merely parroting Father Fernando who often made such ridiculous observations. But I always thought it was an interesting analogy.

Although I was fascinated with the enormous baobab trees and their hollow trunks which were large enough to house a whole family, my favourite was one of the many thorn trees dotting the landscape, the one Lodiya and I regarded as *our* tree. The only other creatures who appreciated it were the donkeys and goats who carefully picked off the tiny leaves clustered around the long slender white thorns.

It was here, squatting on the ground beside me, that Lodiya told me she was going away. 'You have to stay,' she said. 'You are not to follow me.'

Stunned, I looked at her, then overcome with a feeling of utter desolation, I felt the tears springing to my eyes.

'I'll come back soon. I promise,' she said, avoiding my gaze. 'I am going over there across the mountains,' she said, inclining her head towards a hill in the distance.

I couldn't let her go. She was the only connection I had to my past. I loved and trusted her. How could this be happening again? I grabbed hold of her arm and clung to it. She tried to loosen my hold, making an impatient clicking sound with her tongue. I began to cry then, sobbing as though my heart had broken.

'Stop it,' Lodiya hissed. 'Sister Luisa might come . . .'

But even the threat of Sister Luisa couldn't stem my tears. I cried until I was exhausted and all the while Lodiya sat beside me, holding me.

'You will see,' she said, 'I'll be back soon. I'll come to fetch you. Don't cry,' she said gently. 'I have to go. Don't tell Sister Luisa.'

I wanted desperately to believe that 'soon' meant some time before dark. I held on to her hand, reluctant to let her go.

Event ually she pried herself loose from my grip and got to her feet. I tried to grab her legs, but she stepped out of reach. I lay there, face down, tears mingling with the dust. I couldn't even cry out after her. It was as though my tongue had been ripped out. I raised my head and watched her go. She didn't look back. I knew, deep down in my heart, that I would never see her again.

I leaned against the tree trunk, the rough edges of splintered bark cutting deep into my shoulder. I pressed back hard against the bark until the pain became so unbearable that it stilled the greater pain of loss.

I sat under the tree each day keeping watch, but there was no sign of her. She never returned.

Chapter Three

São Lucas had been home to me for a year and ten months, and it was almost eighteen months since Lodiya had left. Although I still missed her terribly, I had found ways of shutting out everything and protecting myself from the outside world, and in particular from Sister Luisa. I had no idea what the future held for me. I assumed that the mission would be my home for the rest of my life and in my young mind that prospect seemed to stretch into infinity.

It occurred to me on several occasions that if life became too unbearable I, like Lodiya, could run away from it all. And always when these thoughts came to me, my gaze would wander in the direction of the hills where Lodiya had gone. Perhaps I thought that if I went that way too, I would eventually be reunited with her. I had no inkling of course that my situation was about to change.

One day when I was sitting under my tree, playing my solitary game, Father Fernando saw me, came over and sat on the ground beside me. For a while he sat in silence, observing me as I continued my game, tossing a pebble into the air and deftly removing another from the pile in the centre of a circle, before catching the descending one. He smiled as I shyly demonstrated my dexterity, tossing one pebble and picking up another until a pile had grown outside the circle.

The priest had a peculiar face: dark, deep-set eyes and a weariness in his expression which made him seem much older than his years. He was a small man and his thick, dark hair was peppered with grey. On this particular day he had a day-old stubble of beard on his chin, and something in his posture, in the way he sat forward with hunched shoulders, indicated his troubled state of mind.

'Child,' he said, finally addressing me. 'We are sending you to the city. We can't do anything more for you here.' With these words spoken, he quickly avoided my startled glance, and looked into the distance.

I followed the direction of his eyes and for a while we both focused our attention on the distant horizon, as though the answer to our problems would miraculously appear from there.

Eventually, with a weary sigh, he turned to me. 'You have not uttered a word since you've come here,' he said. He paused and looked at me sympathetically. 'The sisters at the orphanage in the city have more experience about these things. They may be able to help you. Who knows, perhaps they will even be able to find you a good home? You'd like that, eh?' he said kindly, taking my hand.

With my eyes still fixed on that distant point, I withdrew my hand from his. In a way, I suppose, I blamed him for putting yet another burden on my shoulders. I had, at last, and in my own way, adjusted to life here at São Lucas. Besides, what if Lodiya returned and found me gone, how would she ever locate me?

'I'm sorry for everything that has happened to you, child,' Father Fernando continued. 'But God in his merciful wisdom sets our course for us. He will take care of you,' he said, as he struggled to his feet. 'I have destroyed your history. No one knows who you are and where you came from,' he muttered almost distractedly to himself, while he dusted his trousers. He turned back to me, but I had lowered my head, hiding the hurt and despair.

The decision had been made. I was told later that I would be travelling to the city by bus and that one of the women at the mission was to accompany me. But the weekly bus which plied the route between São Lucas and the city had broken down, and we were told that it would be out of service for a long time.

In the end I journeyed to the city by myself, on the back of a donkey-cart. The owner of the cart was instructed to deliver me, and the letter of explanation from Father Fernando, directly to the orphanage.

'It will be much better in the city,' Sister Domina whispered an assurance to me as she said goodbye. 'If Lodiya returns, I will tell her where to find you.'

I was relieved that there was some hope of Lodiya finding me if she ever returned here. While Sister Domina reassured me, Sister Luisa glowered at us from the church door.

The last two things I saw as I left São Lucas were Sister Luisa's face and the life-size statue of Christ at the entrance to the church.

Life in the city was no better than it had been at São Lucas. In the city too, I was just one more child crippled and orphaned by acts of barbarous violence. Half-starved, ragged and barefoot, a steady stream of children arrived at the orphanage, which was located in the grounds of the mission on the outskirts of town. The orphanage was separated from the mission behind a high stone wall.

Some of the children who came to the orphanage were naked. Others wore only a potato sack with holes cut in it for a neck and arms. Scores of destitute children, considered an eyesore and a nuisance by a government bent on promoting tourism, were picked up by police and brought here. It was like a way-station where they spent some time, were processed and then went elsewhere.

The children, some of them as young as five, were housed in the older part of the orphanage. The rest of us, eleven in all, were in separate quarters. We seemed to fit into a different category because we had all spent time in mission schools and had been sent here in the hope of finding adoptive parents.

The pair of canvas shoes and the two dresses given to me at São Lucas comprised all my worldly possessions, but even this was more than the kids of the streets had.

The orphanage was a large drafty old building with stone floors. A large white cross fixed to the apex of the roof indicated an earlier grandeur. Much of the rest, however, had fallen into disrepair. Some attempt had been made to restore the marble work in the cavernous chapel, but this had been abandoned at various stages of completion.

The building in which the nuns lived and where our dormitory was located had been restored. The old wing occupied by the other orphans was behind us, across an open courtyard in which stood a large statue of Christ. One of the statue's hands, extended in supplication was missing, as was a chunk of the left foot. In this setting, the image of a crippled Christ seemed quite fitting.

The stone floors, cool in summer, were cold in winter. My first winter at the orphanage was also the coldest experienced in decades. In the old wing the other children suffered terribly. There had been rumours about conditions there: fearful whispers in the dark about men who came in the night to cart away the bodies. We'd heard, too, about the filth and disease, and how the floors had to be disinfected daily and doused with pesticides to kill the vermin.

The threat of ending up there was enough to keep those of us who were living in relative comfort, out of trouble. We remained isolated from the others and because of all the stories, none of us dared to venture into the old wing.

The sound of crying from that quarter was a regular occurrence and the sisters at the mission told us that we'd eventually get used to the sound, but I never did. I remember one night I was awakened by a persistent wailing coming from the old building. At first I thought it might be a dog, but as I listened I realised that it was a child crying. I got up, fumbled around in the dark, found the torch which the nuns kept in a drawer outside our room, and crept over to the old wing.

I was afraid of the dark and afraid of being there, yet a relentless curiosity propelled me on. The bolt on the old door was stiff, and I had to struggle with it for a while before I managed to release the latch. Trembling with fear, I almost tripped over a body lying asleep on the floor. The crying appeared to come from one of the interior rooms at the far end of the passage. There was barely enough space for me to step between the bodies which were packed like sardines and huddled together for warmth. Some of them were lying on rags or on pieces of cardboard, the only protection between them and the cold stone floors.

I picked my way through the passage and found the room. It had no door and was absolutely void of any furnishing. I directed the beam of light towards the sound. A girl of about my age, sitting with her back to me, was trying to comfort a younger child. The child, about three or four years old, had her head on the older girl's shoulder. Trembling with cold, her teeth chattering, she was crying out for her mother.

The older girl turned as the light fell on them and the child stopped its crying. As I stood there, all the stories I had heard about this place sprung into my mind and the hair on the back of my neck bristled. My fear was greater than my curiosity and I backed away, slowly at first, and then I ran for the door, leaping over the sleeping bodies, tripping and falling in my haste to get away. I left the old building, bolting and locking the door behind me.

The crying started up again just as I got into bed. It continued all through the night. I couldn't sleep and lay awake in the dark, haunted by the images of the children.

The weather along the coast was usually quite mild and the cold snap had taken everyone by surprise. Daylight, which should have come as a welcome relief, made us more aware of our hunger. Many of us suffered from cramps and diarrhoea, which in turn made it difficult to eat.

The children from the old wing were given tin plates and had to line up for the stiff mealie-meal porridge and stew of vegetable tops. There was never enough. The fare was the same for all of us, but we ate indoors, away from the others. Occasionally there was some dried fish, but most of the time we lived off the ground maze and vegetable tops collected from the market or from the hotels. Sometimes, if we were lucky, a few vegetables, still attached to the tops, arrived with the discards. Kwashiorkor and intestinal parasites were not an uncommon affliction amongst the younger children who came to the orphanage. A number of them died because their condition had gone untreated for such a long time.

The high walls surrounding the grounds were designed to keep the children in, but the older ones scaled over at every opportunity to rummage through rubbish bins for scraps of food. The only deterrent from permanent escape was the fact that they were subject to arrest. Despite the conditions at the orphanage, the nuns told us that it was a lot better than living like animals on the streets. Some said they were like animals anyway, whether they were on the street or whether they were here.

It was a difficult life, but we learnt to survive. We were told that the children in the old wing were sinners. They were shrewd and devious. They lied and they stole. Sometimes I thought that the only thing separating them from me was a pattern of behaviour instilled in me at an early age. At night I prayed, 'Holy Mary, Mother of God, pray for us sinners now and at the hour of our death . . .'

The nuns and staff were under pressure to cope with the influx of street-children. The orphanage, which was supposed to house fifty children, now held two hundred, and with each week these numbers increased. Towards the end of that year the situation had reached crisis proportions. Resources had been stretched to the limit.

We waited patiently for a miracle to change our lot. But there were few miracles in those days. The Governor of Mozambique had promised to provide some assistance for sorely taxed institutions like the orphanage, but none of the promised help materialised.

I hoped that Lodiya would come for me. I waited for her, occupying myself with a piece of string which I held between thumb and index finger of each hand, making little figures and designs by hooking the index finger through and looping it. Eventually I could do it without even looking. It had a tranquillising effect, almost hypnotic, and while I was playing with the string, my mind was a blank. There was no pain, no fear, no joy, just an absence of thought.

I usually sat out on the step, manipulating my magical string. I sat outside hoping that if Lodiya came, she would find me sitting there, waiting. But she never came. Days dragged into weeks and then into months. There was so much misery and desperation in our lives. I wondered in later years how any of us had ever hoped to get away from it.

With the summer rains our supply of food increased slightly. The nuns said it was due to the goodwill and charity of the Red Cross who had responded to requests for assistance. We were told a very generous Senhora had made a substantial donation and that we would be adequately fed over Christmas.

We celebrated Christmas mass. Some of the wealthy Portuguese gave generously to the orphanage over the Christmas season. There had even been a few enquiries about me, about why a European child was living amidst such squalor, but interest waned when it was discovered that I was mute.

Then, one day, a Mozambican woman appeared at the orphanage specifically requesting to see me. I remember I was sitting in my usual spot, on the front steps to the chapel, looking at the statue of Christ, when the nuns brought her over to meet me. Her name, they said, was Mamaria. She was a big woman, so heavy in fact, that it was a struggle for her to lower herself on to the step below me.

Alarmed by the appearance of this woman, my gaze flitted from her to the nuns, who were shaking their heads suspiciously. This was not a reassuring sign, of course. But the nuns did eventually leave us, and when they had gone, the woman smiled at me with a gentleness that I had not seen for a long time.

'It's all right. I'm your friend,' she told me, her face glistening with perspiration. I watched as droplets slid along the side of her face, into her neck and down to the cleavage where a small gold crucifix nestled between her breasts.

She looked at me intently for a few moments and then with a wide grin, reached under her voluminous headscarf to scratch her head.

'Baba,' she said gently, 'Lodiya told me to come here.' She patted the step beside her. 'Come, sit here beside me. It's too hard for Mamaria to get up.'

Only my eyes moved, slowly swivelling from side to side. I sat for a long time watching her from my position on the step above, then inched down until I was sitting beside her.

'You remember Lodiya?' she asked.

My gaze faltered.

'She told me to fetch you. She said Mamaria, you go to fetch Faith and bring her to your house.'

I looked at her again. I wondered why Lodiya had not come here herself.

Mamaria held my gaze and, shaking her head, said: 'She did not come herself. She is far away. She sent a message with Nino. Where she is, is too far to come back.' She paused and glanced around her. 'This place is not a good place, eh? You'll come to live with me. I'll take good care of you.'

She stayed for a while longer, sitting with me and holding my hand as she described the world beyond the orphanage gates. When she left she promised to return again. I was sceptical. I didn't expect to see her again.

But the next day, just as she had promised, she came by. This time she stayed a bit longer. She described her home, the children who lived with her, and the mischief they constantly got into. I was fascinated by everything she had to say.

Mamaria told me she had talked to the sisters about taking me home with her, but that the orphanage could not make the decision independently. Her request had to go through the appropriate channels at the archdiocese. I can only imagine now, years later, what an ordeal it must have been for her to cut through red-tape in a country where the bureaucracy was a nightmare; where the smallest decision could take years. But even as I waited impatiently for things to happen, I knew that, despite the delays, Mamaria never wavered in her determination to take me home with her.

It seemed that the Church's reluctance to release me into Mamaria's care stemmed from the lack of information about me. Father Fernando had not provided any records.

'It seems as if she fell out of the sky,' one of the nuns said, shaking her head in despair. 'This one has a lot of problems.' They always spoke about me, as if I were not there. 'She is ten years old, but she is like a five-year-old,' the nun warned Mamaria. 'She is a lot of trouble. She can't speak and no-one knows why. We don't know what to do with her. No-one wants her. She always has this long face. Afraid of everything.'

'*I* want her,' Mamaria said.

'We will have to wait to see. If she is European there might be more problems.'

'I don't think so,' Mamaria countered. 'I think she is mixed. I know she is mixed.'

'That may be, but it is not our decision to make. We will have to wait for the archbishop to say.'

I watched them walking away from me, intent on their discussion. I ached to go home with Mamaria. I knew that she wanted me. I knew also that no place could be worse than the orphanage.

After months of delay and constant badgering by Mamaria, the director of the orphanage consulted with the archbishop and it was decided that it might, after all, be in my best interest to be released into her care. I suspect that by this time they might have been more than anxious to get rid of me. I was more of a problem than anything else. The next step was to get the written consent. This took several more weeks, but in the end it all came together.

One afternoon when Mamaria came to visit, she was summoned to the director's office. I didn't dare hope for good news, but when I was brought into the office and I saw the broad grin on Mamaria's face, I knew.

'We're letting her go with you,' the director said to Mamaria. 'I hope we're doing the right thing. As you know, we have no records for her at all. I suppose it doesn't really matter what she is. She can't stay here. You are a good Catholic and we know you'll see to it that she is raised in the proper way.'

None of this mattered to me. I didn't understand the significance of having a different skin colour or being Catholic. In fact, apart from my parents, the only white people I knew were those who converted people to Christianity, people like Sister Luisa, Father Fernando and the other nuns.

At that point there was very little difference between the other children and myself. Years in the sun had darkened and scarred my skin, giving me the burnished complexion of some of the mulattoes.

I didn't even know whether I was pretty or not. The nuns told me I was ugly because I never smiled. They said that my sullenness made me even more unattractive and unapproachable. My hair, which had been hacked off by Sister Luisa, had grown back in uneven tufts.

But I didn't care about any of this. I was getting out. I realised that in a way I was luckier than many of the children there, even those whom I had envied, those who would have been considered good prospects for adoption.

On one of her visits Mamaria had told me that all my emotions were reflected in my face and my eyes, which she compared to the colour of golden syrup. I toyed with the notion of having beautiful eyes and dimly recalled a painting of a young child hanging from a wall.

I went home with Mamaria to the township which sprawled along both sides of the ribbon of highway leading into the city. The two-bedroomed house was built of brick with a zinc roof. There were six children living with her, seven including me. We were all orphans. Sometimes our numbers swelled when she provided temporary shelter for children waiting to be taken elsewhere. Everyone knew her and knew of the work she did with the children – she was almost like an institution. Sometimes, when there were more of us, the younger ones like Aesta and Margreta slept with her in the big bed in her room. The rest of us were woven across the spare bed like matting.

This was the first time in years that I had slept in a bed and it took some doing to get used to having all those bodies lying under the same cover as me.

At first the other children were resentful. I was different from them in appearance and they regarded me with suspicion. Rita was the only one who treated me fairly and was kind to me from the moment we met. We became instant friends even though she was a few years older than me. There was no time to ease into my new surroundings. There were so many people around that there was no room to be alone.

On my second day in my new home, Mamaria left the younger children, including me, in the care of Francesca and Rita while she went off with two of the other girls to pick up Senhora Perreira's laundry.

I was sitting on my own, away from the others, when my roving eyes alighted on a doll lying abandoned on the kitchen floor. It was an old rag doll with a missing button-eye and balding head where the wool had been tugged out. No one noticed as I quietly crept over towards it. I had just managed to get to the door with the prize tucked under my arm, when Lena leapt at me, screaming: 'Give me my doll!'

Lena's fury lent her the strength to wrest it from me. When the commotion, which was mainly fanned by the others, eventually died down, I quietly stole out of the house, feeling very sorry for myself. Rita found me sitting on the step, arms wrapped around my legs, face resting on my knees, thinking of the mission at São Lucas and the tree which had provided me with a place of refuge. Here amidst the constant pandemonium there was no place to hide.

'Would you like a doll?' Rita asked.

I was still smarting from the incident and kept my face averted.

Rita repeated the question. When there was still no response from me, she touched my shoulder. I raised my head and looked at her.

'Come with me. I'll make you one,' she said. 'A pretty one with golden hair just like yours.'

I remained on the step. Experience had taught me not to put my trust in others.

'Come, I'll show you how,' Rita coaxed.

I was reluctant to go with her. Not wanting to be hurt again, I was cautious not to allow myself to be drawn into situations which would leave me vulnerable.

But she turned to me with an engaging smile and I got up from the step and followed her to the rubbish heap behind the fowl run. At the top of the heap a scorched and rusted metal bedframe jutted out. I watched as she sorted through the rubbish and retrieved a piece of discarded mattress.

She searched around and found an old stocking which she stuffed with the kapok from the mattress. Then with a deft twist of a piece

41

of string, she defined the head. There were no arms or legs. Just the sausage-like creation which she offered to me.

The doll was a disappointment. There were no eyes or mouth and certainly no hair. It didn't have limbs or even remotely resemble a doll.

Rita saw my disappointment. 'Look, here are the eyes,' she said, placing two small pebbles where eyes ought to have been. 'And here is the mouth. See the red lips?'

All I could see was the kapok which protruded from stocking like a beard. I wouldn't touch the doll and turned away from it.

'Take it,' she urged.

I hesitated, then reluctantly took it.

Mamaria laughed when she saw the doll. 'You are too old to play with dolls, anyway. There are enough real babies out there who need to be cared for.'

I eventually improved the appearance of the doll by sewing on button-eyes, a nose and red woollen-lips and gave the doll to Margreta. Mamaria was right, I decided. I was too old for dolls.

People in the township eventually got used to having me round. Despite Mamaria's attempts to draw me into the close embrace of family life, I remained aloof; afraid of loving and losing again.

Mamaria told me once that she had heard the whole story about my experiences from Nino, who had heard it from Lodiya. I had no idea what the story was. I tried to reach back into that void, but whatever was there was as elusive and ephemeral as a wraith of smoke.

Mamaria was a Barque, a member of a group that had a tradition of resistance to colonial rule. She told us how her people were finally forced to flee the mountains when the Portuguese recruited a large African army and mounted continuous attacks, killing the villagers, burning their homes and crops and stealing their cattle.

'I escaped,' she told us. 'We lived in the rebel camps up in the mountains, but always the soldiers came with their guns and we had to move. Then I came here to the city. And here we are now, one big family, all of us,' she said, laughing. When she laughed her whole body with its enormous rolls of flesh shook like jelly. She always hid her laughter behind her hand, and just when I thought she was all laughed out, she'd reach in under her headscarf, scratch her head and start all over again. I used to sit there in absolute amazement, watching her.

'One day you will find the key to the box which has your laughter,' she said to me. 'Then you will laugh much, much more than me.'

Mamaria was always very protective of me. Once when an officious-looking white woman came to the township to question her about me, she told Rita to take me for a walk and not to return until the woman had left. I knew then that I would be safe with her.

At times when I craved love and attention, I'd quietly go up beside her and stand close to her. She'd put an arm around my shoulder and ask: 'When are you going to speak, child? When are you going to say something again? You have such pretty eyes, such sad, pretty eyes.'

The physical contact with her reassured me. Although she never said so, I knew from the expression in her eyes that she understood. She was the buffer between my real world and the world that emerged from my dreams. When I had nightmares she was always there to comfort me.

Somehow we managed to get through each day with enough to eat for everyone. In addition to Mamaria doing laundry for the *Grandes Familias* – wealthy families of mixed race – she also brewed the inexpensive sorghum beer for the illicit bootleggers in the township. The four-gallon drums of liquor were buried behind the shed in the yard, right next to the rubbish heap in case of a police raid.

The women in the neighbourhood regularly stopped in to visit Mamaria. Sometimes, when they talked in the yard, I'd strain to listen in. Although I couldn't hear the words, their voices, richly resonant, were peppered with whimsy, indignation and laughter. Years later I recognised the same tone in the voices of other women I came across who, despite their hardship, still retained a sense of humour and could laugh and tease each other. This sense of warmth and camaraderie with each other was the basis for strong friendships and many important support systems.

On good days some of us went out to sell roasted corn, boiled peanuts and fried fish to dock workers. The port authorities used to chase us from the area, but we'd go off and wait around the corner until they were out of sight and then we'd return again to hawk the rest of the contents of the baskets.

Francesca and Augusta not only helped at the docks, they also sold food at the train station to mine workers leaving for South Africa.

I remember once when Augusta and I were walking by a Portuguese farm, a chicken scurried across our path, bent on some unknown destination on the other side of the road. The quick-thinking Augusta reached down and snatched it in mid-stride. The startled bird fought back valiantly, kicking and squawking as Augusta stuffed in under her shirt.

'Tomorrow we cook this one and sell it at the docks,' she said, trying to pin down the struggling bird under her arm. I stumbled after her as she half-walked and half-ran down the street. The chicken was making such a din that there was no point pretending we were out for a stroll. We bolted down the street to the corner, expecting at any moment to hear the bellowing voice of the farmer in pursuit.

When we reached safety Augusta took out the chicken from under her shirt. Her stomach and waist were covered in deep painful scratches where the bird had tried to claw its way free. She held it by its legs, shaking it as she gingerly touched her midriff. 'You are going to die tonight,' she said, as she buttoned her shirt.

Augusta and Francesca both eventually left for Beira. I was very sorry to see them go. I had grown quite attached to Augusta. Next to Rita, I liked her best. Fortunately there was no time to dwell on their absence and how much we missed them. Those of us who were left behind, had to assume added responsibilities. There were two newcomers; two little girls who had arrived from the village, both of whom had lost their parents. Despite the extra work, however, Mamaria was determined that all of us would have a chance to be educated. She was particularly concerned about Rita and made sure that Rita and I went to school regularly.

School was more difficult for me because of my inability to communicate and my innate desire to escape attention, but eventually I learnt to use some rudimentary gestures and signs. Most of my responses, however, were written on a slate which I always carried around with me.

For a while things seemed to be going a lot better than they had for a long time. From past experience, though, I knew that one could not take anything for granted. Life had a way of turning on those who were too content and I lived with the constant anxiety that whatever little bit of happiness I had could be wrested away at any time.

I was right. One day, without any prior sign of illness, Mamaria collapsed and went into a diabetic coma. Two days later she was dead. We were devastated. I knew that things had been too good to be true. But why Mamaria? She had given so much. Her whole life had been devoted to taking care of others. I couldn't understand why it was always people like her, who were struck down so easily. What about others? I suppose I wondered about those whom I considered expendable.

But there were no answers, no obvious reason why she had been taken from us. All I knew as I sat out on the backstep, was that I had once again been abandoned. I vowed that I would never let my defences down again.

After the funeral Rita and I clung to one another. I didn't think she would ever overcome her grief. Mamaria had been like a mother to her. Her own mother had died giving birth to her.

In one stroke our safe little world had collapsed. My own misery was further compounded by the fact that the adult relative Ester, who had come to take care of Rita, Aesta and Margreta, had refused to take me in.

I was almost fourteen years old when I returned to the orphanage. The day I left the township and Mamaria's house something inside me died as well.

'Don't hope for a miracle,' Rita said bitterly as we said goodbye. 'There's no such thing.'

She was right. What was the point of hoping for things like my speech, or that someone would come along and take me home with them? If anything were to happen it would only be to provide false hope. I didn't want to contemplate the future, afraid that something would again come along to shatter my dreams.

Conditions at the orphanage had improved since the last time I was there. Although still considered high, the number of children had declined. We heard that many of the children had been sent out of town to other institutions. Later we learnt that they were being used as forced labour on the big Portuguese estates.

45

This time my stay at the orphanage was brief. Thanks to Doña Maria Del Gado Cardoso, a wealthy Portuguese woman, who had heard of my plight.

I was only there for a few months when the director summoned me to her office, asking me to bring my slate in case I needed to respond to questions.

When I opened the door to the small cramped office, I was surprised to find an elegant woman waiting inside. The director beckoned and I went forward, nervously eyeing the woman in hat and gloves peering at me through her glasses. I sensed that this might be a rare opportunity for me to get out of the orphanage and I was determined to make a good impression. Fortunately on that day I was neatly attired in a navy skirt and white blouse from a bundle of old discarded clothes which someone had brought to the convent.

'Doña Maria, this is the child we spoke of,' the director said. Then turning to me she introduced Doña Maria.

I lowered my head, my palms sweaty as I gripped my slate. I stood with my feet together, hands clasped in front of me, head demurely bowed. From beneath lowered lids I watched as she studied me and exchanged glances with the director. I had learnt to play the game.

'That's all, Faith,' the director said, ushering me to the door. 'Please wait outside. I'll talk to you later.'

I was waiting in the corridor when Doña Maria and the director finally emerged from the office. I watched them walking away. Dreading another rejection, I didn't dare hope.

The director returned to where I was waiting and told me that Doña Maria had left instructions for me to be transferred to the convent where I would receive my schooling. This was not what I had expected. I had thought I would be going home with her. She saw the look of disappointment in my face.

'It's a wonderful opportunity for you, child. Be thankful.'

I hadn't the faintest idea what would be involved in attending a convent and I didn't dare irritate the director with questions which I had to write out on my slate.

Sister Claudia reminded me how lucky I was that Doña Maria Del Gado Cardoso had taken an interest in me. The nuns could not praise her enough for her generosity to the orphanage. In the end I felt privileged that such a woman should be concerned about my welfare.

Arrangements went ahead with the nuns at the convent of Santa Teresa, located some way out of town. As the time approached for my departure I became increasingly nervous. I was concerned about the distance from town, and if I would ever see Rita again.

Before I left she came to visit me. I'd missed her more than I realised. She was obviously still deeply affected by Mamaria's death. We climbed up a tree and then on to a wall near the playing field. From our vantage spot we watched some boys playing soccer with a tennis ball. It was hot and dusty and we coughed up the choking dust.

I indicated to Rita that I didn't want to be so far away from her.

'Don't worry, everything will turn out all right.' She paused for a moment and, giving me a sideways glance, said, 'Do you know that a convent is where nuns go for training? If you go there, they will force you to become on of *them*.' She saw the panic in my eyes and added, 'It's not so bad.'

I indicated that I didn't want to go and pleaded with her to take me home to live with her.

'Ester doesn't want you there. She says there'll be trouble because you are European.'

I was hurt. She was the only one who had ever understood me. It seemed to me the she had changed. She had become hard and uncaring. Although I couldn't put my finger on what was different about her, I could sense it. It was there in her rigid posture and in the way her legs stiffly swung back and forth, the worn heels of her shoes drumming against the wall.

I tried to fathom her thoughts, but her round face was devoid of any expression, the smooth, flawless skin glistening in the heat. I touched her arm and she abruptly jumped off the wall. I followed, landing with a jarring thump and waited for her to speak.

'You are lucky. Because you have a white skin there is always someone to help you. The Mozambican children are not so lucky,' she said.

Peeved, I marched beside her, eyes fixed on the ground. My skin colour had never been an issue. Why had it suddenly become one? Seeing that I was hurt, she put a hand on my arm.

The prospect of going into the convent became more appealing as each day passed. In the end it was the only thing I could think of. It was the only place left where I was actually wanted.

BOOK TWO

Chapter Four

Several weeks went by after Doña Maria Del Gado Cardoso's visit. I used to love the sound of that name – it was so elegant, so majestic.

'It is the name of the Portuguese conquerors,' Rita said scornfully when she saw the look on my face each time that name rolled off Sister Claudia's lips.

Years later when the subject of Doña Maria again drew Rita's ire, she said: 'They came with their fancy names, took everything from us, and left thousands of their half-caste offspring with nothing but grand names.'

In the meantime, at the orphanage, Sister Claudia told me that things were going well and that word from the convent was expected imminently. However, time dragged by and nothing further was heard from Doña Maria or from the Sisters of Mercy at Santa Teresa.

Then one morning, just when I had decided that I had been foolish to pin my hopes on strangers, Sister Claudia rushed over to tell me that we were expected at Doña Maria's house that morning and that she was driving me there. Hurriedly, we prepared for the visit, Sister Claudia giving me a last quick inspection before we left.

On our way to Doña Maria's estate, Sister Claudia cautioned. 'I suggest you change your attitude, young lady, and smile. No one likes to look at a sour face.'

Smiling didn't come easily to me and throughout Sister Claudia's lecture, I kept my eyes fixed on the road. I didn't dare to hope. I was so afraid that all of this would amount to nothing and that I would be disappointed yet again.

We drove up to the house, which was located at the top of a narrow winding road. There were only a few homes in the area, all of them large old mansions in enormous grounds. My nose was pressed to the window as we drove past acres of grass so green that I could only gape in disbelief. My first glimpse of the mansion convinced me that I was right not to have high hopes. I could never possibly fit into such palatial surroundings. It was magnificent. Below us lay the turquoise ocean, above us the opalescent sky.

A servant opened the gate for us and Sister Claudia's old car puttered noisily as we drove up to the house. At the front door we were met by a another servant who led us into the enormous entrance hall where all the walls were covered with pictures of frowning men dressed in uniform, smiling ladies in flowing gowns, horses, carriages, gigantic houses, and a smiling Doña Maria posing with dignitaries. The entire wall along the staircase which led upstairs was also lined with pictures. There was so much to see, I doubted that I could take in everything in one day.

We were shown into the drawing room where Doña Maria was waiting for us. Dominating this room from its place above the mantel was a portrait of an exquisitely beautiful young woman with sad eyes and full red lips. Doña Maria noticed my interest in the painting – I was standing right in front of it, staring at it, struggling with my own memories, which seemed so elusive.

'My daughter Isabella,' Doña Maria said. 'She lives in Portugal. In that country from which Mozambique is ruled,' she added, eyes twinkling, as if to make a point about the distance between here and there. 'Another country. Far away, across the ocean.'

This was just the beginning of my education from Doña Maria who told me once how this vast land, ruled from a distant *Metropole*, was bled dry by a faceless government. Although I had been too young to understand, Mamaria had told us the same thing, saying that when it came to the rights of the Mozambicans they were as voiceless as I.

I was overawed by my surroundings and curious about everything. As I stood by the window, I fingered the sheer curtains which billowed like sails filling out in the breeze.

'Please sit down, Faith,' Sister Claudia's voice was irritated.

I came away from the window and Doña Maria smiled indulgently. 'Your eyes are a lot like my daughter's,' she said.

I sat down, carefully placing my feet together so that my shoes would not make contact with the upholstered skirt around the bottom of the chair. Neither of the women seemed to notice how mindful I was being.

'I'm here by myself for a few weeks,' Doña Maria explained to Sister Claudia. 'Senhor Cardoso is away visiting our daughter Isabella.' Her glance strayed to the protrait above the mantel and then returned to us.

'I know that you cannot speak but of course you can hear quite clearly. Can't you, child?' Doña Maria asked. I nodded, ready to lower my eyes, but her gaze held mine. 'How old are you?' she asked.

I indicated fourteen, although I wasn't too sure. There were no records of my birth and I knew that the director had guessed my age and had then fabricated a birth date for me.

'You're a young woman,' Doña Maria remarked, 'but perhaps a bit too inexperienced to make a decision about devoting yourself to a religious order,' she continued thoughtfully. 'In any event, the education you receive at the convent will be invaluable. The nuns will be a good influence, I'm sure. I think it would be best for you to wait until you're eighteen before you decide whether you want to join the order or not.'

The mere mention of leaving the orphanage made my heart beat a bit faster, but I hid my feelings carefully as I studied my hands loosely folded in my lap.

'I suppose we'll have to see how things work out,' Doña Maria said. 'Can you read and write?' she asked.

I nodded.

'Good.' Then to Sister Claudia she said, 'I've arranged for a doctor to see her. I'd like to have her examined once more before she goes into the convent. I want to make sure that everything that could be done has been done about her inability to speak.'

While the two women made the arrangements my attention strayed. I turned as the door opened and the man-servant reappeared. As soon s the door opened a small dog dashed past him and made a bee-line for Doña Maria, skidding to a halt beside her chair. The dog sat up, obviously waiting, its tail thumping, short legs quivering.

'Come here, you little rascal,' she said, leaning over and lifting the little Pekinese on to her lap. The dog, no bigger than a toy, perched on her lap, its snub nose turned up in an expression of disdain.

Such audacity flabbergasted me. The only dogs in my experience

51

were the scrawny mongrels which ran wild in the township, competing with children for scraps of food on the rubbish dumps.

On our way home to the convent Sister Claudia said, 'I'm glad you were so well behaved today. At least you were smiling and showing some appreciation for what Doña Maria is doing for you. I'm sure you'll like it at Santa Teresa.'

She glanced at me, waiting for some reaction, but I gave none. I stared straight ahead of me while she negotiated the small car through the narrow cobbled streets to the orphanage.

'I know you'll make the right decision about joining the order. It's a very rewarding vocation. And I think you should be proud of the fact that God has chosen this path for you. Of course, Doña Maria has been very generous, but we can't ignore the fact that He has guided events. It'll be the best place for you. Besides, you don't need a voice to commune with God,' Sister Claudia said enthusiastically.

Her words brought to mind what Lodiya had said about Him that day at São Lucas when Sister Lucia had strapped me so severly.

The weeks flashed by in a blur and before I realised it, the day of my departure was upon us and Doña Maria's car arrived to pick me up. I had expected to see Rita before I left, but there was no sign of her. In the excitement of leaving, though, everything else was pushed out of my mind. I was on my way out of the orphanage and this time I hoped never to return.

I leaned out of the window as the car pulled away to the jeers and cheers of the other children. Sister Claudia waved from the front step.

The convent of Santa Teresa was located about fifteen miles out of town and it nestled in a valley near a river. Not even this peaceful and pretty setting could still my anxiety as we approached the convent. I was alone again and the initial excitement had worn off. The reality of my situation struck me and suddenly I felt so small and insignificant in the back seat of the enormous limousine. All my old apprehensions surfaced and as we drove through the wrought-iron gates, I could think of nothing else but my fear of starting again in a new place, amongst unfamiliar people.

We approached the grey building with its red-tiled roof and rows of tiny square windows which climbed up the side of it. It was the same building I had seen from the road with the enormous cross on the top of the roof. Sandwiched between this and another grey building was the church of Our Lady of the Immaculate Conception with its enormous belfry. The convent seemed to rise out of the landscape like an oasis in a desert. I slid forward until I was perched on the very edge of my seat. I didn't want to miss a thing.

We pulled up in front of the grey building. At the entrance was the statue of the Blessed Virgin. Two nuns were waiting for me on the front steps. One was a smiling young novice in her mid-twenties – I knew instantly that I would like her. The other, an older woman, looked forbidding. For a moment I felt a surge of panic. I quickly withdrew from the window. The older nun waited patiently with her arms folded in front of her, her hands tucked into her sleeves.

I hesitated about getting out of the car, pressing back into the seat, wishing I could disappear into it. The two faces appeared at the window. The driver saw my anguished expression in the rear-view mirror and winked encouragingly. The young novice, Sister Angelique, opened the door and I got out.

The older nun, I discovered later, was the Mother Superior. She was in her sixties. Her face was deeply tanned and scarred from life in the tropics. Although she seemed kind enough, I was wary of her – there was something about her, in the way she walked and held her head, which reminded me of Sister Luisa.

Sister Angelique showed me to my room, which was large enough only for a narrow bed, a table and a chair. Regardless of the size, however, it was mine and I was thrilled that for the first time I would have a small space to myself. The wall was decorated with a picture of the Sacred Heart and a crucifix hung above the bed. A plastic statue of Our Lady stood on the table.

'You'd better hurry,' Sister Angelique said. 'Mother Superior is waiting.'

I accompanied her to Mother Superior's office. We stood before her desk, feet together, hands clasped before us in an attitude of humility.

'Welcome to the Convent of Santa Teresa,' Mother Superior said. 'Sister Angelique will show you around for the first few days. She will also take you through the catechism and prepare you for

53

confirmation.' I had been told that I had to be confirmed in order to be accepted into the community.

'Sister Angelique has spent many years working with the deaf and so she will also be teaching you sign language. Sister Carmelita and Sister Alphonsus will be your other teachers. Your classes will be as regular as possible, but they will be organised around our schedule. You will also observe all the rules as they apply to our community. Sister Angelique will familiarise you with these.'

I was so nervous I could barely keep my knees from trembling as I stood listening to Mother Superior.

'That's all,' she said, and dismissed us.

It took me about two weeks before I could even begin to grasp the strict convent routine and get used to the heavy black serge uniform I was obliged to wear. The black stockings were hot and I was not accustomed to having my feet encased in shoes all day long.

I had only been there for a month when I was summoned to Mother Superior's office again. I stood across the desk from her, full of anxiety, while she delivered a stern lecture about the virtue of obedience.

I tried to think of a possible transgression that could have warranted such a summons to her office. Had someone seen me falling asleep in chapel? Had I disobeyed one of the rules? If so, which one had I inadvertently violated?

I had swung my arms while walking into chapel the other day. It was considered swaggering and Sister Alphonsus had glared her disapproval. I tried to list my offences, just as I would do when preparing for the confessional. Nothing of a serious nature came to mind though, studying my hands, which were loosely clasped in front of me, my slate tucked under my arm.

'I believe you're doing well in your studies. In a few weeks you'll be ready for confirmation,' Mother Superior said.

I relaxed. I was not going to be chastised after all. Perhaps I'll be praised, I thought hopefully.

'I know you've been through a lot,' she continued. 'We want to help you. But you must obey every one of our rules.'

I kept my head bowed.

'I know you're in there somewhere,' she said, leaning forward to see my expression. 'You're not deaf – you can hear me.' She opened the file on her desk. 'I see here that you lived in the township for about four years with a woman called Mamaria.'

54

I nodded.

'Were you happy there?' she asked.

I nodded again.

'When she died, you returned to the orphanage. I'm sorry about that. It must have been difficult for you.' She paused.

I waited for her to continue.

'But now you are here and life will be quite different for you. There are a few things I'd like to remind you about, though.'

My eyes met hers briefly, and then dropped to my hands again.

'I notice you've become fairly dependent on Sister Angelique. It isn't good for you to be so dependent on one person. Here at the convent we do not allow particular friendships. In communal life one must resist the temptation to become too close to any one person. You must learn to be independent and totally self-sufficient,' she said. 'I have told Sister Angelique that she will be with you only during the hours of religious study, sign language, chapel and recreation,' she said, ticking these off on her fingers. 'You will not be allowed to go out for a walk unless there is a third person present. Is that clear?'

I did not respond and the silence stretched between us.

'Do you understand me, child?' she asked again.

Finally I nodded my head.

'Good. Now I don't wish to discuss this with you again.'

I sensed that she hadn't quite finished with me.

'You will have to forget all about your past and the way you did things before. While you're at the convent, you will not be allowed to visit the township. You will be allowed one visit a month to Doña Maria if she requests this, and the occasional visitor will be allowed, but only with my permission.'

What about Rita? I wrote on my slate.

'She may visit you,' Mother Superior said. 'But I want you to understand that unless you co-operate with us, we might have to curtail such visits.'

I lowered my head again, ashamed of the nasty thoughts I harboured about her.

'The convent is a place of religious study and contemplation. It is a place of silence and introspection. A place of humility and service to God,' she said. 'We all work very hard and there is no time to waste on pampering a young girl. Your duties here will be set out clearly. We expect you to pull your weight. Doña Maria has been a generous benefactress and we'd hate to offend her by sending you away.' She paused waiting for all of this to sink in.

'Doña Maria is counting on us to help you, to educate you the best way we can. The education you receive here will also help you to make up your mind when the time comes for a decision about your future.' She paused again and turned the pages in her file.

I linked and unlinked my fingers and then fidgeted with my slate, keeping my head lowered.

'Both the doctors you have seen feel that eventually you may speak again. They say your condition is curable. It's just a hysterical paralysis of the vocal chords. The cause lies somewhere in here,' she said, tapping her head. 'One day you'll be able to speak again,' she said, smiling.

I glanced up and noted that she was smiling and that the smile had softened her stern countenance and made her look quite beautiful, almost like a madonna.

'It might take days, weeks, or even years for you to recover your speech,' Mother Superior continued. 'Fortunately you don't need your voice here at the convent. Our rule of silence will be well suited to you. You won't find it as much of a hardship as the others might.'

I looked down at my hands again, nervously trying to concentrate on what she was saying. Finally, satisfied that I had understood her concerns, she gave me permission to leave. Like a sleepwalker I headed for the door. I could feel her eyes on me. I turned, expecting that she might have something more to add. She made a small impatient, dismissive gesture of the hand, leaving no doubt that the interview was concluded.

I returned to my room ready to throw myself on to the bed. But I remembered that it was against the rules to do so. Instead, I perched on the edge of the chair. I thought about what Mother Superior had said. I liked it here. I liked Sister Angelique. We were friends and I had started calling her 'Angie', when we were alone.

Later that evening when Sister Angelique slipped into my room, I described what had transpired between Mother Superior and myself.

'It must be hard for you being here,' she said, smiling as I looked down dejectedly at my shoes.

'No,' I signed. 'It's not hard for me. I'm used to silence and isolation.'

'Oh, Faith,' she said, and put her arms around me. She held me like this for a while. At first I was shy and awkward about being embraced, but those loving arms around me displaced all the misery and unhappiness. She touched my hair, caressed my cheek and held me close again. Then quite abruptly she let go of me and hurried out of the room.

I watched her go, realising that we had violated the strictest rule of contact at the convent. If we had been caught in such an embrace, there was no doubt that we would have been in serious trouble.

The following morning I awakened earlier than usual. Our day began before sunrise when we were roused by a bell. We had to dress in a hurry in order to present ourselves at chapel. After that we had breakfast together and started our chores. Later in the morning we had classes. The latter part of the afternoon was spent in spiritual reading and then it was chapel again, supper, recreation and bed. I looked forward to recreation hour, especially when Angie played the guitar.

She never hugged me again. But I craved human contact. I remembered how I used to snuggle up to Mamaria. Occasionally Angie and I talked about our pasts.

She was very good at signing and told me that she had learnt to do it at the Deaf Institute in Portugal. Although originally from Oporto, she had spent much time in Lisbon. She wistfully recalled her life in Portugal, but was always a bit sad when she described the poverty in the *barracas*, the city slums. It was this abject poverty in her home country and her desire to help, which had influenced her decision to join the convent, never dreaming that she would be sent to Mozambique instead. Her stories opened a whole new world for me, a world that I had only glimpsed through my association with Doña Maria.

Most of my formal tutoring in sign language occurred in the morning, after prayers and morning chores. In the afternoon there were more chores. There was a lot to do at the convent. Apart from a small winery, the convent also grew enough food for its own use and for sale to the hotels in town. The six dairy cows provided milk and there were chickens and goats which had to be tended.

One day Rita arrived to see me, having hitched a ride on a

donkey cart. She was so excited about passing her exams and about going into her final year at school that she had to tell me herself. With Mother Superior's permission I took her on a grand tour of the convent and introduced her to Angie. Rita seemed to be her old self again.

'I want to do nursing,' she told me. 'It's the only thing I want to do in life.'

I smiled. She had an amazing drive to accomplish things she believed in. Secretly, I envied her this ability.

'You know how much I've wanted to do this,' she said.

I nodded.

'It's like something in my blood, something that I have to do. I have never wanted to do anything as much as I want to become a nurse,' she said.

We walked on in silence. I didn't understand this passion. I wasn't thinking much further beyond the present. The future stretched too far ahead of me.

'I'm going to apply to the Medical Institute in town,' she said. 'It's the only way to get experience. But maybe I'll have a hard time getting in because I'm black. What do you think?'

I shrugged.

'Maybe I'll have to go to St Bartholomew Hospital, but I don't want to work for the nuns.'

I listened as she considered all her alternatives.

'The thing is if you are black they can send you to the bush or else they make you do all the dirty work in the hospital. For Europeans it's different.'

This talk about black and white and Europeans made me uncomfortable. I was only just beginning to understand the significance of my skin colour and I didn't want to be categorised because of it. I was her friend. In fact, she was the closest person I had to a sister. I smiled, showing her that I had confidence in her ability.

'You look happy here,' she commented.

I nodded. Although I wanted to let her know that I was learning sign language, I felt I couldn't. Instead we walked in silence through the orchard and the vineyard. Some of the vines, I had been told, dated back almost two hundred years and had been brought here by Father De Valera, who had founded the convent. The grapes were used in the convent winery.

She told me that Augusta had married in Beira. I listened to

58

what she had to say, but there was a distance between us. It just didn't feel the same any more. I was conscious too, of the increasing distance between the world of the township and my own here at the convent. I suspected that she sensed it too.

'You must come and visit us,' she said.

I didn't dare tell her that I had been forbidden to visit the township. Instead I indicated that I was not allowed to leave the convent grounds.

'It's like being in prison,' she remarked.

Was this what prison was like? I wondered. Angie had once told me that not being able to speak was like being imprisoned in your own body. She had assured me that sign language would ultimately free me.

Rita and I walked to the gate, arms linked. I hoped that we would not be seen. It was against the rules. We were supposed to pattern ourselves after Him, maintaining an aloof distance from others. We had to place ourselves apart, physically and mentally.

'I won't be coming very often any more,' Rita said. 'This place is too far away. There are no buses. The old man who gave me a ride out here is going back into town so I'll be off. I said I would meet him in the village.'

We said goodbye. I watched her go, briskly striding down the road, arms swinging loosely at her side. I saw her stub her toe on a rock and stumble. She turned and waved to me. I waved back and then returned inside.

Later that afternoon I met Angie before going to our cells for spiritual reading. She was standing behind a tree. It was almost as though she had been waiting for me.

'Did you have a good visit with Rita?' she asked. She reached out and held my chin, her thumb caressing my cheek.

'You've got mud on your cheek,' she said. Our eyes met and for a moment I felt shy and awkward about this unexpected intimacy. She noticed and withdrew her hand.

'You'd better hurry,' she said, 'or you'll be late for reading.'

I hurried away. It took me a long time that day to settle down to my reading. So many questions were beginning to nag me, questions about Angie and the way I felt about her.

We never referred to this incident again and I didn't know whether it had happened by design or by accident.

At first Angie was the only one with whom I could use sign

59

language, but the others learnt merely from watching us and had a great deal of fun communicating like this rather than speaking. It was one way of not breaking the rule of silence and became a game for some of the novices.

After my confirmation I felt more content at the convent. In a way it seemed almost as if convent life was tailor-made for me. I didn't mind being alone.

'Here in this peaceful environment,' I signed to Angie, 'it is as if I have finally come home.'

'Does that mean you're thinking about joining the order?' she asked.

I nodded.

She turned to me abruptly. 'Don't be in a hurry to make such a decision,' she said. 'You're still young. Wait. Leave the convent for a few years, and then decide. Don't do anything that you might regret.'

Before I could respond, she had turned and walked away. I tried to catch up with her, but she was much too quick for me and by the time I turned the corner, she had already disappeared from view.

I had Angie to thank for my ability to speak with my hands, and Sister Carmen, who was an avid gardener, to thank for passing on to me her love for the soil and all that it yielded. I had learnt so much since my arrival at the convent and I found in myself a new enthusiasm for fresh challenges.

The ceremony in which the postulants, dressed as brides, took vows of Poverty, Chastity and Obedience was impressive. I think what fascinated me most was the mystique of the ritual. Had it not been for Doña Maria's insistence that I wait until eighteen to enter the novitiate, I might have thrown caution to the wind and done so right away.

Initially Doña Maria kept her distance and there was no interference from her about the way the nuns were educating me. My ability to read and write progressed in leaps and bounds. But most of all I loved to be outside, particularly in the spring and in autumn. At these times there was a special ambience in the air which evoked in me an intense longing, and yet I had no idea what it was I longed for.

In the autumn Angie and I managed to take some walks together, collecting leaves to press, always careful about taking Sister Carmen along with us. In the summer we picked flowers from the garden for the same purpose – although cynical about preserving memories, Angie ended up saving every one of those pressed leaves and flowers.

At the end of that first year Doña Maria began encouraging regular visits with her. On the last day of each month her car and driver arrived to fetch me.

At first these visit were full of awkward silences and I sensed her frustration at having to read my responses from a sheet of paper. The whole process seemed to interrupt the natural flow of conversation and eventually she did most of the talking, rambling on as if conversing with herself. I nodded politely and shook my head whenever such a response was called for.

On occasion, however, I was able to make myself understood by using hand gestures and now and then by using a sign. I was surprised and pleased when she began to remember the ones I used regularly. At first I started with simple words and progressed to some simple phrases.

Despite our communication problems I actually began to enjoy my visits to her. Sometimes she and I sat outside watching the gardener or one of the groundsmen at work. There were several Mozambican labourers on the estate, doing menial jobs like gardening and cleaning. She didn't think anything of it, neither did the servants, who in those difficult times were grateful just to be working.

Isabella made a few trips to Mozambique to visit her mother, but she preferred the concerts and glitter of life in Lisbon. On both occasions that I met her, she was kind and considerate, although I detected her boredom with me and with being in Mozambique.

The first few times I visited when Senhor Cardoso was home were full of uncomfortable moments. He had a grim, silent countenance, and seemed almost unapproachable. Initially I was a little afraid of him. I kept my distance, standing to one side until he acknowledged me.

Later, when I realised that this was only his manner, I began to let down the barrier between us. Ultimately, I was rewarded for my efforts and the two of us would sit together in quiet, companionable silence, enjoying the ability to make the most out of the silence around us.

'At least you're quiet,' he said to me. 'I don't like people who talk too much and have too little to say.'

One day Rita came to see me at the convent. She arrived in a small beat-up Fiat borrowed from a friend. She brought Aesta with her whom I hadn't seen for two years. She was much taller than I remembered, with sparkling dark eyes in a heart-shaped face.

'I have passed my tests too,' she told me proudly.

'She's doing well at school,' Rita said.

'How are things with Ester?' I asked.

Rita shrugged off the question and I suspected that there were problems with her and Ester. I never liked the woman, not only because of her rejection of me, but because there was something about her that I distrusted.

I showed Aesta around the convent and the grounds. She was quite taken with it, especially the gardens. She loved the flowers. Sister Carmen was in the garden and pointed out the various varieties of flowers she had cultivated.

'Maybe Aesta will become a nun one day, too,' Rita said jokingly. I didn't laugh. I'd learnt not to discount the improbable.

'I saw Nino the other day,' she said. 'He told me that no-one has heard from Lodiya for years. Nino thinks she may be captured or dead.'

'What's the difference?' I wrote on my slate, feeling angry about our helplessness. She didn't say anything and we walked on in silence.

From time to time I still thought of Lodiya, but she had become part of the distant past, quite removed from my life here. I could no longer conjure up a clear picture of her face. All I remembered was the scar on her cheek. We all seemed to have scars. Some of us had them on the inside. Mamaria used to say that my tribal scar was the strawberry mark on my neck, just below my hairline.

Despite my vow that I would never let anyone close enough to hurt me again, I fell into that trap once more with Angie. I had let her into my silent world, never expecting that anything would change. But it did.

One night, just as I was about to fall asleep, Angie appeared in my room. I was startled and my heart pounded with anxiety. We both knew what the penalty would be if she were discovered in my room at this time of night. She sat on the edge of my bed and we both listened for any suspicious sounds from outside. The sisters were encouraged to spy on each other and it was extremely risky for her to be there. My immediate thought was that something was wrong. I propped myself up on one elbow.

She touched my face with that same gentle caress she had used under the tree that day. She kissed me and lay beside me, holding me. I had never experienced anything like this before, yet the feeling this contact opened up inside me, caused me to wonder. It was different – not like being touched by my mother or Mamaria, and yet it brought the same kind of peace. We just lay there for a long time, holding each other. I could sense an infinite sadness about her, as though she had made some monumental decision which was about to alter her life.

She didn't speak, didn't say a word to me. We just lay in each other's arms deriving comfort from the closeness. Yet this closeness awakened something much greater inside me, something that I would never be able to still again. She left my room a few hours before the rising bell went and I lay awake, wondering what had happened to me.

In the morning she and I went out to the field to dig up potatoes. At first neither of us mentioned the previous night. She was digging energetically, and had barely glanced at me all morning. I was on my haunches, picking up the potatoes and tossing them into the wheelbarrow. Now and then she'd pause to wipe perspiration from her brow and would leave a huge smudge on her cheek which extended to the white edge of her cap.

'I'm leaving the convent,' she eventually said in a matter-of-fact way.

Stunned, I gazed at her. My hands felt cold and clammy. She turned away from me and dabbed at her face. I waited for her response, but she avoided my glance.

I remembered a similar scene under a thorn tree many years before and panicked. 'Why?' I signed, still squatting on my haunches.

'I've been thinking about it for a long time,' she said.

'Did you know before you came to my room?'

'Yes, but I couldn't tell you.'

I wanted to get up off the ground, but I was afraid my legs, which had turned to jelly, would not hold my weight.

'Do you want to get up?' she said, smiling. 'You look like a frog on a log!'

'Don't change the subject,' I signed. But I couldn't have got up, even if I'd wanted to. 'Have you told Mother Superior?' I asked.

'No,' she said. 'I'm going to see her this afternoon.'

I was hurt and angry that she was leaving. I couldn't believe that this was happening to me once again. Later, when she stopped by to talk to me, I turned away from her. All I knew was that I wanted to inflict as much pain on her as she had on me. She had brought me a little parting gift, a book.

In flagrant violation of the rules, I sat on the edge of the bed, mutely staring at my hands, barely looking up as she placed her gift on the table and left my room. Afterwards, I curled up on my bed and lay there for a long time. But there was no relief from the wrenching ache inside of me.

Angie left the convent that night, very quietly, without saying anything to the rest of the nuns. Mother Superior and I were the only ones who knew. The next morning at breakfast there was only her empty chair and the questioning glances from the others.

Several weeks after her departure, I picked up the book she had left me, and finally opened it. It was a slim volume of poetry which I had often seen her carrying around. In those lonely days after she had left, the book of poetry was a great comfort to me.

On one of my visits to Doña Maria, Senhor Cardoso must have noticed something different about me. He was a very perceptive man. For a long time he sat with me, not saying anything, finally he asked, 'What do you plan to do with your life?'

Startled by the question, I tried to think of an answer. But I had no idea what I wanted to do. The order no longer held the same appeal for me. The veil of mystique had been ripped away. All I saw now was the way the nuns were oppressed by the Church. A church dominated by priests whose power was absolute. They determined how convents would be run. They determined what nuns would wear. Only they could give Communion, making themselves indispensable. The habit, with all its cumbersome, clumsy features, was designed by nineteenth-century priests who cared nothing for the comfort and well-being of the nuns. They treated them like children, withholding their meagre salaries out of spite, determining that particular friendships would encourage homesexuality while they, themselves, made clumsy sexual advances.

How could human beings be deprived of human companionship and friendship, I wondered. How was it possible to live in isolation?

I found myself unable to answer Senhor Cardoso. I felt ill-equipped to make decisions about my future as I was having difficulty separating the individual threads of my life to make sense of my experiences. My confusion was overwhelming and sometimes I had problems distinguishing fantasy from reality.

With Angie gone, the convent had become my prison, no matter how much I prayed for guidance and some kind of revelation. It seemed the peace I had hoped for would elude me forever. Angie's words, 'Don't be in a hurry,' tormented me.

It had almost been three months since Rita's last visit. And when she came to see me, she had a lot of news.

'I have registered with the Institute to learn sign language. It is because of you, Faith.'

She and I were able to communicate in a way we had never been able to do before. I promised to teach her all I knew.

Despite the pleasant visit, I was subdued and preoccupied.

'I have applied to the *Instituto*,' Rita told me. 'I hope they will accept me to do my nursing there.'

I was pleased, but she seemed to have a few doubts.

'The positions are all for *assimilados*,' she said. 'But I don't know if I can do it. I don't know if I can give up my identity, even for this. Being an *assimilado* means denying my heritage and becoming like the Portuguese. I am black. I am Mozambican. I am not Portuguese.'

'You could pretend to be an *assimilado*,' I suggested. 'It will only be for a while until you are accepted into nursing. No-one will know.'

'I will know,' she replied. 'It'll be like sliding on my belly. I can't do it, even for something I want so badly.' She caught sight of my perplexed expression. 'Don't you see? Our people are showing more pride in who they are. They want to be free of the Portuguese.'

'The Portuguese will never free you,' I signed.

'Then we will die. We will all die. We are already dying,' she said, as though this could be the only acceptable outcome. 'Every night there are police raids in the township and people are dragged off to jail. The police come in big trucks and when they leave the trucks are full, packed to overflowing. Some of those people will never be seen again. They are taken to the Vila Algarve.'

Even I knew about the Vila Algarve, which was the official headquarters of the secret police. When I was living in the township there were many stories about what went on behind those walls. But as far as the rest of it was concerned, I began to realise how far removed the convent was from the reality of what was happening in the country. Being at the convent was like being marooned on a sheltered island in a stormy sea.

When Rita left that afternoon, I had a sinking feeling that I would not be seeing her for a long time.

Chapter Five

I left the convent at the end of that year. Doña Maria used her influence to secure a position for me at the Clinic for the Deaf, where I was to teach sign language.

Although I knew that my decision to leave the convent was the right one, the thought of leaving a place I had come to regard as home saddened me. The only consolation was that I had some good memories to take along with me.

I was fortunate that I had been given another chance to lead a normal existence. Frightening as the prospect of my departure was, it was also exciting that I was journeying beyond the walls of the convent to find a job. I was going to be self-sufficient and independent and for the first time able to support myself.

My decision to leave the convent had obviously been prompted by Angie's abrupt departure. But it took a while for me to realise that I was merely marking time here. The convent was a safe place. It had provided me with a refuge from the world outside which held such terror for me.

Angie had probably known for a long time what had taken years for me to discover: that I was not cut out for convent life. It was why she had advised me to reconsider my intention to take my vows. Doña Maria and Mother Superior were both disappointed, but once I had made up my mind, there was no point in prolonging the agony. I realised much later that if I had entered the religious life feeling the way I did about the Church, I would always have been dissatisfied and restless and would never have done justice to the vocation.

At eighteen I moved into accommodation at the *Instituto de Medicine*. The Clinic for the Deaf was only a small part of a large medical facility. I was to teach sign language to the children who were being treated at the clinic. Doctor Aleda Emmanuel, who was in charge, eventually allowed me the freedom to introduce a few of my own programmes. Initially I worked only two days a week because there were only five children enrolled at the clinic. They were all from well-to-do Portuguese families and were born with congenital hearing impairments which could not be rectified by surgery.

This wasn't enough to keep me totally occupied and so, despite my own speech handicap, I volunteered to work at the hospital during my free days, determined to learn all that I could about the profession that had captured Rita's passion so completely.

To my delight, one of the nursing sisters allowed me to take some of the basic nursing courses. This concession was greater than I had expected and my days, divided between the clinic and the courses, were so full that there was no time for self pity. It was as though my whole life had suddenly opened up.

Rita's life, too, had undergone many changes. By the time I arrived at the Deaf Clinic, she had already started her training as a nurse at the *Instituto*. There was a serious shortage of medical staff, and Mozambican recruits were now being taken on to replace many of the Europeans who were leaving. Rita told me this was why she was one of the first black nurses to be accepted into the new intensive training programme at the faculty.

Hospital authorities were still cautious about letting down too many barriers, except of course in the case of the *assimilados*, confident that they would be loyal to the Portuguese in the event of trouble.

It seemed a bit out of character for Rita to work in a hospital which catered mainly for the Portuguese armed forces. But she seemed quite content with her work and refused to enter into a discussion about her motives. When she first started, she was relegated to many of the menial duties which prevented patient contact or the appliction of her skills, but as the shortage of skilled staff became more acute, her responsibilities increased.

I expected that eventually she would transfer elsewhere to work with her own people, but I was glad to have her so close for moral support. I even considered the possibility of moving back to live in the township with her, but Rita herself discouraged me from doing so. I remember she was sitting across the table from me when we discussed the squalid conditions there.

'You're right,' I signed. 'I can't come back to live here.'

'I told you,' she said. 'This is no place for you. You belong up on the hill. You've changed. You're not eight years old any more. Everything has changed.'

'I don't know what's happened to me. I wish things were different,' I signed.

She looked at me for quite a while, then said: 'Look, you didn't find what you were looking for at the convent and I don't think you'll find it in the township, either.'

'Come with me; we can find a place of our own in town.'

Rita shook her head. 'This is my life. I know of no other. Besides, there are other people here who need me, too.'

'When are you going to start thinking of yourself?'

She laughed and the awkwardness between us vanished.

'Be careful. The secret police are everywhere,' I signed.

'Don't worry. I'll be fine. You take care of yourself as well,' she said, squeezing my hand. 'Anyway, it's not as if you're moving to another town – now that my training is over and we're at the same hospital, we'll often see each other, I promise.'

I nodded, feeling a little more reassured.

Our departments were located in different wings of the building, but I expected to bump into her frequently. In the canteen, perhaps, or in one of the other common areas.

'I still don't understand why you're working in a hospital full of Portuguese soldiers – I know how you feel about the Portuguese,' I signed.

She did not say anything, just sat there for a long time, pensively staring at her hands. Her silence was disconcerting.

'Well,' I persisted, 'why have you taken a job at the *Instituto*?'

Preoccupied with her own thoughts, she hadn't seen my hands moving. I had to touch her arm to get her attention and repeat the question.

'Enough questions now. I don't want to talk about it.' she said, making a small impatient gesture.

'Tell me,' I insisted.

She laughed. 'Don't worry. I'm working here for the right reasons. I have done my training here and I am obligated to work at the Institute for at least two years. As far as I know it's the best surgical hospital in the country . . . especially since I eventually hope to work in the trauma unit. The experience I get there will be valuable

69

for me later on. Now come on,' she said, rousing herself, 'no more questions, eh?'

I studied her for a moment.

'We're both lucky to be here. It was a good thing that Doña Maria got you the job at the clinic. Anyway, I know you are the right person for it. You are good with the children,' Rita said.

'I like working with the children at the Clinic, but most of all I love the childrens' wards. I'm glad they allowed me to do those courses. Who knows, some day it might all come in handy.'

'*Sim*, who knows,' she echoed. 'You'd make a good nurse. Better than most. Even better than those who can speak, eh?'

I knew that there would be many problems, the most insurmountable of which was my inability to speak. How would I communicate with my patients in the event of an emergency? But not even the prospect of this could deter me as I continued in my pursuit of nursing credentials.

In the beginning, the few patients I saw were children under the age of ten. Some of the deafness in children was as a result of congenital or childhood diseases. The most common cause, however, was shrapnel injury from exploding mines.

We were seeing more and more children who, like me, had lost their ability to speak because of traumatic experiences. Some had witnessed their parents or siblings being killed, or had been forced to participate in these atrocities. For these children, too, there was little help, except in assisting them to cope with their day-to-day existence. Specialists who dealt with aberrations of the mind and spirit were virtually unknown in this remote corner of the world. They preferred the fashionable European salons.

Sign language was not a priority for the Mozambicans, either – life-threatening issues like hunger and disease were of much greater concern to them. It took weeks to persuade one of the township parents to send her child to the clinic. It was all a matter of priorities. A matter of survival.

The deaf, unlike the blind, could not show their affliction and had a much harder time begging on the streets. When they did eventually come to the clinic, it was in the hope that they would be rewarded with a meal. If they were lucky they were given something to eat; mostly, however, they went away hungry.

Rita was deeply troubled about the plight of the children. Often

70

after she had finished her shift at the hospital, she'd stop by to see me and invariably we'd discuss these concerns.

'Why is it that it is always the children who pay the price? What have they done to deserve this suffering? Where is your God?' she demanded.

For the second time in my life I heard the same question being asked about a Christian God who would allow such a travesty.

Each time I saw children turning up at the hospital or at the clinic in the township, I thought of Rita's words. They were in a dreadful condition, all either racked with disease or in the advanced stages of starvation, with the distended belly or the pale discoloured hair symptomatic of the malnourished. Their eyes staring out of sunken sockets were stark with expressions of hopelessness, limbs as brittle as twigs. Abandoned infants, whose mothers were no longer able to feed them, died before medical assistance could reach them.

This tragic situation, confined mainly to the black ghettoes and townships of the poor, went largely unnoticed amongst the European population. Doña Maria was right when she said we might as well be living on another planet.

Apart from starvation, abandonment and their dispossession, these young victims, defenceless and vulnerable, were also sacrificed at the altar of war. It was they who suffered debasing cruelty perpetrated on them by the very adults in whom they had unwittingly placed their trust.

Rita told me that there was no food in the countryside. 'Villagers have been driven from their homes and their shambas,' she said. 'I heard the other day from one of the patients that the soldiers are burning cultivated fields so that villagers will not be able to feed the freedom-fighters.'

This only brought home to me how little I knew about the economic and political realities. Life at the convent had sheltered me. In the years since I had left the orphanage, I had virtually forgotten what it was like to be hungry or cold and unwanted – I had been cut off from the mainstream of life for so long. At first it felt as if I was emerging from years of incarceration to find that the world out there had changed. I didn't know how to begin to help these children: it was like trying to use a thimble to bail out water from a sinking canoe. I prayed for them, but my faith in God supplied no ready solutions and I had to wrestle constantly to find some meaning in what was happening.

71

'We have to liberate ourselves from colonial bondage,' Rita said. Her political rhetoric about 'liberation' and 'Imperialist Forces', and the incessant talk about war worried me. Even I knew the dangers of loose talk. The secret police were everywhere.

One day, when I had signed my concern to her, she dismissed it, asking instead, 'Can't you see the difference when you visit Doña Maria? Think for yourself, Faith. Imagine what we feel like when we look up and see, on the hills overlooking the calm waters of the Indian Ocean, the mansions of our oppressors perched like glittering jewels, reminding us of our helplessness and misery.'

I signed that Doña Maria was not like that.

'They are all like that,' she said, cynically.

I didn't agree with her, of course. Doña Maria had always been very critical of the government in Lisbon. She was the one who had told me that Lisbon was responsible for all the trouble in Mozambique.

Senhor Cardoso, too, used to criticise them, bemoaning the fact that Portugal had discouraged industrial development in the colony in order to protect manufacturing interests in Portugal. He told me that agriculture was developed here only to supply cheap raw materials to Portugal. The domestic market, mainly the Portuguese population, provided only a small outlet for Mozambican manufactured products. All the cotton grown in Mozambique was sent to Portugal to be processed and manufactured. It was exactly what the British had done in India prior to independence, he told me, and for the first time I heard the name Mahatma Gandhi.

Senhor Cardoso spoke about many things as we sat in the garden together. It was he who made me aware of the fact that the railway system provided a link to Mozambique's white neighbours, and that the ports serviced the South African and Rhodesian hinterlands. He told me, too, that the railways also provided the means to export black labour to white neighbouring countries, which earned for Portugal a large chunk of its foreign exchange.

Much of what he said surprised me. The history I had learnt at the convent portrayed the colonialists as Messiahs.

It was at about this time that I met David at a dinner party at Doña Maria's house. Prior to this, I had not shown any interest in the opposite sex. I was too self-conscious and awkward, mindful that I had almost taken my vow of chastity. Until I left the convent, my experience of relationships had been mainly with women. Then, when I started work, I was too busy to be romantically involved with anyone.

I met David at a time when I was vulnerable. He was about fifteen years my senior and quite distinguished-looking. He was a tall, lean Englishman with a profusion of freckles which seemed to sprout in the sun, making him appear much darker than he actually was. In some peculiar way which I couldn't quite determine, he seemed to remind me of another man, a shadowy figure who had some dim connection to my distant past . . . a tall man who wore thick glasses.

David said little to me, but I was aware of his gaze following me around the room as Doña Maria introduced me to the rest of her guests. I was so flattered that a man of his obvious sophistication would be interested in someone like me.

Later that evening, when he came over to speak to me, I learnt that he was one of the engineers working on the Cabora Bassa Hydroelectric Power Scheme. He told me all about how this was supposed to be one of the largest man-made lakes in the world.

'The government hopes it will supply twice the amount of electricity of Egypt's Aswan Dam. Enough electricity to sell to seven or eight other countries,' he said.

I gave a non-committal shrug. Rita had told me some time ago that going ahead with the Cabora Bassa project would only increase the conflict. The government's scheme was to encourage increased settlement. There were plans afoot to bring a million Portuguese and other European immigrants to Mozambique to settle the areas around the dam.

But I was more interested in what he had to say about himself. He was an intelligent man and good company. The evening turned out to be a big success. It was the most enjoyable I'd had for a long time.

We didn't see one another again for several weeks after the party. I was rather pleasantly surprised, therefore, when David quite unexpectedly dropped by the hospital one afternoon.

He explained that he'd been away at the construction site since the day after the dinner party. 'I've been busy,' he told me, 'but I've been thinking of you.'

Rita, who was about to join me for her break outside, backed

73

away. I saw her and beckoned frantically, but she hurried away. Afterwards, she teased me about the way my face had glowed in David's presence.

Despite the fact that most of his time was spent up north at the construction site, we saw each other often. One of the bonuses accorded the expatriate professionals at the site was that they could be flown into the cities by helicopter or company plane.

We saw each other whenever he was in town and whenever I was available. This was a good arrangement – I felt relatively free and unencumbered by the relationship. My life could go on as it had done before, except that there was now someone who cared for me.

BOOK THREE

Chapter Six

On several occasions David had asked me to marry him but each time I found some excuse to put him off. Although I wanted to be with him, I wasn't yet ready for such a commitment. There was still so much I had to discover about myself, and with so many of my own needs unfulfilled, how could I hope to fill the needs of someone else?

We had been seeing each other for more than three years when I suggested to him one day that we should try living together for a while. He was incredulous that I would even suggest such an idea. I suspect that he gave my proposal a great deal of thought before agreeing.

David was a good man, interesting and knowledgeable, but very conventional and rigid, qualities which later began to irritate me. We tried to move in quietly with as little fuss as possible, but in a community where everyone knew everyone else's business, it was impossible to keep a secret.

Doña Maria was suspicious about our domestic arrangements and on several occasions asked pointed questions about where David lived and where I lived. In the end I had to tell her the truth. She expressed her disappointment in both of us, but I didn't take any of it too seriously. Those who knew me and knew of the time I had spent in the convent, were surprised too.

Although I wasn't openly rebellious, I had decided that I didn't really care about what others thought. There were, after all, aspects of my life and my personality that few people understood. Much of who I was had been forged in those early years under intolerable conditions, without complaint. With no voice to cry out, there was a slow build-up of rage and resentment which manifested itself in my rebellious attitude towards the Church and its omniscient, invasive control which dictated its own brand of morality.

I was pleased when David and I discovered a small flat in the older part of town, on the *Avenida Vinte e Quatro de Julho*. In this part of the city life was much easier. The earthiness of the population around us indicated their love of life. It was the type of environment in which passions were raw and tempers quick.

At times I wondered if David enjoyed living on the fringes of the old quarter as much as I did. The conventional side to his nature must have been appalled at the way I had decided to disregard conventions. For the time being, however, the arrangement with David coming home only on his days off, suited both of us well.

For the first time in my life, I felt safe and confident about my abilities. I didn't want anything to change, but underlying this semblance of security was the deep-rooted fear of giving too much of myself and in the end being abandoned again. I tried to prepare myself for this outcome by erecting barriers; walls which not only kept others out, but which also locked in all the old fears and anxieties.

Our flat was at the back of the apartment building, on the third floor, overlooking an inner courtyard that was full of energetic life and drama. Here nobody ever closed their curtains. It was a vicarious existence. On hot, steamy nights when sleep seemed impossible, windows were flung wide open and cooking odours mingled with the smell of sweat. I used to lie in the dark listening to voices raised in argument or stand by the window in the darkened room, looking out into neighbouring apartments where bodies glistened with the sheen of frenzied love-making.

This was the nature of life in the tropics. It had always been this way. David yearned for England, but Mozambique was in my blood. It pulsed through my veins with a rhythm of its own even when I grew weary of it and when it sapped my strength. During those hot, torpid days when the air seemed too heavy to breathe, David spoke fondly of England and the cool evening breezes which rustled the lace curtains in his mother's living room.

There were times when I was torn between visions of David's temperate homeland and the steamy lustiness of life here, where passions flared without warning and emotions had an immediacy about them that all the cool English breezes could not extinguish. There were so many layers of existence here, each revealing a little more about the nature of the people.

One evening as I gazed out over the courtyard, the air thick with the smell of wood-smoke, I noticed a child sitting on the doorstep at the house with the blue door, across the way from me. The child was Sofia, daughter of a woman known only by the name of 'Crazy Bella'. For a while I watched her amusing herself with a game, tossing a pebble into the air while picking another out of the circle. The sight of the girl transported me back to São Lucas, reminding me of how I had waited in vain for Lodiya.

When the child spotted her mother coming up the stairs, her whole face lit up. No matter how tired Bella was when she got back at night, she was always overjoyed to see her daughter and swept her up into her arms, showering her with kisses. A single tear gathered in the corner of my eye. In it dissolved an image of a young girl lying on a floor in a dark room.

As the sounds of the courtyard slowly receded, swallowed up by the approaching darkness, my mind ballooned with images from the past. They marched through my thoughts like soldiers on parade. Some of them were crystal clear, others faded, like old photographs. A few of them were splintered fragments of a larger picture. Disjointed images of a gentle face, long blond hair, the fresh scent of lavender against a breast, the soft underside of a woman's arm, the sweet sound of laughter, the smell of antiseptic; a black face wrinkled and marked; Lodiya's face with its butterfly scar, the smell of wood-smoke, fresh dung and decaying vegetation.

Scenes and snippets of conversation buzzed around in my head. Images came to mind of burning huts, faces and scorpion-like creatures entangled amongst vines in the dark, silent jungle. And all around was the oppressive silence, sucking me into its vacuum.

Then as suddenly as these images had appeared they were gone. They vanished like smoke into air. I turned away from the window. I didn't know what all of this meant. Was I going to recover my memory? Was this the first sign? Did it mean that my voice would return?

I was desperate to hold on to what I had uncovered, but all that remained were the same few tantalising images from those early years which had endured and become part of the tapestry of my life. Even these seemed so fragile that I was afraid of losing them.

David told me once that the flat reflected my personality. The front room was an earthy room with straw mats, African artifacts and brass ornaments picked up at the bazaar. For me it stirred remembrances buried deep in my subconsious. The flashes of recollection I had with regular frequency left me confused. I couldn't always perceive whether they were connected with dreams or with reality. There were strong feelings, haunting memories which never crystallised.

I experienced a familiarity about everything, even the painting of a seascape at sunset, which I had done and hung in a simple black wooden frame, seemed as though I had known it all my life. I discovered later that it wasn't the painting which had aroused this feeling in me, but the frame, similar to the ones which my mother had used for her paintings.

The room was an eclectic mixture of baskets which hung like grapes from the ceiling, wooden masks with grotesque expressions leering down from the walls, Indian silks, and cushions which were strewn on the floor. Nothing matched. Like my own life, here, too, bits and pieces had been thrown together.

I sat down on one of the cushions on the floor and drawing my knees up to my chest, buried my face. Once again I could see Lodiya walking away from me. In my mind's eye I saw the old tree with its brittle branches oozing globs of gum. I lowered my knees and curled up on the floor amidst the pillows, warm tears trailing down my cheeks.

After six years at the clinic I was doing a great deal more than just the simple programme initiated when I first started there. I tried to encourage referrals for black children as much as possible. At one time there were four Mozambican children enrolled in the programme, but then two of them stopped coming. I was still called in regularly to do shifts on the ward. Most of the work involved fairly menial duties which did not require verbal skills, but I didn't mind, I enjoyed being on the wards.

Rita, who had at first expressed enthusiasm about the Clinic for the Deaf, became critical of it, saying it had become nothing more than a white elephant catering to the whims of the Europeans.

'You can't sit there in your classroom, waiting for the children to come to you. They will never come because they don't understand what it is you are trying to do,' she told me.

I had noticed that in the past few months Rita had become increasingly concerned about the fate of the children. We had all heard rumours about them being kidnapped in remote villages. But no one seemed able to substantiate these stories. We heard that in some villages there were no children left between the ages of ten and fifteen. It was so bizarre that even those of us who had witnessed some very strange occurrences found this story quite incredible.

I had told her years ago about the children at the orphanage and the stories about them being carted away in the middle of the night and how we later discovered that some of them had been sold to farmers as slave labour. Somehow the orphanage was connected, but I didn't quite know to what extent. There had to be another, more sinister force at work.

'Those children in the orphanage were taken off the street by the police and the soldiers. Maybe the government is involved?' I signed.

She was silent for a moment. 'Maybe,' she said, 'but I'm going to find out for sure. I can't believe that all these children are disappearing and no one knows anything about it.'

It was difficult to believe that this was going on right under our noses.

'So, what do you think, eh?'

I shook my head. I had no idea what was going on. Of course I did not have access to information the way Rita had. At the Clinic for the Deaf, I was fairly isolated, except when I was working at the hospital, where there were always stories going around.

Rita, who had long since worked her way up beyond the menial tasks, was actually nursing on the trauma unit and was in a position to find out more. The unit was the busiest floor of all where most of the Portuguese soldiers, crippled by shrapnel from land-mines or shot by sophisticated Russian-made weapons, were treated. This was where they came after a quick amputation in one of the field hospitals.

In many of the remote outposts staff were recruited from outside the medical discipline. The lack of medical expertise was evident. At one of the field hospitals the chief surgeon was a dentist.

Staff regularly complained that by the time victims reached the hospital, it was too late to correct any damage. The Institute was expected to heal not only the broken bodies, but also the broken spirits of men often too young to understand the extent and significance of what had been done to them.

'I feel so sorry for them,' I signed to Rita as we watched the endless flow of injured.

'In the bush our people are fighting under worse conditions,' she said, irritated by my comment. 'They have nothing to relieve the pain. There are no antibiotics or anti-tetanus toxoid, or serum for snakebite. Bandages and antiseptic are in short supply. In the bush there are no facilities for blood transfusions. How do you think our men feel?'

I had no answer for her. We were all affected in one way or another.

I remember one day witnessing a commotion in the emergency ward. A young soldier about to be discharged had gone berserk, ripping equipment out of sockets and smashing it against the wall. He then turned on the staff who were attempting to subdue him. I was there with one of the children from the clinic and rushed over to assist the nurse who was bleeding from a gash on her brow. For my trouble I received a glancing blow to the side of the head. Eventually it took three burly orderlies to restrain the soldier.

The gash on the nurse's brow required fifteen sutures. My injury was minor compared to hers, but as I sat in the canteen later that morning, nursing a splitting headache, it didn't feel that insignificant. Matron had instructed me to see a doctor, but at the time I hadn't bothered about it.

I was sitting in the canteen having my coffee, replaying the emergency room scene in my mind when Doctor Juan Guerra joined me at my table. I was so preoccupied that I didn't realise anyone was there until he spoke.

'May I?' he asked.

I glanced up and distractedly gestured to the vacant chair.

'I heard what happened,' he said. 'How's your head?'

'Throbbing,' I signed.

'You should have it looked at.'

He sat down and I watched as he unwrapped his sandwich. It wasn't only the attack that had unsettled me, it was also the sight of the young victim of a land-mine explosion who had arrived a short while before the incident.

The boy couldn't have been any older than eighteen. Rita told me later that he was rushed in by helicopter because his injuries were so extensive. His right hand was a pulpy mess, his right leg torn off below the knee. The mutilation was all the more grisly because the camouflage suit had been ripped open all the way to his waist to expose his wounds. I could tell at a glance that he might not make it through surgery.

Juan Guerra, sitting so impassively across the table from me, eating his sandwich, had assisted Doctor Valdez with the operation. The patient had died a few hours later. Someone had suggested that the attack on the ward had been triggered by the news of this soldier's death.

Juan was speaking. He sensed my preoccupation and paused.

'Sorry I'm talking too much.' He smiled wryly as I glanced up. 'Still can't get over it, can you? I remember my first experience with war casualties quite clearly. It's not easy when one is so full of idealism. You have to get used to it though. If you don't, you might as well pull the covers over your head and not bother to come out. This is reality. The reality of war.'

Preoccupied, I stirred my coffee.

'Being caught in the cross-fire the way you were today, is just one of the hazards of our job,' he continued, biting into his sandwich. 'There's nothing wrong with being compassionate, except when it interferes with your ability to make decisions. Sometimes it's better to be like a machine,' he said.

I looked at him steadfastly. The eyes gazing back at me were coldly dispassionate.

Rita had told me about her first experience in the trauma unit. Her gruesome initiation into the brutality of war had occurred when a young peasant boy was brought in, almost disembowelled by an exploding land-mine. She had blamed the government soldiers. Juan had argued that the rebels were just as responsible for the tragedies because they unearthed mines buried by the army and reused them.

Ultimately it didn't matter which side was culpable. The very nature of the act implied a brutality which went way beyond comprehension. I soon learnt that in those wards, amidst the grim reality of the war, was revealed the darker side of human nature. Even the deaf and the mute were not immune to the violence – some of the black children handicapped already by losing a limb or two, were maimed a second time.

Once when I was filling in as an aide on the children's ward, a young boy had come in with his hand blown off by a mine. He was playing in a field. All over the world children play in fields. Here, however, it costs them their lives.

It infuriated Rita that the brutal conflict fought in the bush, away from the cities, was an aspect of life which few tourists ever saw. Travel brochures with glossy pictures of blue oceans and white sandy beaches extolled the virtues of a holiday in Mozambique – a tropical paradise with miles and miles of unspoiled beaches. Soon those beaches, too, would be spoilt with the deadly toys of war.

Despite the festering wounds, the gangrenous stumps and the permanently damaged psyches altered by the inhuman effects of the war, on the surface things appeared to be quite normal. This facet of life in Mozambique bordered on lunacy.

Amidst all this madness I had somehow managed to preserve an island of tranquillity which David shared with me. A few days after the incident with the soldier in the emergency ward, I was standing by the kitchen sink in my flat, thinking of the hospital and my conversation with Juan Guerra.

David, wearing a robe, came from the bathroom, padding bare-foot across the floor. He took my hand and led me to the sitting room, where he collapsed amongst the cushions, drawing me down beside him. I was tired and moody and evaded his embrace. On the ward they cynically referred to this weariness as battle fatigue. Embattled, that's exactly how I felt that day.

'Is something wrong?' David asked.

I gave a small careless shrug and indicated that I was going to make coffee.

'Don't worry about coffee. Sit down and tell me what's bothering you.'

But I was already half way across the room.

'Need any help?' he asked, sauntering over to the record player.

He nodded in time to the music. I was out of sight behind the folding screen which separated the front room from the kitchen. Distractedly, I listened to the music, watching him through a crack in the screen. The twang of guitar chords swooped through the room, jarring me out of my reverie. David returned to the cushions, lying back and listening to the music. I returned with the coffee and handed him a cup. Instead of sitting down I went around the room, tidying up, plumping up cushions and moving things around.

Finally, when there was nothing more to shuffle around or shake loose, I went over to the window to open the curtains. Summer sunlight streamed in. 'We had quite a commotion at work the other day,' I signed.

'What happened?' he asked, lazily watching me from under lowered lids.

'One of the soldiers went berserk. He tried to kill one of the nurses.'

'Why?'

'Combat fatigue.' I deliberately refrained from mentioning the blow to my head.

'I don't like you working under those conditions,' he said.

I shrugged. 'Things like that happen. I work in a hospital.'

With a proprietorial air, he patted the cushion next to him.

I sank down beside him.

'Faith, I've told you; you don't have to work at the hospital. Working with those deaf and dumb children is a depressing job. You'll never get over your own handicap if you stay there,' he said.

'The war is what's depressing,' I signed.

He shook his head, his expression reflecting his disapproval. 'There'd be enough for you to do at home. I'll be coming into town more regularly now that I don't have to be at the site all the time. Maybe I can work out of the office here. We'll be able to get married then.' He paused, a little hopefully.

But I gave no response.

'At least I hope you'll consider it this time. I'm not comfortable with this loose living arrangement,' he continued.

I could see where this discussion was heading and so I nodded absently, only so that we would not have to explore the subject again. I was tired. It was as if we had already beaten this subject of marriage to death.

'If we get married you won't ever have to work. You'll be a lady of leisure, admired by all those poor slobs who have to go out to work every day. You deserve to be spoilt,' he said gazing at me. 'I care for you, my dear, and I've done everything I can possibly do to show you just how much. Look,' he joked, 'I even learnt sign language so we could communicate.'

I was in no mood for his jokes and returned his gaze coldly. His remark about my work had irritated me. 'I enjoy the work. The children challenge me. I want to keep on working,' I signed.

'You're just being obstinate about this. Faith, you should think about others . . .'

I drew my knees up, hugged them and shut off his voice as I pressed my face down. My hair fell to either side, exposing the back of my neck and he reached out to touch me. I was tense and tried to remain motionless as his fingers traced the strawberry mark on my bare neck.

'You have to deal with your past. It's the only way for you to recover your voice,' he said. 'I want to help you.'

I looked up, drew my fingers through my hair and covered the back of my neck. He ignored my irritated reaction.

'I'm offering you a way out of this hell. England is safe. You need that kind of environment if you ever hope to recover your speech. Believe me, once the war escalates, someone like you won't survive out here on her own.'

'What do you mean someone like me?' My hands agitatedly flew as I signed. 'I survived long before you came into my life.'

'Don't get me wrong, my dear. I know that things haven't been easy for you. All that stuff about your past – your inability to speak, being shuffled around from one corner to the other.' He paused; he could see from the way my jaw was set that I was angry. 'Look, I'm not the enemy. I just want to help you. I've talked to a psychologist friend of mine in London. He's very good. He wants to meet you.'

I was dismayed by this comment and furious that he had presumed to make arrangements behind my back.

David gave a long-suffering sigh and tried to draw me back into the circle of his arms, but I was as stiff as a board, my hands clutched between my knees. He sensed that the wall had gone up between us.

'I thought you loved me?' he said.

I drew my legs up to my chest again.

He withdrew his arm and leaned back against the cushions.

'What are your plans for today?' he asked.

'I'm going to the township,' I signed.

'I can't understand you. You have a life here with me; why on earth do you always insist on going back to the township? There's nothing there for you any more.'

Seething, I turned on him. 'I have a past there. The only distant past that I can remember clearly, and it was full of love and happiness.'

'In that stinking hell-hole?'

I nodded vehemently.

84

'You lived there. You know what it was like. You also made a conscious decision not to go back there.'

'I also made a conscious decision to help out at the township clinic whenever I could.'

He glanced away. He never did like the idea of me working at the township clinic with Rita, even though it was for only a couple of days a month. How could I explain my burden of guilt and responsibility? I grasped his arm, forcing him to look at me.

'For the first time in my life I'm living a normal life. I know what I want to do. I feel needed and useful. I won't have anyone telling me how to run my life. It's *my* life.'

David got up and went out of the room.

I remained on the floor, hugging my knees, my expression agonised. A wrenching pain somewhere inside me seemed to fill my whole being.

A while later David slammed out of the house.

For a long time I sat there listening to the silence. I felt not only the dreadful emptiness of a past I could not remember, or one which I wanted to forget, but also a physical emptiness which had spread like a gaping hole inside of me.

Later that afternoon I left the flat and went for a long walk along the beach front. I must have walked for miles. Several ships were anchored in the bay, waiting to get into the harbour. The ocean was so calm. The coastline was famed for its beautiful beaches. One could wade out for almost three hundred yards on some of the beaches and the water would only be deep enough to cover your head.

I sat down and watched the sun dip into the Indian Ocean, its rays lending copper tints to the calm surface of the water. On the beach the waves bubbled and frothed, lapping against the shore, shunting pebbles and forking around obstacles, to scallop the sand with foam edges, before washing back to sea. In their wake they left behind a trail of slimy green seaweed.

So much beauty and so much destruction, I thought, and all of it happening as an indifferent world turns its back.

Chapter Seven

'David, *please*. Help us to find out about the children,' I signed. He looked at me questioningly. 'Some of your contacts might know something,' I continued.

David, back home for a few days after an absence of two months, was standing at the window, gazing at me in astonishment. He didn't say anything for a while and I felt a bit foolish because I had no real plan, and had no idea how he could help. I was desperate, though, and would have resorted to anything.

'Dammit, Faith! What do you expect me to do?' he demanded.

'Help us to find out what they're doing with the children.'

'Who are *they*? Who are you talking about?'

'We think government forces are . . .'

'*We*! *We*! Who's *we*?' he interjected.

'Rita and I.'

'For God's sake, Faith! Are you mad? Can't you let it be? Don't get involved in any of this. Please. It's dangerous, especially with the way things are right now. The secret police are everywhere.' He stood before me, arms spread, appealing to my common sense.

'I thought you dealt with them all the time,' I signed.

'All the time . . .?' he asked. There was an unfamiliar harshness in his tone.

I winced and glanced away.

'What do you think I do?' he asked. He studied me for a moment and shook his head as though exasperated. 'Well, what do you think I do?' he asked again.

'You have contacts with the PIDE,' I signed, stubbornly.

'That's part of my job, dammit! They drop in at the site or at the office whenever they want. What am I supposed to do?' he asked. 'I get reams of paperwork from them; bulletins about the war, new regulations, new directives. My company has shifted all these responsibilities on to my shoulders. It's not just the scientific stuff, it's all the other crap as well.'

'All I'm asking for is your help. Children don't just vanish into thin air.'

'What do you expect me to do?' he asked and walked away to the sideboard where we kept a few bottles of liquor. He poured himself a drink. I watched in silence. I had noticed he had started drinking quite excessively lately. I tried to calm down.

'Why is it so important for you to know about the children?' he asked.

I rolled my eyes in mock frustration. Irritated, he turned away and headed for the kitchen. I followed him.

'Is what I'm asking really that difficult?' I demanded.

'Yes!'

My brows arched, sceptically.

'For God's sake, what do you think I do all day long?' he asked.

'I turned on the tap. He reached over to turn it off.

'OK,' he cried. 'That's it! If you think my life is so easy, come with me. I'll take you around with me for one day. Just one day! You can see for yourself what I have to put up with.'

It was a stupid idea and I indicated so.

'Dammit, you're not going to get out of it that easily,' he said, gripping my wrist until it hurt.

I looked at him calmly. He released my wrists and with an apologetic grimace, said he was sorry.

'All right,' I signed, tossing the dishcloth into the sink. 'As it happens I have the day off on Monday. I'll come with you. Perhaps *I'll* be able to find out about the children.' With that I strode out of the kitchen into the sitting room.

He followed me, shaking his head as though I were some incorrigible child and he watched as I distractedly kicked the cushions scattered on the floor.

'Faith . . .'

'I thought you'd be able to help,' I signed. I was angry and distressed by what I thought was his lack of concern and interest in an important issue.

'I hate dealing with the secret police. They're unpredictable. If you're not with them, you're against them.'

'Well?' I asked.

'Well what?'

'Are you with them?'

My question startled him. 'What kind of question is that?' he demanded, his irritation flaring again.

I sat cross-legged on the floor amongst the cushions.

'I don't know what's got into you,' he said. 'I don't have time for all this cloak-and-dagger stuff. It's crazy enough trying to do business here.' He paused, running his hand through his hair in exasperation. He looked up, and caught me watching him intently. 'I'm sorry,' he muttered. 'Everything's such a mess. You can never get hold of people. It's either lunchtime, siesta time, or else you have to pay to grease the wheels. I'm fed up with having things postponed until tomorrow when they ought to have been done yesterday!'

He paused, threw his hands up, and came to sit on the floor beside me, leaning back against the cushions. 'It's a bit uncharacteristic of me to lose my head like that, isn't it? I've been feeling out of sorts lately.'

I raised my shoulder in a noncommittal gesture.

'It's this country and the way it's all beginning to fall apart. Things are definitely coming to a head. The escudo is worthless outside the country. None of the contractors want to be paid in Mozambican currency. So what are we going to do? The government in Lisbon doesn't seem to give a damn about any of this. All they care about is having the construction completed on schedule. I don't know how they expect us to pay for imported equipment without money.' He fell silent, staring morosely at his hands.

Somehow the senselessness of the war, the brutality, the poverty and the shortages were hardships we had all learnt to endure. Drawn into this way of life, we soon forgot what things were like before.

In the past few months David had become increasingly preoccupied with going home. He had tried to persuade me to go with him. But I had no intention of leaving. Lately we had seemed to be drawn into disagreements about nonsensical issues.

Once when we were having an argument he said, 'Just when I think I know you, you turn into a stranger. One moment you're there, the Faith I know, and then I blink and you're some moody, withdrawn creature who bears no resemblance to the woman I love. I can deal with your nightmares, and all the other terrors that haunt you. I can even take your silence, but what I can't take is the way you suddenly turn everything off. Sometimes when we're making love you lie so perfectly still as if my touch had turned you to stone.'

How could I explain my ambivalent feelings toward him, when I didn't understand them myself? David's hand caressed my back, interrupting my thoughts, making me shudder. He jerked his hand away as though singed by a flame. Whatever had gone wrong between us had crept up so insidiously that neither of us had been aware of it.

On the Monday, as agreed, I accompanied him to the office. I had hoped to get out of my silly promise to him. But David was not the type to take agreements lightly. One's word was one's honour.

When we arrived at his office building, the doors were still locked. He suggested a cup of coffee at a small café around the corner.

It was another beautiful day. The sun was bright even at that early hour and I rifled through my purse looking for my sunglasses. Despite the feeling of promise in the air, all around us there was evidence that the country had gone to pot. I wondered how David would manage without all the little luxuries needed to make his life bearable.

Even Juan had started to complain about the state of the economy and especially about all the shortages. For those of us who had never had much, it didn't matter. When I told him that, he laughed uproariously, calling me naive.

The café was a grubby little hole-in-the-wall with a fly-speckled picture of the president of Portugal prominently displayed on the main wall, a grimy flag draped around it. We sat in upright wooden chairs. The president, with his benevolent expression, stared down at us. Neither of us was much in the mood for conversation and so we sat in silence. The waitress, a hard-faced young Portuguese girl, brought our coffee. She placed David's cup down with a careless clatter, slopping coffee into the saucer and on to the newspaper, staining it. I saw him wince as he glanced at the cup and the paper. I smiled; it was an old paper with old stains and old news.

He asked for a bread roll. She brought it over, disdainfully dropping it on to the plate before him. There was no sugar or butter on the table and she gave him a surly glance when he called her over to point out the omission.

She was full of resentment, her bony hip jutting out impudently as she waited for him to finish his complaint before sauntering off, returning with a chipped sugar bowl. In the heat, the butter which had been standing out all night had become a greasy blob skidding in a layer of oil on the bottom of the dish.

I waited for him to react, but he didn't. I couldn't understand why he had waited for her to return with the sugar. Why hadn't he just got up and marched off?

'This whole country is going to the dogs,' he muttered.

The dogs of war, I thought.

The waitress stood at our table, insolently waiting as he added one carefully rounded teaspoon of sugar to the coffee and stirred it, the spoon clanging noisily against the side of the cup.

David had told me that he often came here for coffee. Why, I wondered, would he keep coming back to this place – a greasy little dive tucked away around a corner? The owner, a loud-mouthed, fat, cigar-smoking slob, cared nothing about the service he provided. The food was the least attractive feature of the place. Then why did David keep coming? Was it convenience, because it was close to his company's office, or was it habit? I settled on the latter.

The other patrons stared dull-wittedly out into the street, as addicted to sameness as he. Were we so weakened by an incompetent system that we could no longer function? Rita had once said that the system had worn us down; had made us acquiescent. She was right.

I drew the paper closer. The front page was filled with reports of the war.

'The war will end soon,' David said. 'It has to. It'll either run out of steam and grind to an unexpected halt, or else the tides of fortune will turn against this colonial power. A day that we will, no doubt, all regret.' David continued to stir his coffee. 'I wish you'd make a decision about coming to England with me,' he said.

I glanced up from reading the news.

'David, I think you should go home to England,' I signed. 'I've told you before, I can't go with you. This is my home.'

'Aren't you war-weary yet?' he asked. 'I know I am. And don't think things will be any better if the rebels come to power. The way things are going now is a good indication of what they'll be like later. You'll have one faction fighting another; there'll never be any peace and stability. The people here are still too traditional – their

90

way of life is quite incompatible with development. It'll take years for them to catch up with the developed countries and when they do they'll be outstripped again and there will be the same imbalance between the needs of the people and the aspirations of the politicians. If you look at the abysmal record elsewhere, you'll see that Africa is dominated by dictatorships, all notorious for their excesses and their lack of integrity and humanity. You mark my words, one day, weakened by war, corruption and famine, we will see Africa recolonised by new masters.'

'You're wrong, David. Dead wrong. I think countries in Africa will survive as independent states.'

'You're too idealistic, Faith. You've spent too much of your time dreaming behind walls. I'm out in the real world. I see what's going on.'

'Where the hell do you think I am?' I demanded. 'I'm on the front line, David. I see evidence of what happens in the real world.'

'I'm not talking about counting bodies. I'm talking about crawling around in the sewer with all the rats . . .' He shuddered and averted his gaze. 'Anyway, let's not get into another argument. I'm tired.'

'I still say you're wrong about the Mozambicans, David. I know them. You forget, I'm one of them.'

'I haven't forgotten. You won't let me. But when it comes to the crunch and they have to choose between you and one of their own, you'll find yourself on the outside. That's why I want you to come away with me.'

'David, colonialism is a white man's concept. For the blacks it means slavery, it means genocide, it means the raping and pillaging of their nation and their culture. As for the white man's concept of morality and humanity, I can tell you that it hasn't impressed me at all. I've encountered more morality and humanity amongst blacks than I have amongst whites. And I've seen both sides of the coin.'

I thought about David's world-weary cynicism and wondered what he really stood for. I studied him from under my lowered lids. I thought I knew him, but it seemed I didn't know him at all. David glanced at his watch and indicated that we should be on our way.

'I have a few things to do at the office. If you like you can go off shopping and I'll meet you back there at twelve o'clock. I have a meeting at lunchtime. I'd like you to meet this fellow.'

91

I nodded. I didn't particularly feel like sitting around the office while he caught up with his work. I had enough errands of my own, and since a day off was a rarity, I was pleased to get out of at least part of my silly obligation. I had only gone along with his plan because I had hoped that the person he was meeting would shed some light on the fate of the children.

As we left the café, our chairs scraped back noisily. A few of the patrons glanced up with weary eyes, but realising that it was nothing of consequence, they slouched back into their chairs.

David threw a few coins on the table to pay for the untouched cup of coffee and the bread roll. He waited for me to gather my bag and my hat.

'See you at noon,' he said as we parted company, he going to the office and I to finish some errands.

At about half-past twelve, David and I arrived at the restaurant. Wynand van der Berg was waiting. 'He's a South African trucker, contracted to transport raw materials to the dam site,' David said as we approached the table where the other man was waiting.

I was disappointed. I had hoped that David would be meeting someone more consequential. David sensed my feelings but said nothing.

When van der Berg saw David, he grinned broadly. He grasped David's hand in his large paw.

'How've you been, man?' the South African demanded.

'Good. How about you?' David asked.

'First class, man. First class,' van der Berg said enthusiastically.

David drew me into the circle of conversation. 'This is my fiancée, Faith,' he said, introducing us.

'Faith, like in faith, hope and . . .?' he asked, gesturing with a flourish of his meaty hand.

We sat down, van der Berg adjusting his crotch. He took a packet of cigarettes from his pocket and ripped it open.

'My last packet,' he said regretfully, offering David and me a cigarette. We both declined. 'South Afiican,' he said. 'Smoking Portuguese cigarettes is like smoking lettuce leaves.'

Apart from a few comments directed at me, most of van der Berg's conversation was with David. We were sitting on the patio of a restaurant on the *Avenida de Janeiro*. It was a busy street and full of wonderful sights. I was quite content to sit and watch the parade of people.

'So, my friend,' van der Berg asked, 'have you been staying out of trouble?'

'Uh huh. What about you?' David replied.

The South African laughed. 'Nothing new with me. I just wish they'd drop a bomb on those bastards. Send the whole effing lot of them to Kingdom Come. So, what's happening, man?'

Startled, my face red with indignation, I flashed an outraged glance at van der Berg. David was embarrassed. He placed a restraining hand over mine and smiled with a look which pleaded for indulgence.

Van der Berg puffed on his cigarette, watching David and me through wraiths of smoke.

'I hear there was some trouble at the site the other day,' he said. This time his glance nervously flitted around the tables.

'Nothing serious. We lost some scaffolding.'

'I heard the bleddy rebels blew it up,' said the other man. 'Christ, I don't know why they don't blow those fuckers right out of the jungle.' He paused and glanced at me, grimacing apologetically.

'Everything's under control,' David muttered, his glance shifting from me back to the other man.

'If those bastards lay one hand on my trucks, I'll show them which side is up,' van der Berg snarled unpleasantly.

'That's exactly what I want to talk to you about, Wynand. Your trucks. We have a deal, remember?'

'Of course we have a deal,' van der Berg laughed mirthlessly.

'Then why is it that you're running behind schedule?'

'Spare parts, man. Spare parts.'

David lapsed into thoughtful silence for a few moments. Eventually he said, 'I can't have your trucks breaking down all the time.'

Van der Berg opened his mouth, but David put up a hand to silence him. 'The delays are becoming too costly.'

'Look, man, it's not my fault. I've had a helluva lot of trouble getting parts for the trucks. The other day we had to fly them in from Jo'burg.'

'We have an agreement, Wynand. And there is nothing in our agreement about the consideration of spare parts. You transport. We build. The maintenance of the trucks is *your* concern. I don't want to hear about it. I just want to see them rolling in with material from the docks.'

'Oh, come on. Don't be such a fucking heartless Englishman,' he said grinning. 'OK, I promise no more delays. But it's not my fault that the trucks keep breaking down on those shitty roads. There's no let up, not enough time to get the trucks serviced properly. Supplies keep coming. Trucks have been rolling twenty-four hours a day from the docks.'

I had lost interest in Wynand van der Berg and watched as a begger with atrophied legs crossed in a lotus position scooted over on his skateboard. David glanced up. The beggar caught David's eye and slowly wheeled over to our table where he produced a pair of lottery tickets from a grubby pouch.

'Buy one, *bwana*,' he pleaded. He was an old man. I saw a look of quiet desperation in his eyes. He tried to smile, but a nervous tick distorted his features.

Van de Berg sneered unpleasantly. Intimidated, the beggar lowered his glance, his posture slumping into an attitude of deference.

'*Voertsek!*' van der Berg muttered as the man reached up to tug at David's sleeve.

The old man hesitated, small, lizard-like eyes darting anxiously. *Bwana*, please . . .'

I opened my wallet.

Van der Berg half-rose out of his chair, cursing loudly.

David placed a restraining hand on his arm. 'Sit down,' he said sharply. The South African sat down.

I took ten escudoes out of my wallet and handed it to the beggar, who promptly kissed my feet. Startled, I drew my feet away. The beggar clapped his hands in gratitude and backed off.

Van der Berg shook his head disapprovingly. 'You shouldn't have done that. It's people like you who spoil them.'

I gave him a contemptuous look which I hoped would silence him. David sat back, studying me and as I met his gaze I understood what he meant about the people he came into contact with. I shook my head, shrugged my shoulders and turned away from him.

'What's wrong with her?' he asked David.

'Your bad manners,' David said.

'Man, I'm sorry if your lady friend is annoyed, but that's the way I am.'

'That's no excuse,' David remarked.

'Damned cripples,' van der Berg muttered under his breath as David and I exchanged glances.

'You should know,' David said to him. 'In this country you can be whole one minute and crippled the next. It's always a matter of being in the wrong place at the wrong time.'

Van der Berg remained silent, gloomily watching the passers-by.

'Let's eat,' David said. 'What would you like, Faith?' he asked me.

I studied the menu in silence. I wasn't particularly hungry and was searching for something light. I thought I'd much rather go home, but I'd got myself into this fix with David and now I had to put up with my exasperation.

I glanced up. David was looking at the menu, but van der Berg was leaning back in his chair, eyes screwed up against the sun. His shirt, stained from previous meals, stretched across his bulging midriff. The straining buttons revealed patches of soft white flesh gleaming like the underbelly of a fish.

'I'm going to order,' he said. He glanced around at the mounds of prawn-shells piled on plates at the tables just vacated. 'How about some prawns?' he asked.

'Fine,' David said as a waiter appeared.

'I'll get it,' van der Berg said, placing a puffy hand on David's arm. 'Waiter!' he called. 'What are you having little lady?' he asked as a black waiter strolled over.

'I want to get the hell out of here,' I signed to David.

David grinned and returned his attention to his menu.

'I'll get some wine and peri-peri prawns,' van der Berg said. He snapped his fingers at the waiter. '*You bring um peri-peri prawns. You bring uno bottle vino. Uno bottle cerveja. Quick, quick.*'

'Too late. Lunch over,' the waiter said blandly.

'*What he got um on that plate?*' van der Berg asked, indicating a plate that one of the other waiters had just brought out.

The man shrugged indifferently. He saw David's embarrassed look. 'I bring for *you* peri-peri prawns, *bwana*,' he said in Portuguese, glancing pointedly at David.

'What did he say?' van der Berg demanded.

'Why don't you learn to speak Portuguese?' David asked when the waiter had left.

'He understood me just fine,' van der Berg said. 'You want to bet that he would have brought the prawns anyway?' He paused and wagged a finger. 'If he hadn't I'd have kicked his arse.'

David shook his head wryly. 'Trying to change people like you,

Wynand, is like trying to turn a thirsty donkey away from the sight of water.'

With that remark ringing in my ears, I picked up my hat and bag and left the restaurant.

A few days after that lunch meeting, van der Berg's body was discovered at the docks, his throat slit. Although there was a great deal of speculation about his death, police claimed thugs were responsible. David suggested that the PIDE might have been behind the killing.

In my opinion, however, Wynand van der Berg had probably opened his big insulting mouth once too often, and had got exactly what he deserved.

Chapter Eight

The war continued. Each day saw a flood of new recruits arriving from Portugal, making it increasingly dangerous for women to be on the streets by themselves at night. Unlike their Portuguese counterparts, Mozambican women went about unchaperoned.

There were uniformed men everywhere: in the parks, along the beaches, in the cafés, in theatres. Even the shy new conscripts strutted like peacocks. Unable to afford the services of prostitutes, they daringly accosted young women, even those who were accompanied. In the meantime, the number of sex-related crimes soared.

For many of the young recruits, it was like going from one boiling pot into another. Encouraged by the government in Portugal, the poor and dispossessed, eager for a better life, came in droves. They left behind friends and family for the promise of a better life.

They were no longer on the lowest rung of the social and economic ladder – in Mozambique, the blacks were much worse off than the poorest of the poor in Portugal.

At first glance, life in the city seemed astonishingly calm. Beyond that first impression, though, one became aware of an undercurrent of tension created by the presence of uniformed men and convoys of army trucks rattling through the streets.

David had returned to the construction site and I was actually glad to be on my own again.

'How come David left so early?' Rita asked.

I shrugged non-committally and went on with my work, and after a few moments I became aware of her intent gaze and looked up from what I was doing.

'What?' I asked her.

'Something's wrong,' she said. 'I can see it.'

97

'It's David,' I signed. 'I don't know what to do about him.'

'He's an Englishman,' she said knowingly.

'What do you know about Englishmen?' I signed.

'Albertina, the nurse on the women's ward, told me. She says they're cold, like fish. All talk, no action.'

In my opinion, Albertina wasn't much of an expert on the subject. Yet, as I thought about it afterwards, David's most irritating feature seemed to be captured in the essence of her remark. David believed in discussion. Everything had to be thrashed out. Spontaneity with him was non-existent. He had beaten it to death.

'Maybe you're looking for a father-figure,' Rita said with characteristic perception.

This remark provoked more thought than I would admit to.

I was recalling my conversation with Rita as I walked to the bus stop one afternoon, shaking my head in amusement, when a car drew up alongside me. Startled, I leaped out of the way. I turned to deal sharply with the driver of the vehicle and found, instead, that it was Juan, the young doctor, following in his jeep. I had been too preoccupied to notice him earlier.

'Get in,' he said.

I indicated that I was going to take the bus home.

'Nonsense, I'm going for a drive. Coming along?' he said. 'I'd like the company.'

I shook my head and continued on briskly. I had a lot to do and no time for drives. He followed alongside. I knew he wasn't going to give up easily. He never did. He'd probably just wear me down.' Finally, I threw up my hands in mock surrender and climbed in beside him.

Juan swung the jeep around into a side street and headed in the direction of the ocean. He was unusually quiet, yawned a lot and seemed preoccupied. He had just come off a thirty-six-hour shift. The top of the jeep was down and the breeze was delightful. I found myself enjoying the outing despite my initial reservations. He had suggested once that whenever I was having a good time, I ended up punishing myself. Perhaps he was right.

We hadn't gone more than a few blocks when he pulled up in one of the side streets.

'You drive,' he said. 'I feel sleepy.'

He got out and came around to my side I slid over and got in behind the wheel, adjusting the seat.

I pulled away from the curb and saw him lean back wearily against the seat. In a few moments his head slumped and he was fast asleep.

It was a pleasant drive through the tree-lined boulevards. Ahead of us was the ocean and above us a pale shimmering expanse of sky. It was as though the sun's rays had been filtered, diminishing its potency.

On the distant horizon a clear line distinguished the dark blue sea from the light blue of the sky. The palm trees lining the street along Ocean Drive rustled gently in the breeze. Juan woke up and smiled, but it wasn't long before he dropped off again.

It was deceptively peaceful as we drove through the city streets with little sign of the guerrilla insurgency. The only evidence of military activity was an army jeep parked at the beach. About a mile further down the road we passed a truck carrying soldiers.

I headed away from the city with all its trappings of sophistication; its tall buildings, side-walk cafés, the cobbled side streets, cathedral and large mansions suspended from cliffs overlooking the ocean.

We could have been driving through any European city. The illusion was complete in every way, except for the black figures scything the grass, sweeping the streets, carrying heavy burdens on their heads, or baskets on their arms.

After a while I turned inland. Outside the city we passed shanty towns where bare-buttocked black children begged alongside a road congested with traffic. Lumbering beasts of burden jostled for right-of-way with sleek city cars; the ancient and the modern juxtaposed, struggling to co-exist.

There was greater evidence of a military presence in this area and for a while we were trapped behind a convoy of military trucks carrying soldiers with machine guns and other heavy artillery. The road was a narrow ribbon of tarmac wide enough for one car only. At the approach of other traffic, each vehicle had to squeeze over on to the shoulder. This manoeuvre meant a drop of almost a foot off the tarmac.

Generally the slow-moving convoys were a nuisance on the roads. The army vehicles travelled close together and one had to pass several of them at once. It was not only hazardous, but also extremely intimidating to be sandwiched between vehicles which had their artillery pointed directly at you. The convoys were frequently used to escort traffic along the main arterial roads, especially in view of recent guerrilla attacks on supply trucks from South Africa.

There was obviously no hope of getting by the long line of military vehicles, and so at the first opportunity I turned off on to a secondary road.

Juan woke up and glanced at his watch. 'Santa Maria!' he exclaimed. 'I've slept for an hour-and-a-half! Where are we?'

I told him, smiled and changed gear to slip in behind a donkey cart. Traffic was heavy even on this road and I was caught behind the cart for almost half a mile. Eventually, I turned off again and we bumped along a dusty track until it joined the main road where it cut through the township.

Juan was gazing at me. 'You're a good driver,' he remarked.

I shrugged. There was no need to tell him that David had taught me. I was tempted to turn off into the township. Rita's house was just a few blocks away, beyond the grove of banana trees which lined the road. One could actually catch a glimpse of it between the trees. She might be home, I thought. I knew that she was off duty that day. She'd told me that she'd promised to take care of Zeca, while his mother, Teresa, went out to look for a job.

Nineteen-year-old Teresa and her baby, Zeca, were two of the strays Rita had picked up and brought home with her. She had virtually plucked them off the streets. It had been a tough life for Teresa, who had survived by selling her body to South African tourists, eager to have a 'black' experience.

There seemed to be ample room in Rita's house now that Ester had gone and Aesta had entered a convent. Margreta, too, had gone off and got married, leaving Rita alone in the house. Absorbed with these thoughts, I hesitated and then it was too late: I had passed the turn-off.

As we neared the city, Juan sat up. 'If you want, you can pull up over there,' he said. 'I'll drive now so we can stop at my place and pick up some papers.'

I pulled over and slid back into the passenger seat. Juan pushed back the seat to accommodate his long legs. I had not been to his flat before and was quite interested as we pulled up in front of the building. He invited me in.

I got out and followed him into the *Pensão Rosa*. The outside wall at the front was covered with a mural intricately laid out in mosaic tiles. It depicted the arrival of sailing ships in the bay, with the black population waiting to welcome them ashore. The *pensão*, now faded and tarnished with age and neglect, was indicative of much earlier grandeur.

Inside the building, the once beautiful marbled staircase was chipped and discoloured. In the entrance hall, faded wallpaper peeled from the top of the walls.

His flat was on the third floor. Despite the flaking paint, the carpets worn almost threadbare in places, the flat was large, bright and airy. It had high ceilings and a charming view of the bay from the balcony. The interior was spartan and the only greenery was a pathetic-looking palm in a ceramic pot on his balcony.

I waited as he riffled through a sheaf of papers on the table, found what he was after, folded it and tucked it into his shirt pocket.

'Would you like something to drink?' he asked.

I nodded.

'*Cerveja?*'

I nodded again.

He returned with a bottle of beer. 'I still think you're a very brave woman to stay here in Mozambique,' he said. 'Especially after what happened to you. You are to be admired for your courage.'

His remark put me on the defensive. Where on earth were people expecting me to go? They spoke as though there was some kind of alternative. I was Mozambican. I was born here. This is where I wanted to be.

Juan noticed my irritation and was at a loss for words. I must have presented quite a picture, standing there with my arms crossed, the bottle of beer clutched to my chest. But even Juan's amused glance could not penetrate my armour. Sometimes I wondered about the paradox that was me: my need for affection and my fear of commitment.

My reaction to his comment had created some awkwardness between us and as soon as I had finished my beer, he indicated that he was ready to leave.

Life was becoming increasingly difficult for everyone. There were long queues at the stores and never enough goods. Shelves were often empty even though supplies were being shipped from South

Africa. In one way or another we were all suffering the effects of shortages. There was petrol rationing and many of the luxury items were available only on the black market.

The currency, worthless outside the country, had very little purchasing power within it. The only thriving sector of the economy was a black market in foreign exchange.

We heard that the war had been stepped up. General Arriaga, who had assumed control of the government forces in Mozambique, was no longer content with merely containing the fighting to the more remote regions. David told me that the strategy and tactics were beginning to mirror American practices in Vietnam.

The PIDE was more active than ever, operating with a network of *bufos* – informers. It was becoming too dangerous to have conversations in public. There was an air of tight-lipped suspicion wherever one went.

The rebel movement had gained momentum. An all-out war was now being conducted from the Liberation headquarters in Dar-es-Salaam.

It was tough for the underground. Many of the early revolutionaries had been killed, their bodies left on display to serve as a warning to others. The deaths had not stopped the guerrilla war. It had only served to create martyrs and to strengthen the revolutionary resolve.

In our apartment building little had changed. Young girls still undressed at uncovered windows or unselfconsciously made love without heed to their voyeuristic audience. My vicarious existence continued – the aroma of food, the sound of voices still drifted in through the open windows and I still shamelessly eavesdropped on lovers, on domestic arguments, or listened to the shrill voices of mothers chastising their offspring. There was a joyous feeling about being part of this community. The tenants had become the family I didn't have.

Life was never dull here and there was a certain earthy richness which seemed to compensate for the despair and the tragedy in these people's lives. Sometimes this meant an inter-dependence which had the potential for all sorts of conflict.

I remember being awakened one night by a commotion from outside. I recognised the squawking of the parrot in the corner flat. The owner, a retired merchant marine with a penchant for foul language, left the parrot out on the balcony at night from time to

time, and although it frequently squawked and screeched obscenities, it usually settled down eventually. This time, however, the
disturbance went on for hours and was unusually raucous.

At about two-thirty I got up out of bed and went to the window
to see what was going on. Lights were on in other flats, too. Some
of the tenants were out on their balconies, hurling insults at the
owner; others, anxious for peace and quiet, shouted for him to take
the parrot inside.

The owner responded with invectives of his own. More people
joined in the clamour and a loud, boisterous altercation developed,
an enthusiastic audience supplying encouragement. Then, quite
abruptly, realising that he was outnumbered, the owner made a
rude sweeping gesture to include everyone in the building, before
taking the parrot indoors.

One by one the lights went out. I remained at the window gazing
down into the courtyard where the ghostly shapes of the frangipane,
loquat and fig trees loomed out of the darkness. Distant sounds of
traffic and voices reached me. Through the open window I could
hear a woman's voice raised in complaint, then a man's cajoling
tones.

I returned to bed and lay in the dark, thinking. I thought of the
parrot, but most of all I thought about the innocents caught up in
this war and their suffering. Suddenly, I was overwhelmed by a
feeling of such utter despair that I had to put all thoughts out of my
mind or succumb to tears.

A few weeks later, Rita and I both had a day off and I headed for
the township. Rita, Teresa and the baby were all at home.

I was standing in the doorway watching the young girl playing
with her baby in the yard, when Rita came up behind me. 'I don't
think she'll ever change,' she remarked. 'The street is like a drug. I
feel sorry for the child, though,' she confided. 'He's such a good
baby. I'd miss him.'

'She's not much more than a child herself,' I responded.

'Nineteen, going on thirty,' Rita said. 'They grow up quickly on
the streets. Do you want to come with me?' she asked. 'I'm going to
see Luzia.'

I hesitated. Luzia was the local healer.

'Why?' I asked.

'She has cancer of the stomach, but she won't let anyone treat her. She's been taking her own remedies. I don't think anything will help, of course, but Margreta has told me that she has had a miraculous recovery.

When Teresa came indoors, Rita told her that we were off to Luzia's.

'*You* are going to see the *bruxa*?' a surprised Teresa asked.

Rita was impatient with Teresa. 'How many times have I told you, Luzia is not a witch. She uses herbal cures. Plants. Things from which medicines are made of.'

I made a wry expression.

'Are you going to let her tell you about the future?' Teresa asked inquisitively.

'She'll drive you mad with questions, this one,' Rita warned.

'I hear she has all kinds of potions,' Teresa said, not in the least bit discouraged by Rita's stern expression. 'Sometimes when the men can't make it work down there,' she continued with a lewd gesture, 'they go to Luzia. She fixes them up with special medicine. The big shot Senhores, they go there all the time in big, fancy cars,' she added.

Rita glanced impatiently at Teresa. 'How do you think people got along in the early days when there were no doctors?' she asked. 'My great-great grandmother was a medicine woman. She was one of the most famous women in our village. The Europeans killed her because she wouldn't give up her traditional ways to embrace theirs.'

I held Zeca for a few minutes, but then he fidgeted and I handed him back to his mother. In the meantime, Teresa begged to accompany us. Eventually, Rita relented.

Rita brought Zeca along, carrying him on her hip. We took the short-cut through the row of shacks behind the house, climbing over piles of rubbish and stepping over squatting children defecating in the narrow alleys between smoke-blackened dwellings. Along the middle of the pathway ran a small stream of blackened stinking water in which bare-bottomed children were playing while their mothers stood gossiping.

In some parts of the township, like the area in which Rita lived, there were a few brick houses built close together, encroaching on each other, walls soot-blackened and pitted by the elements.

But in this area there were only the shanties, constructed of

104

whatever material was handy: sheets of corrugated iron, plastic, cardboard, hessian, anything which would provide shelter. Some of them were so close together that it was hard to determine where one ended and the other began.

We walked across a dry, stubbled field towards another area. Here ruins of once elegant concrete walls stood as silent testimony to a place that had long ago inspired the name *Bela Vista*. Now the alleys were infested with rats and pocked with puddles of stinking water like festering pustules.

There were friendly shouts of *Boa tarde* or *Bom dia* from women who recognised us. Despite the heat, the township hummed with activity.

In places the alleys were so narrow that we were forced to proceed in single file. We stopped to greet an old woman hunched over a washtub, her hands gnarled into two clenched stumps. She saw Zeca on Teresa's hip, smiled and engaged Teresa in a good-humoured exchange, all the while continuing to knead the wash.

'Last week her son and his family were killed when the soldiers burnt their village,' Teresa told me.

The old woman nodded at me as if to confirm what Teresa had said. I glanced into those slow rheumy eyes and saw the pain. But life went on in the slums of *Bela Vista*. Death was commonplace. People were dying all the time. Dying of hunger, dying from violence perpetrated by each other and by the government forces. One couldn't grieve for too long – life had to go on.

We picked our way through rows of billowing laundry pegged on sagging lines, propped up by wooden supports or branches. It was laundry day in the township and everyone was busy. A big woman with enormous hips grinned as she hefted her naked offspring on to her back. People recognised me. Curious glances trailed after us and when it was perceived that we were heading towards the end of the street, they guessed our destination and there were knowing smiles.

When we reached the end of the alley, we turned into a small yard enclosed by a high fence. The house, a small wooden structure, was patched with corrugated iron where the wood had rotted. The only thing that was strong and unyielding was the fence. There was no way through it or over it. We had to walk all the way around to the front gate to enter.

The front door was painted white, but the paint had cracked and peeled away. On either side was a small window. The wooden casements, painted the same colour as the door, had similar signs of weathering. Teresa lifted the tarnished brass knocker and wiped her feet on the coir mat as we waited.

Through the streaked panes I glimpsed a movement. Footsteps shuffled closer. The door opened. First a crack, then as far as the latched chain would allow – before it swung wide open.

An old woman appeared in the open doorway. In the absence of teeth her face had collapsed inward. Her eyes, yellow and veined, stared out through red-rimmed lids. Her skin was ancient and parched. Her one hand with its gnarled fingers, rigid with age, shielded her eyes against the bright light as she peered at us. She recognised Rita instantly and invited us in. She hooked one of her withered hands under Zeca's chin, but he turned his face from her.

'Nice boy,' she cackled, her mouth working ceaselessly on the piece of chewing tobacco which had stained the remaining stumps of teeth.

The old woman was enveloped in the sweet smell of incense and camphor. It was the smell of clothes that had been stored in mothballs for years. She was wearing an outdated floral print dress with a large detachable lace collar which hung from her neck like the loose skin of a turkey.

'Luzia, we have come to see how you are.'

'I'm all right,' she said in a thin, quivering voice.

I was surprised to see her looking so spry.

Rita saw my expression and smiled. 'I told you she has been treating herself with herbs.'

Luzia directed us to walk to the end of the passage. She followed behind, conducting a conversation over our heads with Rita, who was leading the way.

The house held a peculiar mixture of mustiness and pungency. It was crammed to the rafters with boxes and bottles. There were piles of dry leaves and plants hanging in bunches from every conceivable hook and nail in the house. Many of the items in the bottles were quite unrecognisable and sent a shudder down my spine. The linoleum on the floor was worn bare in places. Evidently a well trodden path, I thought, recalling Teresa's explanation about men with problems coming to see the old woman.

We reached a room at the far end of the passage. In this room was a wooden table and four unmatched chairs. Rows of shelves were lined with bottles, tins, bags and an assortment of other containers.

'I came to see if you needed help, Mamaluzia,' Rita said as we sat down.

Luzia shook her head. 'I am all right, Rita.' She pointed a bony finger at her and laughed. 'I told you. I will outlive you.'

Rita smiled. 'If you need my help, send a message. If I'm home I'll come right away. Where is Margreta?' Rita looked around. 'I told her to stay here for a while.'

'She is in the back yard, bathing her little Thomas,' the old woman said, looking over at me.

'How have you been feeling Mamaluzia?' Rita asked.

'Better than I would have been if I had taken your advice and gone to a doctor.'

'Mamaluzia, your medicine won't help. You have cancer of the stomach. If you don't get help, you'll die.'

'I'm ninety years old. I'm going to die anyway. I'm not going to spend the rest of my days in a hospital. I feel fine. My medicine is stronger than the medicine of any doctor. Why do you think people come to me when their doctors have not been able to help them?'

The old woman was unassailable and Rita shook her head. 'What did I tell you?' she said to me.

As Rita spoke to me, Luzia studied my face with those pink-rimmed, watery eyes and I could see a flicker of recognition in them.

Finally, she said: 'I know you.' She spoke in a shrill, excited voice. 'I saw you when you were a little girl living with Mamaria. I know you. You had no voice.'

'The old woman has a good memory, but I don't remember her,' I signed to Rita, who interpreted for Luzia.

She laughed. It was a dry, rasping sound, more like a cough. Then, abruptly, she became serious again. She gazed at me intently. I felt a bit uncomfortable under her scrutiny. 'Your voice will come back some day,' she said.

I was taken aback by the way she said this, with so much strength and assurance.

'You will go on a journey which has a lot of danger, but at the end of that journey you will get your voice back.'

I glanced at Rita as if to say: 'What have you got me into?'

Rita smiled back sweetly.

The old woman continued. 'There will be much death on this journey. You will meet a man who is half-creature, half-man.'

For a moment there was silence. Teresa, round-eyed, sat bouncing Zeca on her knee. Her attention fixed on me. The old woman laughed, breaking the tension.

I shook my head and smiled indulgently at this nonsense. I signalled to Rita that I was ready to leave.

'I'd like to see Margreta before I go,' Rita said.

The old woman led us to the back door. Margreta was seated on the step with her infant on her lap. She had just bathed the child, a chubby little boy who had fared a lot better than other children of the same age. Mother and son were oblivious to us and had eyes only for each other.

We watched as Margreta turned her son on to his stomach, poured olive oil into her palm, coated her hands and then massaged the little body lying so contentedly on her lap. Her hands moved from the shoulders down to the buttocks in slow circular motions until the child's entire back was coated. She then flipped him over and laid him on his back. The child gurgled with pleasure as her hands gently kneaded and rolled the soft flesh, probing and massaging, working the cleft between the thighs, the little penis erect. The child kicked ecstatically in response to her soft murmuring voice, not for one moment taking its eyes off her face.

Margreta's hands returned to the legs and, starting at the feet, worked each individual toe, then worked the arms moving them across the chest and above the head as the child gurgled happily, its skin glistening with oil. The mother laughed and lifted the child into her arms, holding him against her shoulder. Suddenly she turned, saw us and smiled. It was such a touching scene that I was sorry we had interrupted.

The scene had stirred something deep in my memory. Like a familiar scent, the fragment of memory lingered. The softness of a pale hand touching me with that kind of love.

I thought of that ugly doll I had passed on to Margreta when we were living at Mamaria's house.

'Margreta, how goes it?' Teresa asked.

Margreta, a few years older than Teresa, looked up and smiled. 'Good.'

'We came to see Mamaluzia,' Rita told her.

'She told Faith's future,' Teresa chimed in.

'Faith, so why is it we haven't seen you for a long time?' Margreta asked.

I smiled lamely and then glanced away. I felt guilty about having neglected the family. Was it David's doing or had I changed?

'I told Mamaluzia to send for me if she needs me,' Rita said.

Margreta nodded. She heaved her baby on to her back, and then secured him in a sling under her arm. 'There's nothing wrong with that old woman. There is no reason for me to stay here. I want to go to my own home.'

'Soon,' Rita agreed. 'Has she been in pain at all?'

'Not that I know of. She drinks all that stinking medicine all the time.'

Rita turned to me. 'You see what I mean,' she said. 'These people have knowledge about things we know nothing about.'

I was still watching Margreta and saw the softness in her face. Life was such a contradiction. In all this ugliness I had discovered a tiny oasis of beauty. I couldn't take my eyes off the glow on the young woman's face.

Chapter Nine

One afternoon Rita came over to visit me at home. It was my day off and I was glad to see her. David, who was still away at the construction site, had only been home twice in the last three months and I was feeling a bit sorry for myself.

Rita seemed tired and distraught. I'd heard that the trauma unit had been very busy over the past few days, but it was a pleasant afternoon and we were both able to unwind. We listened to music while Rita passed on gossip and news from the township.

'Mamaluzia is feeling much better and Margreta went home last week.' After a long pause Rita asked, 'Faith, what did Mamaluzia mean when she told you about the half-man, half-creature?'

I shrugged. 'I don't know. It's all a lot of nonsense,' I signed.

'Anyway, d'you want to go to a film tonight?' she askd. 'I hear it's a good movie . . . I forget the title . . . something like *A Town Like Alice* I think.'

My expression must have indicated my ignorance about the film because she laughed.

'Well, d'you want to go?'

I thought about it for a moment, then nodded.

'We'll go straight from here. It's easier than first going home.'

I got up and went to the fridge to fetch us another *cerveja*. It was getting dark and I went to the window to glance out. I had expected to see Sofia sitting outside waiting for her mother, but there was no one out there. I presumed that Bella had probably arrived home already. I looked at the clock and then went to sit on the floor amongst the scattered cushions. Rita watched me from under her lowered lids. It looked almost as though she was asleep.

I had just made myself comfortable when we were startled by a loud commotion from outside. A woman's voice was crying out hysterically. Rita and I both leapt up and rushed to the window. I

saw Bella standing out on the step. She was beside herself, screaming obscenities and issuing blood-curdling screams like those of a
wounded animal. Several people were shouting at her to shut up.

'Something's wrong,' I signed to Rita and rushed out of the flat.
My friend followed me down the steps to the next level where Bella
was practically doubled over in front of her door.

'What is it?' Rita asked.

Bella couldn't speak and Rita grabbed her by the shoulders,
shaking her, Bella's head flopping like that of a rag doll.

'Talk to us!' Rita cried.

'My baby! My baby, Sofia! They have taken her!'

'Who's taken her?' Rita demanded.

'I don't know. I don't know! She's gone. She never got back from
school!'

'She might be playing with friends and forgot about the time,' I
signed to Rita. Rita repeated my suspicion to Bella.

'No! She's gone!' Bella held her arms crossed in front of her chest,
her expression was anguished as she swayed from side to side.

'How do you know this?' Rita asked.

'I know. I just know. After school she never turned up at my
friend's place where she waits until it is time for me to come home.
No one has seen her.'

Rita and I exchanged glances. 'Let's go inside.' Rita said. 'We'll
wait with you.'

But Bella didn't want to go inside. She sat on the step, crazy with
grief, making almost inhuman sounds as she cried and screamed
out her agony. The insults stopped when people discovered the
reason for her strange behaviour. When they heard her story,
residents immediately rallied and organised a search party, splitting
up into groups of four, each group going out to scour a pre-
determined area, but without any success.

Rita and I stayed with Bella, trying to comfort her. We never got
to see *A Town Like Alice* – we had our own crisis. The groups
returned, there was no news about Sofia. Even though people tried
to reassure Bella, saying that Sofia would come home in the
morning, no one really believed that would happen. Disappearances
of adults and especially children had become quite commonplace.

Bella's friend arrived and stayed with her that night. Rita and I
returned to my flat, where we speculated about what could possibly
be happening. I kept going back and forth to the window, hoping

each time that I'd see Sofia sitting on the step of the second-floor landing. I knew that it was a vain hope, but I couldn't help myself.

'I can't forget what you told me about children being taken from the orphanage in the middle of the night. Even if government forces were taking children, where would they take them? What would they do with children, eh? What? Kill them?'

I shook my head.

'It doesn't make any sense except if one assumes they are taking them into the bush and training them to fight against their own people. The trouble is no one has seen these children. If they were being used, someone would have seen them.'

I went to the window again and looked out. Bella was silent; her flat was in darkness. I doubted, though, that she was asleep.

'Last month the mothers demonstrated at the government buildings to find out about their lost children. There were no answers. The governor was away, but the women remained there for ten hours, standing in silent protest outside the gate,' Rita told me.

It was late and I suggested Rita should stay the night. Although she expressed concern about Teresa, she seemed quite relieved at not having to go all the way to the township at this late hour. It worked out well because she was only scheduled to go on duty the following afternoon.

'What do you think is happening to these children?' I signed, as I went to the kitchen to make coffee. She thought about my question, focusing her attention on some obscure point on the floor. I waited and eventually she glanced up.

'What if these children were being taken out of the country?' she asked.

'But where would they be taken, and why?' I signed.

Rita shrugged her shoulders. It was obvious that neither of us had a clue about their fate, but I could tell that Rita was not going to rest until she found out what was happening.

Two months went by and despite all attempts to locate Sofia through a much wider search and a police report which we helped Bella to file with police, there was no news about Sofia. Bella sat outside each night, waiting. I watched her from my window and felt the excruciating pain and the despair of hoping, yet knowing that it was hopeless.

One afternoon, while I was in the canteen having lunch with

112

Juan, a heavy-set, scowling man walked in. Juan saw him and let out a quiet groan.

'Not again,' he said uncomfortably.

'What is it?' I signed.

'The PIDE . . .'

I turned to see who he was looking at.

'In the food line. The one in the grey pants and hat, weighing all of three hundred pounds.'

The man was in the process of selecting his meal.

'Do you know him?' I signed, full of curiosity about Juan's association with the PIDE.

'Not really. He's been pestering me for the last few days. Look, if he comes over here, whatever you do, don't leave me alone with him. No matter what he says to you, stay.'

'I can't,' I protested.

'Yes you can. I'll tell him you're a deaf-mute and that you can't hear what we're saying.'

That was ridiculous and I indicated this to him.

'Please.' The laughter in his eyes was replaced by anxiety.

I could only focus on my own fears. The enormity of our situation was clear to me.

'*Please*,' he urged again.

I agreed, pretending to be unaware as the man approached and stood by our table. 'Senhorita,' he said.

I kept my eyes averted.

'What do you want Marcelo?' Juan asked.

'I want to talk to you,' the other man replied.

In spite of the fact that my head was lowered, I could sense his attention was on me.

'Sit down,' Juan said.

'What about her?' the man said, inclining his head toward me.

'For heaven's sake,' Juan exclaimed impatiently, 'she's deaf and dumb. She can't hear a word you're saying.'

'What about lip reading?'

'She's not interested in you. Look at her. She hasn't even seen you yet. She can only communicate by signing,' Juan said. He fixed the newcomer with a frank gaze. 'Look,' he said. 'I don't have much time left for my lunch. So you either sit down or find another table.'

The man sat down. I looked up and tried to smile nonchalantly, but I was afraid I would end up losing my lunch. I felt sick to my

113

stomach at the thought of being at the same table as a PIDE agent. It wasn't that long ago that I had badgered David to get information about the children. Yet, here I was right beside one of them and I couldn't keep from trembling. Perhaps it was because I suspected that they were responsible for what was going on.

I looked over at Juan. It was almost the end of a thirty-six-hour shift for him. His eyes were dull and bloodshot and I could tell that he was beginning to lose patience with the lumpy, heavy-jowled fellow at the table with us.

Juan leaned back in his chair, away from the other man, exhaustion written all over his face. It wasn't surprising – he had just come out of four hours of surgery, trying to save the life of a young village girl brutally raped by a group of soldiers. The first of her attackers, unable to penetrate her, had used his knife to facilitate entry.

I watched as he sighed and drew a hand through his hair. It seemed that today more than ever, being here, being part of the war and the constant stream of mutilated bodies from the front, had got to him. I thought of the advice he had given me about maintaining a professional distance. There were times, however, when even the most seasoned staff broke down. One couldn't always function like a machine.

'I don't like the idea of her being here,' Marcelo said, scowling. I could feel my face slowly changing colour under the intensity of his probing gaze. 'So you say she's deaf, eh?'

'*Sim*,' Juan said, nodding. 'Look, I'm due back in surgery shortly. So . . .?'

Reluctantly, the man stopped looking at me. I waited anxiously and although he turned his attention to Juan, I could still sense some residual suspicion.

'All right,' he said, still scowling, 'but you'll regret it if you're trying anything stupid. You may be under the protection of the Minister of Health now, but one day things will change. That day, my friend, you'd better watch out,' he growled.

Throughout this exchange I kept my head lowered, concentrating on my meal even though my appetite had gone. Silently, I cursed Juan for dragging me into this situation, but it was too late to change my mind. Doubtless, if I got up and left now, of my own volition, it would only arouse suspicion.

Distractedly, I listened to the two talking. This man Marcelo, was an adversary and it seemed to me Juan was involved in an intellectual game of cat-and-mouse with him. I wished that he would not tempt fate. Didn't he know what power the PIDE wielded? Didn't he know that with a snap of his fingers this man could take or spare his life? What in the world did Juan think he was doing, behaving so cavalierly?

My train of thought was suddenly interrupted by the sinister tone in the other man's voice.

'We have a proposition for you, Senhor Doctore,' he said. The way he emphasised Juan's title was overtly sarcastic.

I watched Juan's brows coming together in a question.

'It's about the thefts at this hospital. We know for a fact the supplies stolen here have made their way into the hands of the guerrillas. We discovered some of your missing supplies when we captured one of their bases up north.'

Juan's expression of curiosity dissolved and changed to a look of boredom. He yawned.

'Either you co-operate or . . .'

'Or what?' Juan asked, glancing up.

'You'll find out soon enough,' the other said.

'What do you want from me?' Juan enquired wearily.

'Information.'

For a moment a blank, uncomprehending expression swept over Juan's face.

'I see I still don't have your attention,' the man said.

Juan dropped his eyes and stifled another yawn.

The man's tone of voice became hostile. 'There is a network of thieves operating in all the hospitals. We know that they are staff members. People who have access to supplies. We want you to keep your eyes open and to report anything suspicious.'

Juan glanced at me and perhaps for the first time actually began to realise that by asking me to stay he had unwittingly drawn me into danger, a thought that had long since occurred to me as well.

He scowled at the other man. 'If you think I'm going to do your dirty work, you're mistaken,' he said.

I saw Rita approaching our table. It's possible she read the expression of panic in my eyes, for she behaved quite admirably, standing quietly by the table until she was acknowledged by Juan.

'I beg your pardon, Doctor Guerra,' she said.

'Yes, Nurse Rita,' Juan replied.

'Sister Constance wants you to look in on our new patient.'

He nodded. 'How is Senhor Martins doing?'

'He's been asking for morphine.'

'Thank you, nurse. That'll be all,' he said curtly.

I breathed a silent sigh of relief as Rita left without further question or comment.

Marcelo watched her walk away, his lascivious glance following the movement of her hips. He started his conversation again. He looked restlessly around the room, examining faces, darting in and out of the shadows.

I sat quite still as Juan regarded the man from under half-lowered lids. He drew a hand across his stubbled chin. 'You're wasting your time. I am a doctor, not a spy.'

The other man ate in silence, his heavy jowls moving rhythmically. Gesturing with his fork, he said: 'You must be very happy here. All these girls . . . What more could a man want, eh?'

Juan ignored the remark.

'Except his life,' he said darkly.

Juan's lips drew into a thin angry line.

The man winked and wiped his mouth with a paper serviette. He chuckled as he drew the bowl of dessert closer and plunged his spoon into the chocolate-coloured mound.

'You are a foolish man,' he said, without interrupting the rhythm as he scooped up the food, carried it to his mouth, and masticated with slow ponderous movements.

When the bowl was cleaned out, he pushed it aside and then, giving Juan a long, penetrating gaze, he said: 'Bring us the information and you will have done your duty to your country. That is all we require of you. We'll do the rest. We'll cut off the rebel supplies and tighten the noose until we strangle them. We'll begin right here with the ringleaders of their gang.' He jabbed the table for emphasis.

'Gang? What gang?' Juan asked, his expression full of scornful disbelief. 'We've always had problems with supplies going missing,' Juan said. 'These people are poor. They will steal anything.'

Anger flickered and leapt in the man's eyes. His expression tightened. I trembled apprehensively.

'I think you're crazy . . . This war has driven everyone crazy,' Juan muttered.

'Do you think we're fools?' he demanded.

Juan laughed harshly. 'Why do you need my help if you know so much already?'

'If you don't help us, it means you are an enemy of the state.'

Juan shook his head in disbelief. 'What do you plan to do, shoot everyone who disagrees with you? In the end, after all this,' he said spreading his arms, 'we'll give up and walk away from here, too weary of the fighting.'

The man leaned forward, his face twisted grotesquely. 'Do you want to be driven from this country by a bunch of black savages in animal skins, prancing around like monkeys?' he asked.

Juan lowered his head. 'In the end we'll leave anyway. If people like you don't get out soon, you'll be driven out of this country like dogs. And I say good riddance. In fact, I'll probably leave here too and go back home to open a small clinic in the *barracas*, or go to Europe somewhere. Where will you go?'

'You are lucky to be practising medicine at all,' the other man said, gesturing with his head towards the building which housed the main part of the hospital. 'You are still eligible for conscription,' he said, tauntingly.

Juan glanced up sharply, a small pulse throbbing in his right temple.

The agent laughed harshly. 'We have saved you for bigger and better things,' he said, scraping his chair back.

Juan groaned.

The man gazed at him, his dark brows drawing together. 'We'll be in touch.' He clamped his teeth down on the toothpick jutting from his mouth. He shrugged, pushed his chair back further and got up. '*Adeus*,' he said with a mocking smile.

When the man had gone, I turned to Juan. 'Are you crazy?' I demanded, my hands signing furiously.

'Relax,' he said. 'They can't do anything to me. They need me.'

'You're not indispensable.'

'I've got to go,' he said.

'Juan . . .'

But he had already started to walk away.

Rita came over the moment Juan left.

'What's going on, Faith?' she asked.

'That was the PIDE.'

'I know,' she said.

'How did you know?'

'They are easy to spot. What did he want?' she asked, cautiously seeking out faces in the cafeteria.

I did not respond immediately.

'What is Juan doing with him?'

I turned away, trying to avoid answering.

'Faith, what's going on?' She gripped my arm so tightly that I had to respond. As I signed, describing the conversation, she listened, her hand trembling as she distractedly raised Juan's half-finished cup of coffee to her lips.

I thought of the way Juan had left the canteen, his hands thrust deep into his trouser pockets. He had not given me a second thought. It was as if he had forgotten about my presence. I felt as though the net had been cast and that we would all soon be entangled in it.

Chapter Ten

A few weeks later, I drove out to see Doña Maria. I hadn't seen her for several months. The last I had heard, she had gone to Portugal for the fourth anniversary of the deaths of Senhor Cardoso and Isabella, both of whom had been killed by a car bomb.

Doña Maria returned to Portugal on each year at that time to visit their graves. Despite denials from Lisbon, she was still convinced that government agents were responsible for the deaths of her husband and her daughter.

According to Doña Maria, Senhor Cardoso had been targeted because of his association with the Communist Party. There were many others, both in Mozambique and Portugal, who agreed with her but of course would never say so openly.

The first year had been very difficult for her, but as time passed she showed remarkable strength and somehow managed to come to terms with her tragic loss, but the rhythm of her life had changed drastically. Sometimes it seemed as if the soul had not only gone out of her, but out of the house as well. There were times when she tended to drift off in the middle of a sentence as though distracted by a thought or a memory. But always there was this struggle to keep a tight check on her emotions because she was such a proud woman, and would never make a public display of her personal feelings. My heart went out to her. I knew from my own experience that the violent death of a loved one could leave one crippled for life.

The portrait of the sultry Isabella still fascinated me as much as it had the first time I saw it. Sometimes, depending on the light, the expression in the eyes seemed to alter.

When I arrived at the estate that afternoon, Carlos confirmed that Doña Maria was still away in Portugal. I didn't feel that my journey had been wasted. I enjoyed the fresh air, and the drive had

119

given me an opportunity to think. Although this wasn't technically out in the country, it was far enough out of the city to give one the feeling of being in the countryside.

Carlos went off to prepare a pot of coffee while I sat out on the terrace. He brought the coffee out and joined me. I stole a glance at him and noticed that he, too, had aged. I was so glad that he was still around to keep an eye on my benefactress. She told me once that Carlos had been with them for more than twenty-five years and that he was more like a family member than a servant. I had noticed, more so now than before, that he tended to hover over her like a shadow, whether he was needed or not.

Out on the terrace, sipping coffee with Carlos, I thought of David and wondered what had gone wrong between us. Perhaps we had become a habit – addicted to each other like a drug which lulls one into a false sense of security. I glanced up and noticed that Carlos had gone off somewhere, and had left me to my daydreams.

I thought of my own life and some of the people who had passed through it: Mamaria who had raised us all, and Rita who had carried on her traditions with the same cool determination; Lodiya who had almost slayed the dragon Sister Luisa; Teresa who had survived in the streets and would fight like a tigress for her son Zeca; Doña Maria who had opened so many doors for me, and Angie who had taught me about honesty and fulfilment.

The word fulfilment reminded me of Margreta and her infant and all the tender loving she had given him in the midst of the township squalor. But it also reminded me of Luzia, who had stopped the progression of a terminal disease, and of the nuns, who, despite the oppression and the constant undermining by the Church and the priests, carried on, bound by their unshakable faith.

All of them great women, who each in their own way had braved and fought adversity for the survival of their children, their family and community.

In the absence of men, arrested, beaten, demoralised, maimed and killed in war, the women carried on. In the end they, too, were marched into battle to be arrested, beaten, demoralised, raped, maimed and killed. Most women, though, were veterans of another kind of war, the war of survival fought on the battleground of their homes and in their townships.

One Friday afternoon several weeks after my visit to the estate I was wrestling with thoughts about the war and the children as I finished my report at the clinic. I was feeling sorry for myself, wondering if perhaps my loss of voice had not rendered me impotent and helpless.

The doctor had recently told me that even if my memory returned, I might still be voiceless. My vocal chords had atrophied from lack of use and I would need extensive voice therapy. There were no facilities here for that kind of treatment. I would have to go to Europe.

I opened my mouth as I had done a thousand times to utter a word, any word to validate the hope that my voice would return. But I could manage only a grunt. It was as if my brain and voice lacked co-ordination and would not function in concert.

I felt so useless. I had tried to find out what had happened to the children, but each time we thought we had a good lead, we'd run into a dead-end. All these problems gnawed at me, especially when I had time for reflection.

As I sat there on my own, deep in thought, a light tap on my shoulder almost made me leap out of my chair. Startled, I turned. Juan was standing behind me, smiling apologetically.

'I didn't mean to frighten you,' he said.

I placed a hand on my chest to still my fluttering heart.

'Why are you so jumpy?' he asked.

'I keep thinking about that awful man . . .'

'Marcelo?' he asked, surprised.

'Yes. I expect to find him standing behind me one day, tapping me on my shoulder.'

'Don't be silly,' Juan laughed. 'He has no reason to bother you.'

'Since when do they need a reason?'

'Let's not talk about the PIDE,' he said. 'I came to find out whether you and David have plans for this weekend.' I shrugged. My only interest was in getting home to rest.

'David will be coming home, won't he?' he asked.

I didn't want to talk about David. I wanted to get home. I was tired, but there was still the report to finish.

'If you don't have anything to do, why don't you come to dinner with me tonight?' he suggested. 'I know this little restaurant where the food is magnificent.'

I shook my head.

'Why not?'

I thought of a dozen reasons, but shrugged off the question. I felt

121

vulnerable and had no desire to get involved in something which might get out of hand. I thought I needed to exert more control over events in my life. I was too easily swayed, too easily influenced and seduced by a few tokens of love or affection. Look what had happened with David and now he wanted to take over my life; he thought that because I had no voice I was incapable of making decisions for myself. I wondered how he imagined I had existed before he had come along.

After months of bitter quarrelling he had finally yielded and had given me some space. So why would I clutter up that space again? God, I was tired. It felt as if my energy had been syphoned away. All I wanted was to be left alone for a while to lick my wounds and to heal myself.

Juan waited. I didn't want to explain any of this to him.

'It's Friday. Do you want to sit at home alone tonight?' he asked. 'You know what your trouble is?' he continued as I gazed at him questioningly. 'You don't know how to relax. Come with me,' he said, smiling that boyishly charming smile. 'I'll show you how.'

I indicated that I wasn't interested and that my only concern was to go home and have a bath and relax.

'So?' he asked, as if this was of no consequence.

I busied myself clearing the clutter off my desk.

'Oh, come on, what harm is there in having a simple dinner with me?'

I thought about David and glanced up. Through the window I watched an old man shuffle across the crowded courtyard.

Was anything in life ever simple?

'Come on,' Juan urged.

He had worn me down. I didn't have the strength to resist and nodded my assent.

'Good, I'll pick you up at eight o'clock,' he said.

A light rain had drizzled down earlier and although one could still see it trailing in some areas of the city, the sky was clearing. It was so fresh out that I left my car and went for a walk in the *Jardim Botanico* – the botanical gardens.

A network of asphalted paths meandered under trees burdened with vines, with ferns and a breathtaking variety of plants. Nestled in the moss-covered limbs of trees were an infinite variety of orchids.

The trees were tall and leafy, arching high above my head to form a canopy which trailed twisted ropes of vines. The rain had left a steamy muskiness and as the air stirred through the trees, it spread a wonderful earthy odour of decay. For a fleeting moment I caught a glimpse of an image from my past.

In the distance, hardly intruding on this tranquil oasis, came the faint noise of the traffic. Insulated here in this paradisiacal enclave, the only sounds were the twitterings of colourful birds soaring to their nests or the chattering of monkeys as they swung between the trees.

There was an uncanny feeling of unreality about this place. It had the ethereal quality of a dream. My dream. I leaned back against the bench and closed my eyes. The shrill sound of a woman's voice startled me and I glanced around. An overweight Portuguese matron, dressed in black and wearing a dark headscarf, was remonstrating loudly with her older daughter, who was ignoring her younger siblings.

There were other people in the garden: young couples, some of whom were in school uniform, surreptitiously holding hands; a crazy old man, brandishing a cane, yelled at a pair who were kissing; a few black women hurried by, one of them carrying a heavy load on her head. At the far end, near the exit, three businessmen carrying briefcases were engrossed in conversation.

I got up and returned to the exit. The clouds had dispersed, the sun was shining brightly and the wet pavements and streets were already steaming in the heat.

Juan picked me up at exactly eight o'clock. Right up to the last moment I was still vacillating about going to dinner with him. I enjoyed his friendship and as illogical as it might sound, I felt that if I went out to dinner with him, it would jeopardise the comfortable relationship we had. I thought that eventually we'd end up like David and me. Juan referred to our dinner engagement as a *date* but I saw it as a purely platonic arrangement.

I can't believe how prudish and foolish I was in those days. It seems to me that I could never let myself go. Perhaps I was afraid of what I would discover about myself. In the end, however, a perverse curiosity drove me into Juan's arms.

In the car, his conversation was halting and awkward. We were both conscious of a current of energy which intensified as the evening wore on. Communication between us had always revolved around basic issues at work, but tonight there was a sense, perhaps more than that, perhaps an awareness that there would be much to say, if only we could find a common ground for communication.

Over dinner he handed me a gift-wrapped box. 'Open it,' he urged.

I hesitated, afraid that whatever it was would seal a fate which awaited me somewhere in the shadows.

'Here, let me help you,' he said eagerly.

I was moving into the black world of the cave again. The cave of silence in which unreality was more tangible, more hard-edged than reality itself.

I lifted the lid off the box. A pair of earrings nestled in a bed of cotton wool. Each earring had two transparent amber-coloured teardrops edged in silver.

I couldn't take the gift from him.

'They're not valuable,' he said. 'I liked them because they reminded me of your eyes.'

In the end I took them to please him. So far it had been a wonderful evening and I didn't want to spoil any part of it over a few pieces of amber glass. For the first time in weeks I felt relaxed. Juan was good company and I was glad I had come after all.

We were the last couple in the restaurant and left around one o'clock, neither of us anxious to end the evening. Instead of taking me straight home, we went for a drive and eventually ended up at his flat. I offered no protest when he led me into the darkened building. It was inevitable that we would make love.

At first my responses were forced and mechanical, holding on to my will, afraid of letting go.

Juan's love-making was passionate. There was none of the cautious tentativeness characteristic of David. Eventually, I responded, despite my reservations. In the heat, sweat trickled between our hot, clammy bodies. I thought of Gina, who lived in the flat across from me, giving herself in such lusty abandon.

Giving. It was all part of being a woman. I thought of Gina again, draped over the bed like a sacrifice in some ancient ritual. To give; giving. In women it suggested more than merely providing, it implied sacrifice. All that giving, the emptying out. In the end how much, and what part of us, remained for ourselves?

*

124

I awakened early the next morning and got out of bed quietly, hoping not to disturb Juan. But he stirred and reached for me.

'Where are you going?' he asked sleepily.

I slipped into his dressing gown and left the room, ignoring the question as though I hadn't heard it. He got up, and came after me, drawing a hand through his dishevelled hair. I drew the robe even closer, wrapping myself in it like a cocoon.

I had to maintain control. I was afraid that if I didn't, I'd end up hurtling over the edge of the precipice.

Chapter Eleven

Helia de Souza was about three years older than me. I remember her as being exquisitely beautiful. Her dignity and graciousness reflected something of her Indian ancestry. Her parents had come to Mozambique from Goa. It was during the time when Goa was still under Portuguese rule.

Helia and I had met when she came to the clinic to enrol her seven-year-old son Manuel, who had been born deaf.

'I will come here, too,' Helia said. 'I want to learn also, so I can speak to my son through sign language.'

To accomplish this goal, she volunteered to help out at the clinic three mornings a week. We became good friends, but there were always clearly drawn parameters to our friendship. As soon as I crossed those boundaries to probe into her personal life, she'd become distant and aloof. We were getting along very well, and Helia was very helpful when the first indication of a problem appeared.

Manuel had only been undergoing treatment for a year when we began to hear that all special programmes for the blind and the deaf were to be cancelled. It came as quite a shock to us.

The government, it was said, was cutting back and closing many of the facilities regarded as non-essential in order to pay for the war. Ironically, the people who had least benefited from government programmes were going to be the first to suffer, and the hardest hit, by these cut-backs. The already small budget for Mozambican education, health care and social welfare, it seemed, would be decimated even further.

Despite all assurances to the contrary from the director, I suspected that it would only be a matter of months before the axe fell on our projects, too. The clinic for the blind, which catered mostly to Mozambicans, was scheduled to close at the end of the year. We were all surprised that they had managed to last for so long already, but it was all due to the resourcefulness of the director of the Institute for the Blind.

Helia told me not to worry. That nothing would happen to the clinic.

'Why not?' I asked.

She shrugged her shoulders. 'I know.'

'How do you know?'

'Don't ask so many questions, Faith. I'll come and help you every morning now,' she said.

'What about your job at the museum?'

'I told you, don't worry,' she said, her eyes glazing over. I knew that look. It meant no more questions. Story over.

Helia had been employed as a guide at the museum, working three afternoons a week. It was still a mystery to me how she had managed to survive so comfortably on such a paltry salary, or how she would manage now without a job.

She never talked about that aspect of her personal life, and one could only speculate about how she was able to live in an expensive, luxury flat near the beach and to own a car.

'What'll happen to these children if the clinic closes?' I signed.

'I told you, don't worry.'

This didn't stop me from being concerned. I even said a few 'Hail Marys'.

Helia was right. By October the clinic was still open and it really seemed more like a miracle. It was as if our prayers had been answered. Yet, as that year drew to a close, one couldn't help reflecting on how bizarre it had been.

Apart from the war, the rains had come late and were much lighter than usual. There was talk of another drought in the interior. The charismatic leader of the liberation movement had been killed by a parcel bomb. In Portugal, the president, who had fallen while on holiday the previous year and had sustained a blood clot on the brain, was now totally incapacitated. The prospect of Portugal without its president seemed odd, but the possibility of his dying from his injury was quite likely. The man whom everyone had thought of as immortal now lay on the brink of death.

His successor declared that change, except within the framework of the earlier system, was inconceivable. 'Evolution within continuity' became the new political slogan.

'All of this means people will continue to die,' Helia remarked. 'This will be a country of cripples. Crazy, isn't it?' she said, as she read the latest casualty figures reported in the paper.

While she tallied the casualties, I worried about how much longer I was going to be employed. Rita had told me not to worry. 'They need people like you. Your training will come in handy,' she had said. 'You'll see.'

Helia agreed. But I wasn't so sure. There was an atmosphere of abandonment here in the colonies. It was as if we were being eased towards the edge of an abyss; the country, already balanced very precariously, was ready to tip over the edge.

Portuguese forces were pummelling the guerrillas. The guerrillas stubbornly continued their fight almost as though victory for them was imminent. With all this going on, though, people from the rural areas were still being forced into *aldeamentos* – armed camps ostensibly built to protect the villagers from rebels. The *aldeamentos*, however, were nothing less than concentration camps, complete with guard towers and barbed wire. People were forced to relocate, their lives disrupted, their property abandoned or confiscated.

Farmers had left their *shambas*, which were small garden plots; they had left their wells, irrigation ditches, crops and livestock. They had been forced out of an existence that had taken some of them a lifetime to establish.

There was no news about Sofia, who, like the rest of the lost children, had fallen off the face of the earth. Bella still waited on the step, peering out as though she expected to see her little girl running out of the darkness. I was convinced that Sofia was dead and that Bella would wait in vain for the return of her daughter.

One afternoon as I was leaving the hospital, debating whether or not to visit Rita in the township, one of the children from the clinic ran over and handed me a note from Helia. The note, hastily scribbled, asked me to meet her at the Taj Cinema on Martinez Street in the second-class trading area, at half-past seven.

I knew where the place was, but was mystified by Helia's request to meet her at that spot. The area around Martinez Street was rough and it was dangerous to be there at night, especially alone. But in the end I went. I suspected that the request had something to do with the children because we had been discussing the issue not so long ago. At the time she had dismissed my concerns, suggesting that they were probably dead already and buried in mass graves somewhere. A lot of this kind of thing had been happening in Vietnam and papers had reported some of it, so the likelihood of similar incidents here could not be discounted.

My car had broken down again and I ended up taking the bus. Martinez Street was in an area that used to be part of the old Asian trading district. A few Indian stores still remained, but many of the Indians, fearing Portuguese reprisals, had left after India seized control of Goa.

I crossed the crowded street. A car hooted and sped by. My step involuntarily quickened as I turned a corner at a busy junction into a poorly-lit street. I must have walked for about ten minutes before reaching Martinez Street. I remembered that the cinema was about half-way down the block. Not much had changed since the last time I was there, except that the area was generally more run-down than before.

I glanced at my watch. It was only seven o'clock. I was early. I took my time, pausing to read a poster tacked to a lamppost. It was a revolutionary message calling for the overthrow of the Portuguese government. I was surprised that the security forces had missed this one.

Sensing that I was being watched, I glanced up. In the flat above the cinema, two young children peered down at me, their faces pressed against the cracked window, the tattered lace curtains falling around their shoulders like bridal veils. From the open window came the odour of cooking: spices, curry, and the smell of slightly rancid ghee. Then, as mysteriously as they had appeared at the window, the children vanished.

I tried the door to the cinema but it was locked. No need to panic, I told myself, there was still time. Without appearing obvious I dawdled, reading the notice-board.

Against the outside wall of the building with its jagged cracks and flaking paint was a sandwich-board advertising an Indian film. The picture looked familiar. I'd seen the same round-faced-voluptuous-lipped leading man on a picture before. His lustrous eyes were clouded with despair. A lock of black hair, falling over part of his brow, gave him a disarmingly roguish look. The object of his fancy was a woman in a vibrant red sari and a matching cast mark, disdainfully staring into the distance.

A solitary light bulb, painted yellow, shed an eerie light on a tattered poster for sweets and cigarettes.

The door to the cinema remained locked. I waited for half-an-hour. I tried the door again and walked to the other side of the building. I pushed against another entrance door, but this would not open either. While I stood there trying to decide what to do, a young Hindu boy hurried across the street to where I waited.

Smiling ruefully, he said, 'No movie tonight.'

I shrugged and turned to walk away.

'Wait! Wait!' he called.

I turned again.

'What's your name?' he asked.

I reached into my handbag for the pad I always carried with me and wrote my name.

'Uh huh,' he said.

I scribbled another message, asking why the cinema was closed.

'Soldiers close place down. No movie,' he said. He peered at me through slitted eyes. 'Your name is Faith?' he whispered.

I nodded.

'I have a message for you,' he said, handing me a slip of paper. 'Go now quickly,' he said.

I started to unfold the note but he stopped me.

'Go!' he urged.

Responding to the anxiety in his voice, I hurried down the street, glancing back once as I neared the corner. There was no sign of him.

Once safely ensconced in my flat, I opened the note. It was a hastily scribbled message from Helia, who apologised for not waiting. According to the note, she had left because she suspected she had been followed.

I, of course, couldn't imagine why anyone would want to follow her, unless it had to do with the information she had for me. It seemed that no matter how innocuous the activity, there was always an element of danger.

First Rita, now her. I wondered where all of this would end. I tried to put these thoughts out of my mind. I was exhausted and anxious to get into bed. But despite the comfort of my bed and my complete and utter exhaustion, I spent a restless night, battling with nightmare images.

At one point in an attempt to relax myself, I tried to focus on the faces of my parents. But all I could muster was a composite which seemed to be glued together from slivers of thought and impressions.

Sometimes the picture was distorted, like a reflection in a cracked mirror.

When I eventually did fall asleep, my dreams were not of my parents, but of Angie and the convent, or some other place which resembled it. I dreamt that I had been injured and that Angie was taking care of me. She was holding a bowl to my mouth, feeding me.

In the dream there was a large old vine at the entrance to the building. It was so thick that I couldn't reach around to encircle it. It stood out like the gnarled finger of an old crone invoking a curse on heaven.

Its tangled branches wove all around the building. The view was almost like that from Doña Maria's place, except that the grounds were terraced towards the cliff edge and surrounded by a low protective wall.

On one of the terraced slopes the vine which had snaked around the building was threaded through a wire frame to form an arbour. Through the openings hung small bunches of grapes, of the variety from which Portugal's famous port-wine was made.

I was sitting in an old, slatted garden chair. The early morning dew formed sluggish drops which slipped through the tangled foliage and fell into my lap.

Suddenly the peacefulness of the dream turned into the kind of turmoil which accompanies a nightmare. The drops of dew turned into enormous caterpillars which plopped into my lap. Horrified, I tried to cry out, but I couldn't. I had no voice. My mouth moved, but no sound issued. Angie tried to reach me, but Mother Superior held her back.

Then, quite unexpectedly, Margreta marched into my dream, carrying her baby in a laundry basket. She walked across the patio, her bare feet splayed on the flagstones. There were caterpillars everywhere. I wanted to warn her about them, but I couldn't. I saw her pushing aside the sheets which billowed on the line.

I managed to get up off the chair and as I stepped on to the ground, the caterpillars were transformed into scorpions. I ran to the stone wall around the lower terrace. The sun was disappearing behind a bank of clouds, below me the ocean turned a dull grey, churning as it sent huge waves crashing against the cliffs. Margreta ran to gather the washing, struggling to reach the sheets as they fluttered in the wind. I tried to assist her. Our hands brushed. The touch transformed her into Angie.

Stones the size of small pebbles clattered on to the patio, but as they hit the patio, they, too, became scorpions. I heard a cry, turned and saw that Angie had slipped and was toppling over the edge. I rushed back to the wall in time to see her tumbling through the air, followed absurdly, by the wicker basket which held the child. The two plummeted to the ocean below.

The grey clouds over the ocean had thinned and were tearing away. The sun was coming through, but I was crying.

Startled into wakefulness, my eyes flew open. The dampness on my cheek was real. I lay staring into the darkness, trying to remember the dream. I got up and went into the kitchen for a glass of water. The building was very quiet. It was three o'clock, I noted. I went back to bed and for the first time I wanted to be held, held close. I thought of Juan, who had awakened such exquisite feelings in me, and I wanted to place my head on his chest, to feel his arms around me. My heart was still pounding and I thanked God that it was only a dream.

Several days later Helia came to see me and explained that she had managed to arrange a meeting with a woman known only by the name of Rhonica. She explained that I was first to meet an old woman who would be waiting for me in front of the fish-market at exactly five o'clock on Friday afternoon. Helia told me that the old woman would be identified by a purple shawl and rimless glasses and that she'd escort me to an address in the old part of the city. It was that part of the city covered by a maze of narrow, winding cobbled streets lined with creaking doorways and foul smelling courtyards.

All this secrecy struck me as being a bit ridiculous. But Helia assured me that it was necessary. She advised me to take all the instructions very seriously.

'It's dangerous. It could mean your life as well as that of countless others,' she warned.

'What do you know about this?' I signed.

'Nothing,' she said abruptly. 'Just take my advice and no more questions, please.'

She had managed to put the fear of the devil in me. I even had second thoughts about going. I had never thought of myself as courageous. Often what I did was only out of necessity.

My years at the convent, where I had been schooled in the art of sacrifice, self-denial and endurance, had been quite ineffective. It was the kind of education which equipped one to suffer in silence, a form of passive endurance. But for me it was more like self-immolation which in a way relieved one of the responsibility to change things.

Chapter Twelve

On Friday afternoon as arranged, I was at the fish-market a few minutes before five o'clock to meet the contact. I had gone there directly from the clinic.

The old woman in the purple shawl and rimless glasses was standing at the far end of a row of stalls, waiting for me. The moment she saw me, she gestured for me to follow her. Even before I reached her, she started off, striding briskly up the street.

I had difficulty keeping up with her. Fortunately, no one paid attention to us as we hastened along the narrow winding streets, stepping over the fetid puddles of water trapped between slime-covered cobbled stones.

At a busy junction, we turned into another narrow street which led up a steep incline, both of us leaning forward a bit to take the uphill slope.

We crossed a square, passed under an archway and entered an enclosed area lined with old buildings. From the crumbling façades and balustrades laundry gently flapped in the breeze. The stench of rotting fish was everywhere. Donkeys, dogs, chickens and pigs foraged in the piles of decaying rubbish and wandered amongst the children playing in the streets.

Most of the houses in this area were dark, dank structures which had survived for more than a century. I followed the old woman as she hurried along. No one paid attention to us.

At the end of the road a burly black Mozambican, dressed in work clothes and wearing a sailor's cap, was quarrelling noisily with someone driving a small van. The man in the van had barricaded himself inside the vehicle, his windows tightly shut and the doors locked. The other was pounding on the roof in frustration. A noisy crowd had gathered in the narrow street to egg on the contenders. I noticed a change in the old woman. She became alert, adjusted the shawl as if to free her arms, and paused briefly. I glimpsed her arms – they were not those of an elderly woman. I glanced away quickly before she could see that I had noticed.

To our left was a doorway. She moved towards it. I followed. She opened it and stepped into the gloomy courtyard. A group of children involved in a noisy game looked up indifferently and then continued with their play. At the far end was another doorway through which we went into another street bordered on either side by heavy doors. Like the one we had just come through, they creaked inward to dark, mysterious passageways.

I followed her through one of these grime-encrusted doors. The building beyond was gloomy and I hung back uncertainly as she scurried across the damp floor. She beckoned and I followed. We crept up the stairs, the old woman attentive and alert.

On the second floor landing we heard raised voices and stopped to listen as a woman screamed obscenities. A man's muffled voice answered, carrying through the thin walls. There was a loud thwack followed by the sound of a woman whimpering. I glanced around nervously as we continued up the stairs to the third floor.

This rat-infested fire trap was obviously home to the destitute. A place for addicts and prostitutes to congregate and share their misery. On the third floor landing my guide stopped and cocked her head to listen. She placed a finger on her lips and beckoned. I followed behind her. By this time my heart was pounding so furiously I could hardly breathe.

She pressed herself against the wall and indicated that I should do the same. We crept towards one of the doors which stood ajar. When she reached it, she paused and peered through the crack, gingerly pushing the door until it opened a fraction of an inch wider.

Dreading what we might find, I watched as she stepped back, again flattening herself against the wall. I did likewise. When we were both in position she leaped forward, swung the door wide open and stepped inside. I saw the back of a man's head. He was bent over a small suitcase on the bed, trying to prise open the lock.

'Chacolo,' she said, softly, almost triumphantly.

Startled, the man swung around. Everything happened in a flash. I heard the door shutting behind us. I don't remember whether she had shut it or if I had.

She was in the centre of the room when the man reached into his jacket pocket. In that instant she stepped right into him, delivering what I thought to be a blow to his solar plexus. It seemed to knock the wind right out of him.

She stepped back. The man crumpled and fell, his head hitting the side of the bed. He never got his wind back – he was dead even before he hit the floor. From the position of the knife one could tell that it had entered at an angle between his ribs and had probably penetrated his heart, killing him instantly. I knelt beside him feeling for a pulse. She pulled me to my feet.

'Come,' she said, 'we've got to get out of here.'

I hesitated.

'Now!' she snapped. There was no longer any pretence about her being an old woman.

I gestured at the body on the floor.

She shook her head. Then, to my astonishment, she bent over the body and removed the knife embedded in his chest. The slender blade, about five inches long, withdrew as easily as if it had cut through butter. She wiped the knife on the dead man's T-shirt, unlocked the suitcase, tossed in the knife and checked its contents. Before she shut the case I noticed a gun and the characteristic pineapple shape of a hand-grenade inside.

She picked up the suitcase and saw the bemused expression on my face.

'I am Rhonica,' she said, stepping over the body. 'I know this man. He was in my squad. He betrayed us. Many good men were killed because of him. I shed no tears for his death. Come.'

Slightly dazed, I followed her. She opened the door, peered out, then gestured for me to go ahead of her. The hallway was deserted and as we left she locked the door behind her. Adjusting her glasses and the shawl, she once again assumed the guise of an old woman.

'We have to go to the docks to meet the man who has information about the children. That's good, eh?' she said.

I shook my head. At that point I was willing to forego the information. I had this awful feeling that it was the end for us as well. A man lay dead in the room upstairs and I had witnessed it. I was an accomplice.

Almost inadvertently, I was being sucked into the horrifying reality of the world around me. All my life I'd been on the outside looking in and now that I was on the inside I wanted to escape. My heart was still thumping as we left the building.

'We have gone through all this,' she said, irritated. 'It's too late for you to change your mind. You will have to come.'

There was something about her, something in the way she spoke, and in the way she looked at me, which confirmed my own feelings that I was being drawn, albeit reluctantly, into the maelstrom of the conflict.

When I thought of the dead man's surprised expression and the swift, efficient way she had dispatched him, I felt physically ill.

'We'll meet our contact at the docks,' she told me as we hurried through the streets, trying to find a taxi. 'He's a seaman. He was working on one of the ships which took thirty children aboard. Unfortunately, when the ship docked at Zanzibar, he was ordered off, but he has proof that it sailed to the Emirates. We are convinced that some of the Portuguese military are abducting the children and selling them as slaves to the Arabs. We think there are some high ranking officials involved. They are destroying our people and profiting from it,' she said. 'I came because I was told that you will help us to expose all of this and bring it to world attention. We have heard about your friend Doña Maria who has powerful connections in London.'

She flagged down a taxi and attempted no further conversation until the taxi driver dropped us a few blocks from the docks. She paid him and then shuffled alongside me with her exaggerated gait. She watched as the driver turned his taxi around and sped away. The wind was chilly and I turned my collar up. She didn't notice the cold. I was at a loss – there seemed to be no way I could communicate with her.

We arrived at the docks to find that there were several patrols out. I knew the area well from the days when I was living with Mamaria, and could find my way around without much difficulty. I took her to a spot where we could climb through the fence undetected.

'Are you sure this is the right way?' she asked.

I nodded.

'How do you know all this?' she asked, surprised.

I walked ahead without responding. Reassured by my confidence, she allowed me to lead the way to the place where she said the sailor would meet us. Not for one moment, though, did her vigilance relax. We climbed through the gap in the fence and she followed me to an abandoned shed, entering cautiously, gun in hand. Then, half-

137

crouching, she slid in through the open door, still carrying her suitcase in the other hand.

Once she was certain that we were safe, she relaxed slightly. 'We have about two hours to wait,' she said. 'Better make ourselves comfortable.'

We sat down on some old packing crates.

'You seem to know this place well,' she said. 'You've been here many times before, eh?'

I nodded.

'I'm sorry; I forgot you cannot speak . . .' she said and fell silent. After a while she spoke again.

'We will help you to get the proof you need about the children. The information must be taken to someone outside the country who will help us. We think that because of your friendship with Doña Maria and because of what happened to her husband and her daughter, she will be willing to help us expose what these people are doing here.

I shrugged my shoulders non-committally. First I wanted to see the proof. I was still more inclined to believe that the children were dead. I knew that there was no point leaking the information to the local press; all the local newspapers were government-controlled. It would be much better to try to get the information to the British press and they could pursue it further.

'I know,' Rhonica said, 'we need positive proof, but I will get that for you tonight.'

Rhonica and I waited in the dark, dank shed, our only companions the rats which scampered around in the darkness. Once we heard voices and froze, but the voices disappeared into the distance.

'I suppose you are still thinking about Chacolo,' Rhonica said after a while. She paused briefly as if half-expecting a response from me. 'I'll tell you a story which might be of interest to you . . . Many years ago when I was training to be a soldier with the liberation army, my instructor used to tell us to be tough. When you are out in the field, it is kill or be killed. I didn't want to kill. I didn't have the heart or the stomach for it. But he was a hard man, that one. When he spoke about *enemies*, it was as if he were speaking about the sand or the stones. Enemies were nothing. They were not people.

'In my mind, they *were* still people. Flesh and blood. At the mission school I was taught about the Christian spirit of love and

138

forgiveness. I believed in the sanctity of life. I believed in it even after the soldiers had come to our village and poured kerosene over my brother and set him alight.'

There was just the faintest tremor in her voice as she recalled the horror of this memory. After a moment, she continued. 'I dreaded the day that some confrontation would require me to kill someone. How could I do it? I mean that person is alive, a person just like you and me. How could I look into their eyes, see their soul and then kill them in cold blood?' She paused and in the darkness I sensed her wry smile. 'But that's exactly what happened. One day our patrol walked right into an ambush. It was lucky that there were more of us than there were of them or we would all have been dead. We put up a good fight. But on that day I confronted my worst nightmare. I shot one man, but another one I bayonetted and it was terrible because I could see his eyes as the knife went into his body. There was such a look of surprise on his face and then nothing.' Her voice trailed away and then, with a shrug, as if to dismiss the memory, she became matter-of-fact again. 'I have killed many times since then. It becomes easier. Some day someone will come along and kill me. None of us lives forever. If your time is up, it's up.'

I thought about what I'd seen: the man's expression when she knifed him. The silent 'O' he'd made with his lips. I shuddered, my whole body trembling, but not with cold alone.

Rhonica struck a match and, cupping the flame in her one hand, glanced at her wristwatch. It's half-past nine,' she said. 'I'll go and see where he is. You stay here.'

I groped for her arm in the darkness and held on, indicating that I wasn't going to stay there by myself. She understood. After a moment's hesitation, she said, 'OK, but be careful.'

Although there was no sign of a patrol, we took no chances. In the darkness we crept over to the far side of the dock where an Egyptian freighter was anchored.

'This is the one,' she said. 'If anyone finds us here, we'll pretend to be prostitutes. You wait here. I will give you a signal. A sharp whistle and you will know to come out and join me.'

I waited in the darkness, in a state of high tension. Eventually I heard the whistle and crept along the side of the shed. I saw her quite clearly, she was with her contact. The man led the way on board. We could not risk a light and so we had to feel our way along

139

the deck, fumbling in the darkness. We stopped frequently to listen, but nothing moved on board the ship. It was as though it had been abandoned.

'The ship leaves in the morning,' the man said. 'The children were brought aboard earlier. There is only one guard and he is asleep.'

Our way seemed to be clear and we hurried across the deck to the hold. We waited for a few moments and then the man opened the hatch and shone his bright flashlight into the darkness.

I almost wept. There were so many children and all of them started to cry with quiet sobs. Some of them were so young, they could barely have been older than four or five.

Even Rhonica, who had been hardened, could not believe such inhumanity. 'My God,' she whispered, 'where are they taking them?'

'To the Middle-East – Bahrain, Kuwait and so on. For a tidy profit they will be sold as slaves.'

Rhonica leaned forward, 'We have to do something about the youngest ones, right now,' she said.

'If we're discovered here, we'll be killed,' said the man.

'No,' Rhonica said as she got on to her stomach and leaned over the edge of the hatch. The children started to cry, but she told them to remain quiet. They obeyed and fell silent. She told them that they were brave and that she was proud of them, and that she couldn't help all of them at that moment, but that help would come soon, before they reached their destination. She explained that she could only help four of them. She asked the children to pass the youngest and the weakest to her. One of the older boys picked out four of the youngest children and instructed the others to move them over their heads towards the hatch.

Rhonica leaned as far forward as she could, lowered the ladder and then the four chosen children climbed up. She helped them and passed them along to us. I took two from her.

The other children knew that the hatch would be closed again. For a moment there was a look of such utter despair and terror that I couldn't bear to watch.

'Don't be afraid,' Rhonica said to them. 'Be prepared for the time when we come to take you to safety.' The sailor shut the hatch. Rhonica couldn't speak. She picked up a little boy and hugged him to her. When she looked up, I saw her eyes were glistening with tears.

The children didn't make a sound. Young as they were, they knew the dangers we faced. I carried one of them, Rhonica another and the man carried two.

'Let's get out of here,' Rhonica said. 'But first I have to get rid of this. I don't want to be caught with it,' she said, indicating the suitcase which she still had in one hand.

Once we were off the ship, we hid in the darkness while Rhonica opened the case and took out the gun which she tucked into her waistband. She then wrapped her shawl around herself to conceal it. At a secluded spot along the wharf, she dropped the suitcase over the edge. It sank immediately.

I couldn't go home that night. I couldn't bear to be alone and so I found myself at Juan's flat, hoping that he would be there. Fortunately it was one of his rare nights off and the instant he saw me, he drew me into his arms. I felt so ashamed of this need for him. He sensed my mood, scooped me up into his arms and carried me to his room. We made love for hours. It was the only way I could put out of my mind what I had seen on the boat.

Chapter Thirteen

'We have come a long way since the days of Ressano Garcia,' Rita remarked as she stepped away from the window. In the grounds below the Mozambicans waited patiently to see the doctor.

Ressano Garcia was the small town which had gained its notoriety from the number of prostitutes who waited there for miners returning from South Africa. It took a while for me to realise that Rita was referring to her people, and the renewed sense of pride they had in who they were. It was especially evident amongst the younger generation who were joining the liberation movement in droves. Rita alluded to this phenomenon as 'black consciousness'.

She came away from the window. 'The children are doing well. I went to see them yesterday. I'm so glad you brought them to safety.'

'I hope Rhonica can do something about the others, too,' I signed.

'What can they do? Those children are already halfway to their destinations by now,' she said.

I had no idea what could be done. I had feared, that night as we came away from the ship, that it would be an impossible feat to save the rest of the children.

'I'm so glad you were able to find a safe place for the ones we brought back. They've been through so much already.'

Rita didn't say anything. She stretched languidly and I could see that she was exhausted. I was tired, too, and ready to go home.

When I got back to the flat later that afternoon, Helia was sitting on my doorstep, waiting for me.

'I'm so glad you're here. I was just about to leave,' she said.

'Come on in. I'm dying of thirst,' I signed.

She followed me indoors. It was as hot inside as it was out. We were all hoping for rain to cool things down, but there wasn't a cloud in sight.

'I was worried about you,' she said.

'I was worried about you, too,' I signed. I hadn't seen her since that eventful encounter with Rhonica. Except for hurriedly dropping her son off, she hadn't spent any time at the clinic and I had no idea what she was doing all day long. This was one subject she refused to discuss.

'Did you find out anything about the children?' she asked.

I nodded. 'They are being smuggled out of the country to Arab countries where they are sold as slaves.'

'Dear God,' Helia muttered. 'Are you sure?'

'I saw them, Helia. I saw them with my own eyes. They were stuffed into the hold of the ship. There was no room for them to move. We brought four of them out. We couldn't manage any more than that.'

Helia shook her head in disbelief. 'Where are they now?'

'They're at a safe house in the township.'

'What about the others?'

I repeated what Rhonica had said about rescuing the others.

'Damn,' she muttered, despairingly. 'It'll be impossible.'

'Helia, how well do you know Rhonica?' I signed, curious about her relationship with the other woman.

'That's not important,' she said, a little off-handedly, then realising that she had been abrupt, she smiled apologetically. 'I'm sorry. I didn't mean to be so sharp. It's just that I'd rather not say. Sometimes the less one knows, the better off one is. Why do you ask?'

I told her a bit about the events of that day. I did not mention the dead man or the suitcase with its incriminating contents.

We talked for a long time until eventually she said that she had to pick up her son who was playing at a friend's house. I watched her go and couldn't help wondering about her strange existence.

Rita was waiting for me when I got to her place on Saturday. I wanted to see the children, but she told me it was too dangerous. She was afraid that someone might follow us and endanger not only the little ones, but the family taking care of them. She was alone with Zeca. Teresa had gone off somewhere. We lounged around talking for hours. It was almost like old times again. When Teresa returned she came rushing in with news that she had found a job.

'What kind of job?' Rita asked.

'A maid. Cleaning up rooms at the hotel,' she said, sitting down on the bed where we were sitting.

'Which hotel?' Rita asked. She had got up off the bed to hang her dress in the small curtained alcove in the corner of the room and turned her surprised glance on Teresa.

Teresa hesitated. Rita looked at me. It was obvious to both of us that Teresa was being evasive.

'Which hotel?' Rita repeated the question and went to sit down beside her. Zeca, who had been crawling around on the kitchen floor, quickened his pace when he heard his mother's voice. I picked him up.

'Do I have to drag every word out of you?' Rita asked. Teresa became impatient, but Rita placed a restraining hand on her arm. 'Sit down and tell me everything,' she said.

'There's nothing to tell. I will be working at the Hotel Presidente,' Teresa replied. She withdrew her arm from Rita's grasp, got up off the bed and sauntered out of the room into the kitchen.

'Who got you the job?' Rita called. 'It's one of the best hotels in town. It's very hard to find work there. What did you have to do to get the job?' she asked suspiciously.

'Nothing,' Teresa called back at her. 'Stop worrying about me. I'm not a child. I'm nineteen years old.'

Rita studied her hands pensively. She was probably beginning to realise that the battle to keep Teresa off the streets might be a losing one.

Teresa came back into the room, saw Rita sitting there dejectedly, and said: 'Everything has a price. When there is nothing left with which to pay, we pay with our lives.' With that she turned away and went back into the kitchen.

'Hey, Teresa. Come back here,' Rita called.

'What for?'

'Just come here,' Rita said, dragging a battered suitcase out from under the bed. Teresa and I watched as she opened it and took out a dress folded in tissue paper. We watched as she carefully unwrapped it.

'How would you like this dress?' she asked Teresa.

The dress was a black strapless affair of rustling taffeta with enormous frills and bows.

'You want to give that to me?' Teresa asked in wide-eyed astonishment.

144

'Of course. Did I not say so?'

'It's so beautiful.' She held the dress up before her and pirouetted into the kitchen. 'What do you think?' she asked me, but before I could answer she was off at another tangent again.

'Where did you get it, Rita?' Teresa asked.

'Feta gave it to me.'

'Who is Feta?' Teresa asked.

'One of the nurses as the hospital. She bought it to catch the eye of Dr Alfonso Henriques. It didn't work. He is engaged to that singer Maria-Paula. They are going to be married.'

Teresa laughed. 'Is he handsome?'

'Sort of. He's not my type, though. Neither is the dress,' she said winking at me.

Teresa laughed gaily. 'Don't you like it?' she asked, peering at her reflection in the small framed mirror on the dresser.

'Not on me.'

'Are you sure?' Teresa asked, turning to face Rita, the dress clutched to her body.

'Yes.'

Rita took the dress and slipped it over Teresa's head. 'You might have to take it in a bit . . . here and . . . here.' Rita said. But Teresa was too excited to worry about a bit of fullness on the waist and hips. She preened and primped before the mirror and then flung her arms around Rita's neck. 'I don't know what I'd do without you.'

It didn't take much to distract Teresa, I thought.

'Now tell me all about your new job. How did you get it?'

'I heard they were looking for young girls,' she said. 'I went to see Julio, the boss. He told me I could start soon.'

'What work will you be doing?'

'I told you. I will be cleaning rooms. Today I go in for training. Julio . . .'

'Julio . . . You call your boss by his first name?' Rita asked.

'Well, he's not the big boss. He's Mozambican, but he has a big say, just like a boss.'

'What is this job costing you?'

'Nothing,' Teresa said lightly.

But Rita knew better.

'I'm glad you have a job,' Rita said. 'But what are you going to do about Zeca? Who will take care of your son?'

Teresa's face fell.

'I will not permit you to leave him here at home by himself. If you want to work, you'll have to find someone to take care of him.'

Rita's words were sobering and Teresa looked a bit bewildered by the question. She reflected for a moment and glanced at me as though searching for an answer. I made a slight movement with my shoulder which was meant to be encouraging.

'I will find someone to take care of my son.'

Rita smiled and I thought that perhaps there was still some hope for Teresa.

The summer was unbearably hot. It brought with it death and disease. The flow of civilian casualties continued unabated, many of them bearing wounds created by a whole new variety of weapons of unimaginable destruction.

On the one hand, the Mozambicans were convinced that they would ultimately have independence, on the other, the government seemed determined to quash such expectations and stepped up their action. Fighting intensified. New military units were formed. One of these was a paramilitary unit called the *flechas* – the arrows – which was comprised mostly of black Mozambicans.

The cycle of provocation and reprisals continued unabated; and caught in the middle were the innocent villagers. I was kept very busy during this time: when I wasn't at the clinic, I was in the wards helping as best I could.

The majority of the Europeans in Mozambique continued with their lives much as before, refusing to believe that independence was imminent. They clung to the hope that the tide of war would be turned against the rebels, especially since we were being told that government forces were making daily gains on rebel-held territory.

December crept up and talk of war turned to talk of the Christmas ball. David and I had tried to patch things up between us and although we still shared the flat, we saw very little of each other. He was deliberately spending more time at the site. From my point of view, whatever we had was either dead or dying.

As a creature of habit, David found it difficult not only to contemplate the consequence of change, but the simple thought of change itself.

When he told me that he might be going to South Africa for Christmas, I considered accepting Juan's invitation to the Christmas ball.

Juan and the ball were on my mind one night when I popped in to see Rita, who was working that evening. It was about half-an-hour before the end of her shift and it was most unusual that she was not on the unit. I looked around for her, but she was nowhere in sight. Eventually, as I passed the stock-room, I saw a light shining under the door. I hesitated, not wanting to barge in, in case one of the doctors or the nursing sister was inside. I listened. There was no sound of movement from within and I quietly pushed the door.

It swung open and I saw Rita at the cabinet filling a small laundry bag with bandages and drugs. Startled, she spun around, dropping the bag.

For a moment there was a stunned silence as we both tried to collect our wits. She bent over to retrieve the bag of drugs from the floor. She straightened up and I waited for her to say something. Instead, she glared at me, her eyes glittering with defiance. After a long pause full of awkwardness, I turned and left the room.

The scene with Rita standing at the drug cabinet with the incriminating bag in her hand was a painful reminder of how things had changed between us.

Somehow, in my half-dazed state, I found my car and drove home in a kind of stupor, Rita's expression with me for the entire drive. I realised that Rita was in grave danger, but there was no use talking to her. She was much too determined to be discouraged by warnings from me.

I began to see the significance of her peculiar behaviour: her staying on at the institute despite the fact that she despised the Portuguese, and her reaction to the PIDE agent visiting Juan at the hospital.

Except for a muttered 'thank you' from her the next day, for not telling anyone, neither of us mentioned the incident again. She behaved as if it had never happened. But it *had* happened and the awareness was there, bubbling up between us.

I worried about her safety as there were informers everywhere. One didn't have to be guilty of anything. Anyone with a grudge could easily have wreaked havoc with another's life. I feared that it would only be a matter of time before she was caught.

When Helia came to see me, she wanted to know why I couldn't make up my mind about the ball. I tried to explain that I wasn't in the mood to celebrate.

'What is this not in the mood business? What's going on? Is it you and David?' she demanded.

Eventually I made up my mind and informed Juan that I would accept his invitation.

That evening we heard that an Egyptian cargo vessel had been attacked off the coast of Tanzania. The report claimed that the ship had been torpedoed and sunk after having been boarded by guerrillas. There was no news of the children. To those of us familiar with the way the government operated, it was fairly obvious that whoever was trading in children was doing so with the tacit support of some very well-placed officials.

The following week, however, we got word from Rhonica that eighty of the children had been rescued. Twenty-five of them had drowned in the rescue attempt. Those who had successfully been taken off the ship were being housed in refugee camps in Tanzania. The news about the children lost at sea was very disheartening. I thought of how the parents would feel when they heard about their children's fate.

After all this time, Bella still waited for Sofia to come home. Both Rita and I expressed our hopes that Sofia might, by some stroke of good fortune, have been amongst the children rescued. We didn't say anything to Bella because we didn't want to get her hopes up fruitlessly.

Chapter Fourteen

One morning, in early November, just as everyone was starting to breathe more easily about the situation at the clinic, orders arrived for me to dismiss the children. No explanations or answers were provided to our questions. With a sinking feeling I realised that it was all over for us. We had finally fallen prey to the vagaries of unstable economic and political conditions. Despite Helia's assurances, I had expected the clinic to close months earlier. The end came as an anti-climax, almost bringing relief from all the tension.

My immediate concern was for the children whose lessons had been interrupted, perhaps never to be resumed again. I was told that arrangements had been made to get the children home. The only problem was Manuel. He had nowhere to go at that hour of the day. The relative who usually took care of him in the afternoons after his class was not expected home until two o'clock. And Helia, I understood, could not be reached by telephone.

Exasperated by the way the situation had been handled, I decided to drive out to Helia's place despite the clinic's inability to locate her. I assumed that she had probably gone out for a short while. If not, Manuel and I would wait. He had a spare key to the flat. I wanted to tell her personally about the closure. After all, she was the one who had assured me that nothing like this would happen.

It took about half an hour to get there and as I pulled up in the street in front of her *pensão*, a black Mercedes-Benz pulled up ahead of me. It was an official-looking car and I was curious to see who was in it. I delayed getting out of the car, much to the chagrin of a very cranky and irritable Manuel.

The occupant was a high-ranking government official. I recognised him from his pictures in the paper. He entered the building and we got out of my car. In the lobby we caught up with the

149

official, who was waiting for the lift. When it came he politely stepped aside to allow Manuel and me ahead of him.

We arrived on the fifth floor where he got off as well. While I waited for Manuel who had stopped to tie his shoelaces, the man passed us and walked ahead. I glanced up casually and to my astonishment discovered that he had stopped at Helia's door.

As Manuel started to straighten up, I took hold of his arm to distract him, manoeuvring him around so that he had his back to their front door half-way down the hall as it opened. From where I stood, I could see quite clearly and caught a glimpse of Helia in the doorway, wearing a white negligee.

The man stepped inside and the door shut behind him. I had to get Manuel away from the flat, having no doubt about what was going on in Helia's bedroom.

'Manuel, let's you and I go for a drive,' I signed. 'I feel like having an ice-cream. What about you?'

He made a reluctant face.

'Come on,' I urged. 'I'd like one.'

'I'll put my books away and tell Mama . . .' he signed in reply.

'No, Manuel,' I responded, tugging him in the opposite direction. 'I just remembered that your mother told me she wouldn't be home until later on. Bring your books along with you. You and I will go for a nice drive, eh?'

He showed more reluctance. He didn't want to carry his books, but I finally persuaded him to go with me. I couldn't think what else to do with him because I didn't want him walking in on his mother.

We went for a drive and got him the ice-cream. On the way to my flat I stopped off and left a note on the relative's door so everyone would know that Manuel was at my place.

Helia got the message and came by to pick him up later that afternoon. She was in a good mood. 'I'm so thankful you were able to take care of him. I don't know what I would've done,' she added, hugging him. But her mood soon changed when she heard about the closure. With an air of preoccupation, she said, 'Don't worry. It won't be closed for long. I promise you.'

'Oh, yes, of course. You have the power to keep it open,' I signed with a touch of sarcasm.

'You'll see. Don't worry.'

I wanted to believe her so badly that even those few words were reassuring. As she was leaving I indicated to her that I had tried to drop Manuel at home, but had come away when I found that she had a visitor. She gazed up with a start and then flushed. There was a brief, awkward moment between us and I regretted mentioning it to her.

'*Muito obrigado*,' she said, thanking me again. She offered no explanation. In the doorway she turned and called, '*Adeus*.'

This time Helia was right. A week later the clinic reopened. I was relieved, but I couldn't help wondering if she had actually been responsible for getting it reopened or whether some bureaucrat had had a change of heart. Still, I couldn't dismiss the fact that she had been entertaining one of the government officials and in all probability, had used some of her influence. She never said anything to me about it. Neither of us discussed it. It was part of the understanding we had between us. It didn't take long for an air of normality to return to the clinic and nothing more was mentioned about its fate.

The date of the long-awaited Christmas ball arrived on the second Friday of December. As arranged, Juan picked me up in his jeep in the evening. I was in a gloomy mood, berating myself for accepting his invitation. It was as though I had some premonition of disaster. Rita was probably right, I thought, when she advised me not to go. But then what was the use? I hadn't spoken to either her or David for weeks.

It was safe to assume that David had already left for South Africa. Funny, I reflected, how I had tried to put him out of my mind, and now here I was thinking of him again. I was the one who had wanted my freedom from him, yet I felt quite disconsolate. Life was such a contradiction.

We had only been there for a couple of hours, but the ballroom was hot and crowded. To escape the noise and the stifling atmosphere, I decided to go for a walk. Despite my efforts to get away by myself, Juan insisted on accompanying me. We walked around the flower beds. It was a beautiful night and the grounds were lit up for the festive occasion. Across the bay the lights blinked against a clear sky.

Rita had said she would never condone such extravagance when people were starving elsewhere.

'Is anything wrong?' Juan asked.

What was the use of explaining all of this to him, when he knew what it was all about. There was a certain attitude amongst the

151

Portuguese and other expatriates. A preoccupation with pleasure and diversion.

'Tell me what's bothering you,' he persisted. 'You know you can trust me.'

Disengaging my arm from his, I walked on ahead of him.

'Are you and David having trouble?' he asked. 'Did you tell him about us?'

I picked a flower from the hedge and gazed out at the distant flickering lights.

'Are you going to tell him or do you want me to?' he asked.

My attention remained fixed on the distant lights.

'Faith, I know that you don't love him. Don't you think it's time you told him so?' he asked.

He sensed my irritation with his question and fell silent. At a loss for words he turned away. 'I'll get you a glass of wine.'

While he went off, I strolled towards the terrace. I was glad to be alone. I thought how my life had assumed the same quality of darkness as the night sky.

'Are you all right?' a voice enquired.

Jolted out of my preoccupation, I swung around. David was standing behind me.

'What are you doing here?' I signed. 'I thought you'd gone to South Africa.'

'I decided not to go. I had to speak to you. I saw you walking with Juan,' he added, a note of reproach in his tone.

Too tired for a confrontation, I turned away.

'Faith, what has gone wrong between us? Why can't we have a reasonable discussion any more?' he asked. 'I'll be going back to England soon. It could've been so good between us. I care very deeply for you, Faith. I have cared for you from the first moment I saw you at Doña Maria's place. Come back to England with me.'

'David, I'm not the same person you met at Doña Maria's dinner party. I've changed.'

A look of incomprehension passed over his face.

'Can't you see that I've changed, that I'm not the same person?'

He looked at me intently, as if searching for something familiar to latch on to, then not finding anything there, he turned away.

'I'm not leaving immediately . . .' he said. 'Think about what I've said.'

'There's nothing to think about,' I signed. 'Actually, it might be better if I moved out of the flat. I'll find another place.'

'That won't be necessary,' he said quickly. 'It's your flat. I'm the one who ought to move out. I'll pick up my stuff tomorrow.'

Suddenly, overwhelmed by a feeling of such devastating sadness, I felt like weeping. What was wrong with me? I wondered. Was this not what I had wanted? Yet, at that moment, the prospect of ending that particular phase of my life created a strange longing, a nostalgia for something that had never existed.

Shivering, I drew my shawl closer. He placed an arm around me as strains of a Latin love song drifted out from the ballroom.

'Does Juan have anything to do with your decision?'

I shook my head.

'Faith . . .'

I turned wearily, resting my head on his shoulder. The silence was heavy between us, full of unspoken thoughts and feelings.

Juan returning with the drinks, saw us like this, and turned away.

The following afternoon David arrived to pick up his belongings. The contents of the flat belonged to me or were things that we had acquired together and which he had no need of now.

'I'll be at the Esplanada Hotel for a few days,' he said, inviting me to come by for a drink later on. 'This may be the last time we see each other. Come for a drink, please.'

I agreed to meet him, 'for old times' sake'.

When he left he took only his clothes. Two suitcases-full. The sum total of his life with me. I watched as he carried them down the stairs and across the street to his car.

Later that afternoon he was waiting for me in the bar of his hotel. The place was unusually crowded. He was at a table in the middle of the room. It was quite noisy and everyone seemed to be full of Christmas cheer. Gradually as more wine and beer was consumed, some of the patrons became argumentative and threatening, as discussions about the progress of the war became more heated.

Two men at the next table argued furiously about the state of the country. The noisy dispute spilled over and gained support from the other patrons. Then, in the midst of the commotion, the outside door of the bar was flung open. For a moment every voice was hushed. A fresh clamour broke out as the newcomer was recognised.

'It's Senhor Morais,' someone answered in response to David's question. The cause of all the acclamation was a tall, well-built man with sun-bleached hair which peeped out from under his air-force cap.

The news about his successful bombing mission against the rebel camps up north had preceded him. Armando Morais, only surviving son of Raul Morais, strode up to the bar like a conquering hero. On all sides men pressed forward, shaking his hand, interspersing their salutations with orders to the barman to fix him a drink.

The man downed the drinks as fast as they were poured. Drink after drink arrived, paid for by the admiring company who continued to jostle one another for the privilege of patting him on the back and saying to him, rather pointedly, 'Good work, hope you get the rest of the bastards next time.'

David and I stayed on for a while longer. Eventually David said, 'It's late already, why don't you join me for dinner? I'm meeting a bloke who just recently returned from Brazil.'

'Don't worry,' he said, chuckling when he saw my expression. 'This one's not like Wynand van der Berg. He's very pleasant. You'll like him. Besides, he's planned an interesting outing for the evening. You might as well join us for dinner,' he said, grinning, 'for old times' sake.'

We had dinner in a quiet café in the hotel where David's friend Eduardo Domingo joined us. Eduardo regaled us throughout dinner with anecdotes. On the whole it was quite an interesting evening and I enjoyed myself.

After dinner Eduardo said, 'I was going to take David to a bar down near the docks. I hear they've got the best music in town. I'd be honoured if you would accompany us.'

The two men interpreted my hesitation as assent. There seemed no point in arguing. It was still early and I had no other plans for the evening.

We left the hotel a short while later, passing by the bar David and I had been in earlier. It was still noisy. A rowdy crowd from the afternoon's celebrations in honour of Armando Morais was still going strong. They were probably too inebriated to remember the original reason for their merry-making.

It was pleasant out and the streets were noisy with boisterous pedestrians. We took a taxi and then walked several blocks in the old quarter, passing through narrow alleys which bustled with activity. It was amazing that amidst all the misery, there was so much obvious joy in being alive.

Eduardo, with his light-hearted banter, had unwittingly smoothed over whatever residual strain there had been between David and me.

The early evening drizzle had petered out and the wind had died down. After the rain there was a smell of damp earth in the air. The stars seemed obscured by a gauzy film of cloud. A perfect evening. A night for lovers, and everywhere they were in evidence: along the crowded boulevards, sauntering through the streets, peering into store windows.

Our destination was a small bar near the wharf. When we entered the smoky room the barman gestured to a vacant table by the stage. We squeezed between the tables pushed together to jam in as many people as possible.

We had just sat down when the lights dimmed. The corpulent barman clapped his hands loudly and a young girl appeared from behind a black shabby curtain and stepped on to the raised dais. She was accompanied by a guitarist. I groaned inwardly, expecting an exotic female act – perhaps a stripper of sorts.

But the girl was a *fadista*.

Without much ado, the young man tuned his guitar and plucked out a melody. The girl began to sing and the patrons, drawn by the plaintive quality of the *fado*, fell silent, staring into their drinks, glassy-eyed with melancholia. It was almost as if they could see reflected in their glasses images of shattered dreams, of former times and bygone loves.

I imagined they were wondering about their future when the unspeakable happened in this country. Some were ready to flee to South Africa, but the majority would return to their country of origin. For many of them, born in Mozambique, it meant returning to their ancestral home in Portugal, thousands of miles away on another continent; a world as remote to them as it was to the black Mozambicans.

The singer's dark eyes flashed seductively, holding the gaze of first one man, then another until none of them could resist her. Young and old alike succumbed. The men, still in work clothes, were dockers. David emptied his glass and lowered his eyes. The singer tried to catch his attention, her voice rising and falling, creating an intimacy which no one could ignore. The audience, most of whom were men, applauded enthusiastically, calling her name – shouting bravo.

155

But it was as if she were singing for David alone, as if he were the only person in that room. Her voice evoked an excruciating sadness, like a drug bridging the gap between light and darkness. She touched a part of my soul which held the tragedy of my life, opening it up like a festering wound. I closed my eyes. It felt as though time had ceased. All my pain and sorrow became focused in that moment of time.

Suddenly the song ended. I opened my eyes. The spell was broken. We were back in the reality of the present. The girl took a sip of water from the glass beside her and there was a momentary pause as if the audience were pulling themselves together before they broke into wild applause. She smiled, her expression confident.

The lights came on and for the first time I saw the hard lines on her face. The gaunt, hollowed cheeks, the brows tweezed and pencilled into tight arches, her thin lips painted bright red with a brashness that defied comment.

I watched with a feeling of disappointment as she strolled through the bar allowing the men to fondle her. Eduardo saw the expression on my face and shrugged apologetically. David looked terribly sad.

The girl walked away from us. There was something in her lazy, laconic stride, in the way her buttocks were outlined beneath her flimsy skirt, which reminded me of Teresa.

I was ready to go home now. The evening was over for me, but I knew that it had only begun for the two men. David wanted to take me back to the flat, but I indicated that I'd take a taxi.

He hailed a taxi and gave the driver the address. He leaned through the window and kissed me lightly. He squeezed my hand and without another word, stepped back on to the pavement. As the taxi drove off, I glanced back. David was standing on the pavement, gazing after me. Then he turned and walked away.

BOOK FOUR

Chapter Fifteen

Over Christmas our hopes for a cessation of hostilities were dashed by new confrontations between government troops and guerrillas. No one escaped. Not even Armando Morais. A few days before Christmas he was killed by a land mine planted along a quiet stretch of road about fifteen miles from the Morais estate.

The incident made front-page news. The report claimed that the mine had been planted deliberately. The death was being viewed as an assassination and special agents were investigating.

For the rest of us – the living – life had to go on and fortunately it was a time of year when there were many distractions for those who wanted them.

The segments of society in the cities who could afford to, threw themselves into the New Year celebrations with a zeal and gusto not seen before, but so did those who could least afford to. There seemed to be an undercurrent of hysteria in the air.

Apart from the anarchy around me, my personal life appeared more settled. For the first time in a long while I felt that I had the power to take charge of my life again. But there wasn't much time to dwell on such issues. Other, more pressing problems created by war, disease, pestilence, drought and now the flooding, took precedence.

The two-year drought had broken with torrential rains, swelling rivers in the north. Refugees brought news of homes being swept away, of people and animals drowning. When water levels subsided, bloated carcasses were beached and lay decomposing in the sun. Lisbon failed to respond to appeals for assistance, despite the threat of disease. The only aid came via the Red Cross, who set up emergency relief programmes. With the help of two local social agencies they opened a mobile medical facility to halt the spread of cholera and typhoid.

For a while nature herself had intervened to provide a respite from the fighting in the north. Hindered by the muddy conditions, the conflict on both sides had ground to a halt. The Red Cross asked for local volunteers. Rita and I both offered our services, but were denied permits to travel.

As soon as this crisis eased, hostilities between the two sides flared up once again. A large contingency of the International Red Cross, suspected of providing medical assistance to the rebels, was expelled. Security at the hospital was stepped up. Draconian measures, which included the death penalty, were introduced to stop the flow of stolen medical supplies from reaching the rebels.

During this period twenty-three hospital employees were arrested, fifteen of them nurses. I was concerned that Rita would eventually be caught, too. Everyone, it seemed, fearing the wrath of the PIDE, took a keen interest in the supply records. But inevitably with the furore about the expulsion of the Red Cross workers over, and no further reports of thefts from the hospital, security relaxed. The shortage of manpower, however, increased the PIDE dependency on informers.

One afternoon Doña Maria and I met at the Hotel Polana for lunch. She was planning a trip to Lisbon and wanted to find out whether we'd been able to get hold of some of the documentation she needed to start an investigation into the illegal trade in children. Helia had assured me she'd be able to get hold of a copy of the ship's manifesto, but her contact hadn't come through. As usual Doña Maria was passionate about what was happening in Mozambique and especially about what was happening to the children.

Life here was such a contradiction, I reflected on my way home. On the one hand you had people like Doña Maria, compassionate and caring, on the other hand there were those who had no concern about the people in this country.

Rita's opinion, however, was that no matter how well intentioned the Europeans were, they never quite measured up. According to her, this concern for the Mozambicans from people like Doña Maria, although commendable, was a mere drop in the ocean when compared with the reality of life, in which blacks were tortured, plundered, pillaged, burnt, raped, emasculated, drowned, decapitated, eviscerated, abducted and slowly but surely decimated.

I had told her many times about the circumstances surrounding Senhor Cardoso and Isabella's death.

158

'Things aren't always what they appear to be,' she had said, sceptically. 'What about Juan? What do you think he'd do if it came to the crunch?'

I couldn't answer for Juan and told her so.

With a dismissive shrug, she said, 'Who cares about us, anyway? We're only blacks.' Her manner was so off-hand, she might have said, 'We're only sand, or we're only stone.'

Doña Maria was disappointed when I told her that we had not got any of the information yet.

'We must have the proof,' she said impatiently. 'We must have proof. I cannot present our case for the children if I am empty-handed.'

'But I saw the children in the hold . . .' I protested.

She shook her head. 'It doesn't help. We need pictures and pieces of paper with official stamps on them. Documents, my dear. Documents.'

I felt quite helpless. Getting these documents sounded like an impossible task.

We parted with a promise from me that I would visit her soon. Unfortunately, I didn't have a chance to do so for several weeks.

In the meantime, David returned to England. There was a letter from him in which he hinted at having found someone else. I didn't know whether to be glad or sad that he'd landed on his feet so easily.

Helia laughed when I told her about my inadequacies with men. She obviously had none. 'You're over-cautious,' she told me. 'Where's your spirit of adventure? Jump into the river and worry about the crocodiles afterwards.'

The thought that I had become over-cautious was disconcerting, especially since this was the quality I least admired about David. But my caution sprang from the fear of being hurt. I had built an impenetrable wall around myself and within that wall my life was relatively safe. There were, however, always attempts by others to break through my reserve.

I remember, one Monday, several months after David had left, and after a particularly vexatious day at work, Juan invited me to have dinner with him at his flat. We had come straight from the hospital. The roads to his place were a mess. Some time ago major road construction had started a few blocks from where he lived. For

159

some reason or other the work had been interrupted and never resumed.

By the time we reached the large scar in the roadway the rain had let up a bit and the sky had brightened. Muddy water had collected in shallow lakes on either side of the road and even though he drove carefully, the windscreen was spattered with mud, the wipers ineffectually spreading a brown glaze over the glass.

Juan pulled over, reached into the back for a cloth and found an old sweater. He climbed out of the jeep and stepped right into a puddle, sheepishly watching as water seeped into his shoes. He cleaned the windscreen and drove carefully along the detour where a smooth layer of mud formed a slippery trap.

The road-making equipment stood to one side. It had been there for months already, rusting in the salt air. The economy was in a mess; the currency was so low that it was worthless anywhere outside the country. No one cared any more about the condition of the roads.

'This stuff will probably lie here forever,' Juan said as we passed the yellow hulks of graders and caterpillars. 'No one cares. You'll see, if they leave this country, they'll make sure there's nothing left to hand over. There'll be nothing for Portugal to cry about. In the end they will say let the devils have that mess!'

Juan leaned over and pointed to a caterpillar. 'My father used to drive one of those. He and my grandfather were both employed by the Public Works Department in Lisbon. I can still see my father astride that monster, manoeuvring it over banks and ditches, moving mounds of earth and lifting rocks. I used to spend hours watching him work. They expected me to follow in his footsteps. But then my grandfather retired and bought a plot of land to grow grapes for a local co-operative. He made a big success of it. A few years later when he died, my father, encouraged by the family, gave up his job in the city and took over the running of the farm. He knew nothing of farming and it didn't take long before we lost everything. My father died a few years later and the farm and everything we owned was seized by the creditors. We ended up squatting on neighbouring lands, living like peasants.'

I listened with keen interest. The windscreen was spattered again, but he drove on, peering through the gaps, reluctant to interrupt his story.

'My mother, who had always been frail and completely dependent

160

on my father, toughened up after his death. She fought ferociously to keep us all going. Pity, my father didn't live long enough to hear the villagers saying: 'Old man Guerra's son is a doctor. He will take good care of his mother.' Here I am, thousands of miles away. Who will take care of her if anything should happen to me? My brother is too young. What will happen to both of them if I am sent to the front?'

For the first time Juan was actually being honest with me and I began to realise that he wasn't as detached as he wanted everyone to believe. The visit from the PIDE agent had obviously unsettled him more than he'd ever admit to.

'Have you heard from Marcelo again?' I asked.

'No. But that doesn't mean that I won't.'

We turned into his street. A dark green Citröen was carelessly parked, leaving barely enough room for him to manoeuvre into the space.

Juan's jeep was open and when we stopped I realised that we were both soaked with mud. We removed our dirty shoes in the front of the building and walked barefoot up the stairs. 'We'll clean up and have a drink before dinner,' he said.

When we reached the top of the stairs Juan was surprised to find his maid, Lena, waiting for us.

'Lena, I thought you'd gone home already,' said Juan.

'Senhor.' She was agitatedly wringing her hands as she spoke. 'You have some people. I told them that you weren't home, but they insisted on waiting.'

'Who are they?'

She shrugged and took our muddy shoes from us.

I followed Juan into the apartment, where we found Marcelo seated in the armchair, legs comfortably crossed. He had helped himself to a drink. The other man was seated by the window.

'Senhor Doctore,' he said, cheerfully raising his glass.

Juan nodded. Although repulsed by this familiarity, he tried not to show it. The man by the window was powerfully built, tall, angular and balding. Both men were staring at me. The police agent grinned.

'Would you like to clean up?' Juan signed.

I nodded. I understood the unspoken message in his eyes. I remembered him telling Marcelo that I was a deaf-mute.

I was about to leave the room when Marcelo said, 'This is Lieutenant Santos Lopes.'

Juan didn't say anything. I imagined he didn't want to know their names because it would only add to the dreaded familiarity. Juan ignored Marcelo's proffered hand and waited for an explanation.

'We need to talk,' Marcelo said.

'I told you I couldn't help you,' Juan replied.

Marcelo and Lopes exchanged glances. They waited for me to leave the room. I obliged. Lena had placed our muddy shoes in the kitchen, which was next to the sitting room. She signalled that she was leaving. I nodded, vaguely aware of the door closing behind her.

I heard Marcelo saying, 'And I told you that if you don't co-operate we'll ship you up north to the war.'

Juan laughed derisively. 'The war won't go on for much longer.'

'That's what you think,' Marcelo retorted.

Juan did not respond.

From the kitchen I could see into the sitting room.

'Pour yourself a drink,' I heard Marcelo saying as if the flat belonged to him. 'What about you, Lieutenant?'

I couldn't hear the other man's reply and although I was quaking inwardly, I gave the impression of disinterest as I busied myself in the kitchen. There was a moment's silence. Juan was at the bar, his back to the others, and facing me. I saw him pouring himself a drink. He was deliberately drawing out the process, giving himself time to think. He saw me and gave a reassuring wink and then went back to his chair.

'What is it you want?' Juan asked.

'The lieutenant has something to discuss with you.'

'Can she hear us?' Marcelo asked.

There was no reply from Juan. I guessed that he had shaken his head.

'We have reason to believe that someone at the hospital was connected to the death of Armando Morais.'

'What has this to do with me?' Juan asked, perplexed.

'We think one of the nurses at the hospital may be connected.'

'Who?' Juan demanded.

The silence was ominous. I plugged in the electric kettle and held my breath as I waited for a response.

'Who is it?' Juan asked again.

'Her name is Rita Alfai.'

There was a pause and then Juan's chuckle of disbelief. My stomach tightened into a sickening knot.

'You may laugh, but we know better,' Marcelo said sharply.

'That's impossible. I know her. She's a good nurse. One of the best.'

'That may be so,' the lieutenant said, 'but the evidence speaks for itself. We are investigating the other one, too.'

'Who?' Juan asked sharply.

Once again silence. Then I heard Juan's incredulous exclamation and my stomach churned even more.

'You're crazy!' Juan said. 'You can see for yourself. She's incapable of such a thing. Here, you want me to bring her into the room so you can ask her?'

I held my breath.

'Yes,' Marcelo growled, bring her in here. 'You must think I'm some kind of idiot to believe everything you tell me about her being deaf and dumb. I know about her.'

There was no point hiding any longer. I came out of the kitchen and went into the sitting room. Marcelo had a look of triumph on his face.

'The markings on the explosives indicate that it came from the dam site. Your boyfriend used to work there, didn't he?'

I nodded. I could barely still my trembling hands.

Juan said, 'I don't believe this! The dynamite came from the rebels who raided the site many times. You should be chasing them instead of wasting your time here.'

'You are a very stupid man,' Marcelo said coldly.

I forgot all about the boiling kettle, until finally I smelt the burnt element and rushed back into the kitchen. As I took the plug out, all I could think of was Rita and the danger she faced.

I came back into the room.

'We know who is stealing the drugs and medical supplies and very soon now we will catch them,' Marcelo was saying.

'This woman Rita Alfai is only a small fish, but we will use her to catch bigger ones.'

'Why involve me when you have all this information already?' Juan asked.

Marcelo cleared his throat. He was the type of person who enjoyed making others squirm. I stood aside, silent and apprehensive, as I waited for his response.

'Lieutenant, I think you can best explain it,' he said, turning to the other man.

'We don't quite have everything yet, but we will soon. We have not arrested the Alfai woman because we had hoped that she would take us to the ringleaders,' Lopes said.

'What does it have to do with me?'

'It has everything to do with you now, since you lied to me at the hospital about this woman being deaf and dumb. Now you are all involved.'

'How?' Juan demanded.

'Are you so stupid that I have to explain everything to you?' Marcelo asked.

'I tell you, you're wasting your time,' Juan said angrily.

'We will trap the woman,' Lopes said. 'Morphine is in big demand at the front. The rebels are hurting,' Marcelo added.

'Why are you telling me all of this? I don't want to hear about it,' Juan said. 'She doesn't want to hear it either,' he added, pointing at me.

'Whether you like it or not, you are both going to hear what we have to say, my dear – Doctore. We are not asking either of you to do anything, we are *ordering* you – unless you want to end up dead,' he said to me.

I lowered my head.

'And unless *you* wish to end up at the front, you will both obey,' Marcelo said grimly to Juan.

'You wouldn't dare,' Juan cried. 'What about my patients? Are you going to drag people off the street to do my job? Dentists and shopkeepers performing surgery?'

'We've done worse.'

I needed to get out of the room and I signed at Juan.

'What does she want?' Marcelo demanded, while Lopez's glance slowly roved over me, making me more nervous.

'She wants to make coffee,' Juan explained.

'Let her go,' he said with a dismissive gesture. 'Just remember we'll be watching every move you make,' he added to me.

164

I hurried out of the room, feeling as though I was about to suffocate.

'We'll be leaving now anyway,' I heard Lopes saying.

The men went into the hallway. I looked up to watch them go.

'Don't be a fool,' Lopes remarked, baring his teeth at Juan as he and Marcelo stood at the door.

Marcelo said nothing, but his eyes were as sharp as a lizard's. 'We'll offer you a deal, Doctore,' he said.

'What kind of a deal?'

'In return for giving us information, we will make sure that you and your young brother do not go to the front,' the other man said.

'My brother? What does this have to do with him?'

'His conscription papers are with me.'

Juan reeled back as if he had been struck.

'Do you get my meaning now?' Lopes smirked.

There was no need for Juan to say anything. It was all there in his expression. In the way he shut the door after them and stood leaning against it, a glazed look in his eyes. I took his hand sympathetically. He seemed totally oblivious to my presence.

'I should go home,' I said.

He nodded absently. 'I'll take a shower and clean up and then I'll drive you.'

We had a cup of coffee before we left. We were both still shaken. 'My brother and I can't go to the front,' he said.

I felt sorry for him. It didn't matter which side you were on. It was a dark, cavernous world in which young boys with lost limbs groped around in the dark, dreading the next step which might be on a land-mine or into a booby trap. It was a world of death. No one came out of it unscathed. It was a world in which you either lived or died. It was kill or be killed.

Chapter Sixteen

Rita had not been to work for three days. I went to the township to try to find out what was going on. Teresa, who hadn't heard from her either, was frantic with worry. I spent some time reassuring her and when I left I promised to let her know as soon as I heard anything. I made her promise to do the same for me. Although I made no mention of it to Teresa, I feared that Rita might already have been arrested.

When I got home later that evening, Helia stopped by to find out whether we'd heard from Rita yet. She'd been making some enquiries, too, but without much success. The one good thing, though, was that she brought an envelope with her, which contained the long-awaited information from Rhonica.

She had sent a copy of a ship's manifesto showing its human cargo and pictures of the children. The photographs were a bit blurred, but there was no doubt about what they revealed. The document was for an earlier shipment of children and Helia said that the Liberation Government in exile was in the process of talking to the Arab state involved in that particular transaction. The Arabs, of course, denied all knowledge about such a slave-trade.

During our conversation, I confided my anxiety about Rita to Helia and asked her advice. I didn't know what to do any more. There was no place one could go to enquire about missing people and there was no one else I could consult with.

'Don't do anything,' Helia cautioned. 'Don't arouse any suspicions. Just wait,' she told me. 'Whatever you do will only serve to implicate you.'

'I'm implicated already.'

'What do you mean?'

Briefly, I explained what had transpired with the medical supplies. I didn't dare tell her about the conversation Marcelo and his lieutenant had had with Juan. She asked several questions about Rita. Afterwards she sat in silence, studying her nails. 'You know what this means?' she said finally.

I was too distraught to respond.

'It means Rita might be dead by now and that you may be next. You've got to get away,' she said. 'You've got to leave right away.'

'I can't. Where will I go?'

She thought for a moment.

'I'll see what I can do.'

'What about your friend the minister . . . Can't he help?'

'Don't even consider that,' she said sharply. Then, seeing my crestfallen expression, she got up out of the chair and came over to me. 'I'm sorry,' she said and put an arm around me. 'I know how scared you must be for Rita. I'll see what I can do to help. Sit tight and for goodness' sake, be careful.'

Helia left and I had the sickening feeling as I went to bed that Friday night that everything was tumbling down around my head. Luckily I didn't have to go into work over the weekend. At least I'd have some time to think of a plan.

I couldn't sleep. I don't know how long I lay awake in the dark, but it was quite late, around two o'clock when I heard a tap at the door. For a while I ignored it, thinking one of the drunks might have wandered in off the street. They sometimes did that.

When it came again I lay quite rigid listening, wondering if it might be the police. The next time it was much louder and more persistent. I got out of bed and went to the door, opening it a crack. There was Soza, one of the nurses on the female surgical unit, and a good friend of Rita's.

Surprised to see her, and still somewhat disorientated by being disturbed so late, I kept her standing in the doorway for a few moments. She seemed agitated and looked about her nervously. I immediately suspected trouble and drew her inside, shutting the door behind her.

Instinctively I knew that something had happened to Rita. Why else would Soza be here at this hour of the night? I was right. As if to confirm my suspicions, she said, 'There is big trouble. You've got to come right away. It's Rita; she's been shot.'

Bewildered, I stared at her. 'Where? When?' I gestured.

'Tonight. The police followed her to the house where the children were staying. She ran out the back, but they chased her and she was shot in the shoulder. She managed to get away and came to my house.'

My bemused glance tried to focus on Soza.

'Where is she now?' I scribbled on a pad.

'I had to leave her in an alley. I couldn't take her any further,' Soza said.

'How bad is she?'

'Bad. But she'll be safe here with you,' Soza said.

I shook my head. It would be the first place they'd come to look.

'The PIDE are watching me, too,' Soza said.

I crossed to the window and peered out, but the courtyard was deserted. 'Wait here,' I indicated and disappeared into the bedroom. I returned a few minutes later, dressed and ready to go. 'Do you know if Dr Guerra is working tonight?' I wrote.

'No,' Soza said. He had left the institute around eight o'clock. I saw him go.

'How did you manage to get her this far?' I wrote.

'We got a ride as far as the alley. Come on, we have to hurry,' she added urgently.

I rushed back to the bathroom and stuffed a few bandages into my coat pocket.

'My car is round the corner,' I said. I don't know why I did so, but as I left I grabbed the envelope of material given to me by Helia. Perhaps I thought that it would be safer hidden in the car than in the flat, but there was no rational explanation for my actions. It was just as well that I had taken them because, as events later developed, I might have lost them.

Soza directed me to the alley where she had left Rita lying behind some packing crates. When I saw Rita I realised that she was going to need a lot more help than either Soza or I could provide. Juan was our only hope. I'd have to trust him.

I wrote out a message for Soza, asking her to wait with Rita while I went to get help.

The streets were almost deserted. There were a few army trucks and some traffic but it didn't take long to get to Juan's place. I parked across the street and could just see part of the French doors over the top of the balcony wall. I thought I saw a light on and prayed he was still awake.

I slipped into the building, using the stairs instead of the lift.

168

There was no one around at this hour and it was very quiet. He was obviously asleep because I had to knock three times before he opened.

Bewildered and groggy, he appeared at the door. 'What's wrong?' he asked, surprised to see me. I slipped by him and shut the door behind me. He turned on the lights, the sleepy expression turning to one of alarm.

'What is it, Faith?' he demanded.

'Rita's been shot.'

'Dear God,' he muttered, sinking into a chair. 'I knew this would happen. Where is she?' he asked, his glance wearily searching my face.

'In an alley.'

'How bad is she?' he asked.

'Unconscious. Blood loss. Weak pulse,' I indicated.

Without hesitation, Juan got up out of the chair and went off to his room, leaving me to pace. He returned a few minutes later, dressed and carrying his medical bag.

'Let's go,' he said.

I drove. It took longer to get back to the alley because I took a wrong turning. Soza had covered Rita with a piece of sacking she had found in the alley. She was kneeling beside Rita's prone body, comforting her.

Juan removed the cover and turned his flashlight on Rita, shaking his head in disbelief. 'How the hell did this happen?'

Rita moaned. I indicated her right shoulder.

Juan gave the injury a cursory examination and shook his head. 'I can't treat her here,' he said.

'Where else can we go?' Soza asked.

'I don't know,' he said. 'She's in bad shape. Seems she's lost a lot of blood.'

'The police are searching for her. We can't go to the township and it's not safe at Faith's place,' Soza said.

My gaze met Juan's. He knew instantly what I was thinking and glanced away quickly.

'Not my place,' he said, shaking his head.

'It's the only alternative. We can't leave her here to die,' Soza pleaded. 'As soon as it's safe we'll move her from there.'

'No! That's crazy!' said Juan. 'My flat is one of the first places they'll come. Isn't there anywhere else we can take her?'

Soza and I thought about possible alternatives. I knew of none other. Soza glanced at me and shook her head. She obviously didn't know either. We had no alternative.

'We'll be in and out,' Soza assured him. 'I'll find somewhere else tomorrow.'

He looked down at the prone figure with a mixture of alarm and apprehension. Rita regained consciousness and opened her eyes for a moment. He tried to stem the bleeding, but it was too awkward and dangerous to work in the alley. We were not going to accomplish anything here. I gestured for him to hurry and he seemed to rouse himself. Soza and I gently started to lift Rita, determined to move her out of harm's way. He had no choice now but to help. The act of moving her was so excruciatingly painful that by the time we reached the car, Rita had lost consciousness again.

We managed to smuggle her into Juan's flat through the back. I had gone ahead to open the door while he and Soza half-carried her out of the old lift cage. We had tried to be quiet, but had accidentally slammed the gate shut behind us and now listened nervously for the consequences. There were none. Most of the tenants in this building were older, and unlike those in my building were sound asleep already. I put an arm out to steady Rita as we helped her through the door.

'Let's get her on to the bed,' said Juan.

A sling fashioned from a piece of cloth, and soaked with blood, hung uselessly from her neck.

Rita winced as I eased the sling over her neck. She swayed and we lowered her on to the bed.

'Take it easy, Rita,' Soza urged.

Her gaze flitted to Juan and then to me. I nodded encouragingly.

'What happened?' Juan asked.

'Don't talk,' Soza said to Rita. 'Everything is all right now. You'll be safe.' Her expression was calm and gave no indication of our anxiety.

'What happened?' Juan asked again.

'She was shot by the police,' Soza said quietly.

'Why?' Juan demanded, aghast.

'No more questions,' Soza said.

'I want to know,' he persisted.

'You know why,' she said, testily.

I tugged at his sleeve, indicating the patient.

Gently he turned her over to look at her shoulder. 'The bullets are still lodged in there,' he said, probing the wounds. One of these was large and the tissue around it torn and oozing blood, the second was smaller.

'She's going to need blood,' Juan said, straightening up. 'Anyone know what her blood type is?'

Rita managed to give him the information he wanted.

'I'll see what I can do,' Soza said.

'You wait here, I'll go,' Juan instructed. 'I need more than just blood.'

Soza and I exchanged troubled glances, neither of us wanting to think of the possible consequences of misplacing our trust in Juan.

'My children are alone at home,' Soza said. 'I must go back soon.'

'Wait here until I get back,' Juan replied. 'I'm going to need your help as well. Shut the curtains and if anyone should come to the door, don't open it. I have the key, so I'll let myself in. I don't know what good all these precautions are; we're all going to end up in jail anyway. You've certainly got us all into a bloody mess!' he added.

I ignored his outburst, touching Rita's brow and checking her pulse. She felt cold and clammy to the touch and her pulse was weak.

'All right,' Juan said, his jaw drawn into a tight, angry line. 'Get some towels and apply pressure to the wound to slow the bleeding. I'll see what I can find at the hospital and God help us if we're caught.'

I hurried off to find the towels.

While Juan was gone, Soza and I tried to make Rita as comfortable as possible. Each time she tried to speak, I placed a finger to her lips to stop her from wasting her strength.

Juan was gone for less than an hour. For the two of us alone with Rita, it felt like ages. It was a relief when we finally heard his key in the door.

'Her breathing is shallow,' he said as he stooped over the inert body and listened. 'Let's get the blood going. Compress the upper arm so I can find a vein.'

I obeyed at once.

'How did you manage to get the blood?' Soza asked.

'Never mind.' He unfolded the bundle which he carried into the room and took out a bottle of saline solution. He expertly ripped off

171

the top and connected a drip. He searched around for some place to hang the bottle, pushed the bed towards the dressing chest and secured the IV bottle from a hook by the mirror.

'Damn,' he muttered. It was difficult to find a vein, but finally he managed to slip in the needle.

'Open the stopper,' he commanded.

I carried out this instruction while Soza held on to Rita's arm.

'Keep the needle in place so I can get the blood going,' he told Soza.

I hung the blood beside the saline bottle and opened the plastic stop-cock.

'Any change in the pulse?' he asked Soza.

She reached out with her free hand to check.

'I'd better take a look at the wound. We'll end up losing the blood as fast as we put it in, and we don't have much of it. Get me some sticking plaster from the bathroom.'

I found a roll in the cabinet and after taping the needle in place, he went to the bathroom to scrub up.

Rita stirred, her breathing was slightly more even.

Juan returned. 'I've brought some ether. We'll give her a whiff of it, but from the look of her, she might not even need it.' He cleaned the skin around the wound with alcohol. 'I'll have to remove the bullet first,' he said. The large wound was at a mid-point just below the scapula. 'Lucky the bone stopped it,' he added.

'Nasty wound,' Soza said, peering over his shoulder.

'Without the proper equipment it's going to be tricky,' he said swabbing away the dried blood around the wound. The second wound was smaller and clean, the edges slightly raised like a pair of pouting lips.

It took a few moments of careful probing with the forceps, but he was able to find the bullet. Rita groaned and Soza and I held her down firmly. Juan stitched up the blood vessels and closed the wound.

It was much more difficult with the second, smaller wound. We had to give her another whiff of ether to keep her under while Juan worked on her. He eventually located the second bullet.

Even though Juan had managed to treat the wounds, Rita wasn't out of danger yet. Far from it. She'd lost a lot of blood and there was the possibility of infection. She slept soundly while we kept

172

vigil. Several hours later, just as the sun came up, Rita opened her eyes.

'I think she'll be OK now, but she needs proper care in a hospital,' Juan said. He left the room wearily. Soza and I followed him to the front room, quietly closing the door behind us.

'Now what?' he asked, caustically.

I shrugged.

'How long do you think it will be before the police make the connection between you and Rita?' he continued.

I glanced away.

'And how long before they make the connection between us? For God's sake! I thought you were smart enough to stay out of trouble,' he remarked.

'What were we to do? Just leave her to die?' Soza demanded. 'Anyway, I must go now. My children . . .'

'Thank you,' I signed.

'For heaven's sake be careful and make sure you're not followed,' Juan added.

Soza left and Juan locked the door behind her.

'In and out, eh?' Juan said, turning away from me. 'Where the hell are we going to hide her? Tell me. What happens when the PIDE arrive on my doorstep?'

He paced around the front room. 'This is crazy. You're crazy. We'll all be shot for this and God alone knows what else they'll do. I have a family. A mother who is sick and a young brother who'll end up at the front.' He took a deep breath. 'Mother Maria,' he groaned. 'Do you realise how serious this is? We've got to get her to a safe place.' I could tell that he wanted to say 'Anywhere but here'.

'We can't move her now,' I signed, putting up a protesting hand. 'Tomorrow.'

'Are you mad? We won't be able to move her tomorrow either.'

I glanced away, hoping that Rita couldn't hear any of this.

'This is my house.' He ground the words through clenched teeth. 'If you want to take the risk it's your bloody neck, but if you're caught, I will not be implicated.' He paused and swung on his heels, running his hand through his hair in a gesture of frustration.

I watched him.

'Faith, don't you understand? They know that we're friends. I'm a doctor . . . two and two.'

'That is why we have to be careful,' I signed.

173

'They're not all fools,' he said.

Rita was indeed too weak to be moved. Juan's biggest fear was that the neighbours would be suspicious. I thought he was being ridiculous. There was no reason for them to be suspicious. But this didn't stop him from worrying. Neither of us left the flat the next day. Juan paced up and down all day long, occasionally fixing me with an accusing glance as if blaming me for his troubles.

'She can't stay here,' he said over and over again. 'What'll happen when we have to go to work tomorrow?' he asked. He was slumped in the easy chair. Suddenly, as if struck by an idea, he got up abruptly and went over to the cupboard in the hallway. I watched curiously as he knelt down and pulled away a loose board inside it. He called me over and sat back on his haunches, shining a torch into the space behind the wall.

'There's enough room here,' he said. 'It'll be a tight fit, but it'll have to do until we can move her.'

I was reluctant to put Rita through this. I could see from the size of the space behind the wall that there would be hardly enough room for her to move.

'It's either that, or she goes,' Juan said emphatically.

It seemed that we had no choice.

On Monday morning before leaving for work we moved Rita into the space behind the wall. For three days we hid her like this. As an added precaution Juan had sent his maid Lena away, telling her to take a few days' paid holiday. She might have argued this point, had she not caught a glimpse of me in Juan's dressing gown. She went away smiling.

We both continued with our work at the hospital as though nothing had happened. But every call for Juan over the intercom, every footstep in the corridor, every clang of the old lift doors in his building, was enough to make us both break out into a cold, clammy sweat.

Chapter Seventeen

On the fourth day, the Thursday after Rita was shot, she was fully conscious and aware of what was happening. She was still in a great deal of pain, but well on her way to recovery. Juan was pleased because it meant we'd be able to move her to another location soon. As far as possible, we kept to our routine, going to work as usual after making sure that Rita was safely tucked away behind the panel.

One morning, however, while we were at work, Marcelo arrived at the flat accompanied by two agents. He had apparently knocked several times, expecting the maid to open the door. When there was no response he lost patience and, according to Rita, started pounding loudly on the front door.

We were lucky that they hadn't broken it down and that instead they had gone to find the owner, who lived on the first floor. Rita said that when she heard the commotion, she quickly pulled the wall panel into place and held her breath as the men were let into the flat. She heard voices in the doorway; footsteps crossing to the adjoining room. Suddenly the closet door was flung open. Paralysed with fear, she waited. Her shoulder had started to throb again. Her long legs cramped into the confined space went numb.

They were moving around in the closet, inches away from her head. Hangers rattled noisily as clothes were shuffled aside. There were more footsteps, this time going into the bathroom. She panicked, wondering if we had remembered to dispose of the soiled bandages. By that time, she said, she could hardly breathe in her confined space.

She heard them in the kitchen next. From the sound of the heavy tread of feet marching back and forth she reckoned that there were three of them. Finally, when the footsteps ended somewhere near the front door, she heard muffled voices and then the door closing.

She let out her breath quietly, tentatively. Waiting for the unexpected. But the flat was silent. She moved her legs into a more comfortable position and straightened her shoulder. The police were next door questioning Juan's neighbours. She heard the woman saying she had not seen any strangers entering the flat next door, except for Juan's girlfriend.

Rita listened as the footsteps continued down the corridor. They were leaving. She breathed a sigh of relief and pushed against the panel, anxious to get some air, but nothing happened. She pushed a bit harder; still nothing. She lay back, gripped by a new panic as she realised that she was trapped. She told me later she was convinced we would find her dead behind the wall, stretched out on her back, hands folded across her chest as though she were laid out in a coffin.

The first inkling that anything was wrong came when Marcelo arrived at the hospital later that morning to question Juan and me. He seemed concerned about the fact that no one had answered the door. He wanted to know where the maid was.

Juan explained that he had given Lena a few days off because we had wanted to spend some time together. Marcelo laughed uproariously at the absurdity of the explanation. It was as though he were playing a game with us.

Marcelo questioned me concerning Rita's whereabouts. He wasn't satisfied with my answers and got quite angry. Twice during my interrogation he pounded on the desk, threatening to have me thrown in prison. Juan interpreted my responses and I merely confirmed what Juan had already told him. Juan and I had rehearsed what we would say thoroughly. It was impossible to read Marcelo's thoughts because he vacillated between angry disbelief and consideration for my well-being. It was as though he were constantly stalking, waiting for a weakness on which to pounce.

Outwardly I might have projected a calm professionalism, but inwardly I was a quaking mass. After the interrogation, I had to find a quiet spot so that I could steady my nerves. The look in Marcelo's eyes had terrified me. We were taking enormous risks. The PIDE were known to have committed countless atrocities under the pretext of interrogating prisoners. It was rumoured that many of the agents were involved with the death squads.

The rest of the day was a loss – I couldn't concentrate on anything. I tried to picture the flat, tried to remember whether I had left any tell-tale clues. Had we shut the panel properly? What if we'd left something lying around: a bandage, medication, anything that might have aroused his suspicions?

After I left the room, Marcelo asked Juan to remain. I wondered anxiously what they were discussing. Juan and I did not have another chance to speak again until later that afternoon when he stopped me in the corridor to tell me that he would be home late that evening.

I didn't know what to expect when I returned to the flat but the end of my day could not come soon enough. On my way back I took a few precautions, driving around for a while to make certain that I was not being followed.

So far we had been lucky, but I knew that our luck would not last forever. I feared for Rita and the consequences for all of us if we were caught. As I drove away, I prayed, 'Holy Mary, Mother of God, pray for us sinners now and at the hour of our death . . .'

Juan was right of course. It would only be a matter of time before we were caught. I felt the ampules of morphine and penicillin in my pocket. It had all happened so quickly. The cabinet had been left open for just a few moments while the nursing sister had turned her back. Without even thinking, I had reached in and had taken the ampules.

Sister would recall that I had been the only other person in the room at the time. I drew in a shuddering breath and turned into the street where Juan lived.

I unlocked the door to the flat with the extra key he had given me, and stood in the doorway surveying the room. There was ample evidence that the place had been searched. I locked the door behind me and went directly to the closet, giving the prearranged signal.

There was a muffled response from within. Kneeling down, I reached for the panel and tugged, but it wouldn't budge. I tried again and then realised that it was stuck.

I managed to prise the panel off with a knife. Rita crawled out, weeping with relief. 'When they left I couldn't get the board out. It was jammed.'

I sat on the floor, comforting her. Eventually, when she had calmed down, I examined her shoulder. I changed the dressing and gave her a shot of penicillin. The day's events had convinced me that it was no longer safe to be there. We had to get away.

I threw some supplies into a bag. Several rolls of bandages had been hidden in the secret space; I took all of these, some aspirin and antiseptic from Juan's bathroom cabinet, and I riffled through his kitchen cupboard for something to eat and drink in case we needed it.

At first I was going to leave a message for Juan, but I had second thoughts about that. We waited until the building was quiet before we crept downstairs, leaving through the back door. Rita waited for me behind a hedge while I went to get the car.

We drove around aimlessly for more than an hour, avoiding the main traffic arteries. Neither of us had any idea what to do next. Our biggest concern was at all costs to avoid a patrol.

Eventually I went out of the city towards the beach where I pulled in amongst the trees. It was very dark outside. Rita was silent – asleep or unconscious – I didn't know which.

I rolled my window down. In the distance I could hear the sound of waves pounding against the rocks. Rita stirred beside me. I didn't want to dwell on the danger we faced. Instead I filled my head with the sound of the waves crashing against the rocks and imagined how the water frothed and parted before flowing back into the dark ocean.

'Where are we?' Rita asked, waking up suddenly. 'I can hear the ocean. Are we at the beach?'

I nodded. A light swept across the landscape in a wide arc.

'We're at the lighthouse,' she said. 'We can't stay here, Faith. If one of the patrols should find us it'll be the end.'

I squeezed her hand reassuringly.

'I'm sorry about what happened between us,' Rita said. 'I should have known you were my sister.' Rita leaned back. I didn't say anything, just held her hand.

After a while she spoke again. 'I was just thinking . . .' she said, but she was interrupted by the loud clap of the seventh wave hitting the rocks. When the sound had died down, she spoke again. 'I was just thinking, my friend, we only have this one chance at life. We must make the best of it. It would be a shame to waste it.'

She fell silent again and I listened to the ocean. In the darkness it was hard to read the expression on her face. Eventually with a sigh she leaned her head back against the seat and fell asleep.

I also slept but fitfully, awakened by every little sound from outside. At one point I heard a dog sniffing outside the car and I panicked, sitting bolt upright. But there were no other sounds and

178

I concluded that the dog was a stray scrounging for food. It took some time to fall asleep again, half-listening for any hint of danger.

In the first rosy glow of morning, I awakened Rita and glanced at my watch. It was a quarter to five. The tide was in and the thundering from the cliffs below had increased to a deafening roar.

I checked the dressing on her shoulder and found that the wound was oozing again. We couldn't stay here. In another hour or so the patrols would start. Our only hope was to find a safe place to hide.

I got out of the car and came around to help Rita, leaning her up against the side of the car while I took a brisk walk down the road to get some exercise. By the time I returned Rita had managed to get back into the car on her own. For a while I stood outside stretching my sore limbs.

The wind had come up and I could feel the spray against my face and the taste of salt on my lips. I peered out across the ever-brightening sky, consumed by a longing for security and comfort. I missed my own place and the comfort of my own bed. Quite inexplicably an image of French doors and billowing curtains came to mind. Then the solution hit me. It was all so clear I couldn't imagine why I hadn't thought of it before. Excitedly, I got back into the car.

'What's going on?' Rita asked, startled. 'Where are we going?'

'You'll see. Just wait,' I signed as I started the car, backed out of the trees and drove away.

Although there was just a trickle of early morning traffic, I stuck to the deserted roads until we were out of town. We had no trouble reaching the winding road to Doña Maria's cliff-top home.

I rang the bell at the gate, persistently keeping my finger on it until a sleepy Carlos appeared in the driveway. When he recognised my car, he hurried over to unlock the gate, waving me through. I waited for him to hop into the back seat for the short drive to the front door.

With uncanny instinct he knew instantly that there had been trouble. 'Police?' he asked.

I nodded.

He clambered out as I stopped at the front door and helped me to get Rita inside. Doña Maria, who had heard the bell, was still tying the sash of her robe as she hurried downstairs. She watched in astonishment as we assisted Rita into the house.

'What's happened?' she asked.

'She's hurt, Senhora,' Carlos said, as we gingerly lowered Rita into a chair.

Doña Maria glanced from Rita to me, waiting for an explanation.

'I think she's been shot,' Carlos said.

'Dear God!' Doña Maria, exclaimed in horror. 'How bad is she?' But before either Carlos or I could answer, she said, 'Get her upstairs into bed immediately.'

We helped Rita upstairs to one of the spare rooms where I again examined her shoulder. The dressing was stained with blood. Carlos got the antiseptic and we cleaned off the wound. I used another ampule of penicillin. There were just two left.

I changed the dressing and made Rita as comfortable as possible, sitting with her for a while before going downstairs to join Doña Maria.

'What happened?' Doña Maria asked.

I took the pad Carlos handed me and scribbled hurriedly while Doña Maria peered over my shoulder, her glasses held to her one eye like a monocle. Doña Maria read aloud getting the gist of the story.

'How could you possibly have got yourselves into so much trouble?' she asked. She stood by the window, gazing out at the expanse of ocean. 'Good God, child, they must all be out there searching for the two of you by now,' she said, turning back to me.

I nodded.

'Does anyone know that you're here?'

I shrugged and then shook my head. I slid forward in the chair, sitting on the edge, elbows supported on my knees, hands cupping my face.

'We need a plan, Carlos,' Doña Maria said.

Carlos contemplatively studied a pattern in the carpet.

'What are we going to do?' Doña Maria asked again.

'I don't know, Senhora. I'm trying to think of something.'

'It's too risky for them to be here. What if they find out that she knows me? They'll come here to ask questions. I am on their list, too,' she said as she paced the floor, pensively tapping her cheek with her glasses. 'First thing is to get rid of Faith's car. If they do come . . .'

'Yes, Senhora,' Carlos said and left the room before she could finish her sentence.

I leapt up to go after him.

180

'Stay here,' Doña Maria said sharply.

Reluctant to give up the car in case we still needed it, I hesitated. But Doña Maria was firm. She was afraid that the police would put out a description of the car. 'The papers are in the car,' I scribbled on the pad.

'What papers?'

'The proof we need about the children.'

'Hurry up and get them,' she said.

I returned with the envelope, quite distressed about the fact that my car was going to be destroyed.

'It's necessary,' she said. 'Now go upstairs and rest. You look exhausted. Carlos and I will take care of everything.'

I handed her the envelope and went upstairs obediently. Instead of going to bed, however, I went to sit with Rita and dozed off in the chair beside her.

Some time later I was awakened by the sound of voices coming from downstairs. Slightly dazed from sleep, I sat up listening, but the voices were low and even – conversational rather than threatening.

I went downstairs and found Juan sitting with Doña Maria. When they saw me, Doña Maria beckoned, but my instinctive reaction, when I saw Juan, was to step back out of sight. He noticed and with a few long strides crossed the room, taking both my hands in his.

'Are you all right?' he asked.

I was still unsure and suspicious about his presence. How had he known where to find us?

'Don't worry, my dear,' Doña Maria said, 'He's in as much trouble as you are. Sit down.' She gestured to a chair with her cigarette holder. The inlaid mother-of-pearl glinted as it caught the light from the window. Vasco, lying at her feet, leapt up when I entered but a sharp word from her returned him to her feet where he curled up again, snuffling the warm, woollen carpet.

I sat down with them and Doña Maria rang for Carlos to bring tea. While we waited for it, Doña Maria told me that Juan had filled in some of the missing details. I still wondered how he had known where to find me. Juan explained that it had been a fairly simple guess that we would come to Doña Maria for help. It was the first thought that had come to his mind when he got home around midnight and had found us gone. He had arrived here at around eight o'clock that morning.

He suspected that it would only be a matter of hours before the police would return to interrogate him about my absence. He had read the nursing sister's report about the missing drugs. If they came to question him again, what explanation could he give?

'We are all in the same boat now,' said Juan despondently.

Doña Maria asked many questions. I studied Juan trying to discern whether his coming here was a trick or not. But he didn't look like a man capable of treachery. Instead he looked defeated and a little helpless.

Doña Maria said, 'Of course they will put all this together. It won't be long before they come here to question me about Faith. They know everything, those secret police.'

Juan agreed.

'Where shall we go?' I signed.

'I don't know,' Juan said.

'Carlos will help you,' Doña Maria said reassuringly. 'We have used escape plans before. He will plot a route for you.' She paused, studying the two of us. 'But for now you must have a good rest. We can discuss these plans tonight and you will leave early in the morning. I hope Rita is well enough to travel.'

'I'll take a look at her,' said Juan.

'Carlos has got rid of your car,' she said, turning to me. 'He drove it over the cliff. They will not find it.'

Dismayed, I got up out of my chair and went to the window.

'It's easy to trace a car,' she told me. 'Incidentally, the evidence in that envelope is very good. We'll have to find a way of getting it out of the country safely.'

I became aware of Juan scrutinising me. I looked past him to Isabella's portrait above the mantel. He turned his head slightly and followed my gaze to the image of the young girl with the dark, sultry eyes and full, sensuous lips.

'My daughter, Isabella,' Doña Maria remarked to Juan. 'She and my husband Christiano were both killed by the secret police who planted a bomb in his car.'

'Why?' he asked.

'Christiano was a member of the Communist Party in Lisbon. They killed them both. He and my daughter,' she said bitterly.

182

'I'm sorry,' Juan muttered inadequately.

She smiled graciously. 'It would be best for you to have a good rest. I have told Carlos to prepare two rooms for you. Tonight you can stay here, but tomorrow, very early in the morning, you must leave.'

I nodded.

'You must be gone before the sun comes up,' she added.

'We'll be ready by then,' Juan assured her.

'Carlos will have a plan for you later.'

We were about to get up and go when she asked Juan: 'What will you do if you get away safely?'

He shrugged. 'All I know is that from now on I will be a hunted man.'

'It would be best for you to go elsewhere. I will make arrangements for you in France,' she said. Juan nodded, but he seemed dazed by the events. She watched him in silence for a while and then turned her attention to me. 'What about you, Faith? What about you, my dear?'

I hadn't thought any further than the first step, which was to get to safety. I had no idea where I could go afterwards. This was my home. 'I really don't want to leave Mozambique. I'd like to stay until Rita recovers.'

'Then what?' Juan demanded.

'I don't know,' I indicated, turning my head from his interrogative gaze. 'This country is my home.'

'They'll hound you to the ends of the earth if necessary. I know these people,' Doña Maria said. 'I will make arrangements for you to go to France with Juan,' she said.

Juan sat silent for a long time. When he spoke, his voice was subdued and filled with weariness. 'I am so tired of the war, so tired of trying to hold together shattered bodies only so they can be returned to the insanity of the front again. I'm a healer, not a mechanic. I can't do it any more. I can't,' he said, holding his head in his hands.

I went over to him and placed an arm on his shoulder. We had all grown weary of the war, but it surprised me to see him coming apart like this. It had never occurred to me that beneath his calm, composed exterior, was so much vulnerability.

How radically our lives had altered. With one little twist of fate, nothing would ever be the same again.

183

Doña Maria lowered her eyes and for a moment her attention focused on Vasco. She stroked him under the chin and with a contented sigh he put his head down on his forepaws to watch us.

'I do hope things will turn out well for you, my dear,' she said to me. 'You've had enough to contend with in your life already.'

Who knows how things will turn out? I thought. I had learnt early in life not to count on anything. I withdrew my arm from Juan's shoulder.

Doña Maria could see what I was thinking and smiled wryly. 'Strange how one can spend a whole lifetime anticipating something. Then suddenly one day it's wrested from you and nothing is the same any more.'

We sat in silence, each preoccupied with his or her thoughts. I stifled a yawn.

'I think Carlos has prepared your rooms. You'd better go and get some rest now,' she said.

Juan got up and stretched his long limbs.

'Is there anything you'd like?' Doña Maria asked.

'It would be very nice to have a bath,' I indicated.

'Of course. There are some fresh clothes in the closet. Some trousers which might fit. They belonged to Isabella. There are some of my husband's clothes too; you can see if anything there fits you,' she said to Juan. 'Please make yourselves at home.'

Afterwards, lying back in the tub of hot water, I realised how totally exhausted I was. The bath was a welcome luxury. I ran more hot water into the tub and poured in some of Doña Maria's scented oil.

I thought about our conversation downstairs and wondered if I would ever see this house again or, for that matter, my own flat. I thought of David and his English breezes and Mamaria and her soft lap and imagined what my mother might have been like.

The water soaked away my aching tiredness and it was with great reluctance that I climbed out and stood surveying my luxurious surroundings. In the fogged mirrors, I caught a glimpse of the blurred outline of my naked body. Here amidst the bottles of perfume and the soft towels I became aware of my own sexuality. I had never considered myself beautiful, always wondering what men saw in me. I thought myself cold and sexually unresponsive. It was as though desire had shrivelled even before it had had a chance to blossom.

As I gazed at myself in the mirror, I wondered if there was something in me that others saw, but that I wasn't aware of. I touched myself, caressing my breasts; my hands, dipped in Doña Maria's body lotion, slid over my belly with a feathery touch. I admired myself, turning this way and that. I studied my body, hands absently sliding down to still the persistent tingling between my thighs.

I needed to be held, to be cherished, even if only for a short while. I wanted to feel safe, to feel loved no matter how fleeting the moment. I slipped into the robe provided by Doña Maria and padded quietly to Juan's room.

BOOK FIVE

Chapter Eighteen

When I woke up, Juan had gone and I was alone in his bed. I had slept for about two hours. The rest of the house was silent and I assumed that Doña Maria was having her siesta as well.

I returned to my own room and took a while to get dressed. By the time I got downstairs Juan was already having tea with Doña Maria and Rita, who still looked quite washed out. They were sitting around the table examining a map.

Carlos moved over to make room for me at the table and then went over the plans, explaining the route to us. He made an 'X' on the map just below Porto Amelia and drew a circle around it.

'Here,' he said, pointing to the spot. 'About fifty kilometres away from Porto Amelia is a small fishing village. You will be picked up there by a ship which will take you to Dar-es-Salaam.'

All eyes except mine were rivetted to that spot on the map. Dulled by my long sleep, it seemed to take a while for any of it to register with me. I looked up and caught Juan's eyes. My gaze then turned to Doña Maria who had intercepted the exchange between us. I concentrated on the map but with difficulty as my head felt heavy – as if I'd been drugged. At that moment our plans seemed so far removed from reality.

The events of the past few days had only compounded our predicament. It had complicated and disrupted our lives, turning everything topsy-turvy.

'We'll never make it,' remarked Juan, who apparently shared my misgivings about moving Rita.

'Don't worry about Rita,' Doña Maria replied. 'Carlos will take all of you as far as the convent at Santa Teresa. She will stay with the sisters while you continue your journey. She'll be safe there. I have spoken to Mother Superior. By the way, she's anxious to see you again, Faith. I must warn you, however, not to delay. It's

186

important that you start your journey immediately. Soon after you arrive at the convent, you'll be picked up by a man disguised as a peasant. Your transportation will be primitive,' she added. 'A donkey cart will be less conspicuous and you'll be taken part-way to Manhica. You'll have to leave before sunrise. Time is of the essence.'

'I'll try to get someone to meet you at Machanga as well,' Carlos added. Juan and I listened without comment, acutely aware of the danger.

'You'll have to cross the river at Machanga,' Carlos went on. 'If you get to the coast in time, the freighter *Santa Monica* will pick you up.' He pointed at the cross he had drawn on the map. 'Exactly two weeks from today – January 21st at eight p.m. the *Santa Monica* will call at this point. You *must* be there,' he urged. His finger, long and slender, jabbed at the cross on the map. By that time the cross was branded not only on to the map, but into our minds as well.

The three of us gazed at it, as if mesmerised. Juan glanced at me and leaned forward thoughtfully.

'The *Santa Monica* will take you out of the country. But if your contact is unable to meet you at Machanga one week from Thursday, then you'll have to make your way north,' Carlos said, moving his finger over the map. 'You will be safe there. It is an area held by the Liberation Army.'

One was immediately struck by the extent of Doña Maria's involvement with the rebels. As I glanced at Rita, I noticed that she was viewing Doña Maria with a look of new respect and appreciation. The rest of us sat around, silenced by a growing anxiety. All of us were uneasy about what lay ahead.

'Don't worry,' Carlos said. 'If you get up north, things will be a lot easier. You are both fit,' he said, gazing at Juan and me in turn. 'It might work to your advantage if you stick together, but if something happens you'll have to split up and meet later.'

Rita was slumped in her chair – it was just as well that she was only going as far as Santa Teresa. The prospect of a long journey was daunting for all of us, but for someone in a weakened condition, it would be an almost impossible feat. She caught my eye and made a valiant effort to rally, but even that effort was too much for her.

'What about you?' she asked me. 'Will you be all right?'

I nodded, reached over and squeezed her hand.

We were all tired. The tension and anxiety had worn us all out.

Doña Maria's attention shifted away from us to Isabella's portrait and then back to me. Although obviously weary, she made an effort to pull herself together.

'Carlos,' she said, 'please fetch the newspaper. I want to see if there is report about the girls.'

The newspaper had been delivered at the gate and while Carlos went off to get it, Juan and Doña Maria prepared a list of things that had to be done. Carlos returned quite shortly.

'Give it to Faith,' Doña Maria said. 'I want Juan to help me with the first-aid kit. Too bad you didn't bring your medical bag,' she told him.

'I didn't want to arouse any suspicions,' he said.

I half-listened to this exchange as I unfolded the paper, glanced at the front page and drew in a startled breath, for there was picture of Helia. The enlargement was slightly distorted, but quite evidently her. There was another picture of the man I had seen going up to her apartment that day. I looked at the headlines:

SEX SCANDAL IMPLICATES DEPUTY MINISTER IN SPY RING

The report alleged that Helia had been passing information on to the Cubans. Doña Maria had joined Juan behind my chair and was reading the paper over my shoulder.

'Isn't that your friend, Helia de Souza?' Doña Maria asked.

I nodded.

'A Cuban spy . . . Did you know anything about this?' Doña Maria enquired.

I shook my head.

For a moment she looked troubled. 'There will be a much bigger search for you now, my dear. This whole situation has got out of control.' Her troubled gaze met mine and then she smiled.

'Never mind,' she said. 'There's nothing we can do about it now. I just hope you understand why it is even more important that you leave here tomorrow.'

It was impossible to believe that Helia was a spy. I had long suspected that she might have connections with the rebels because of her association with Rhonica, but a Cuban spy . . . Such an allegation might have been ludicrous at any other time or in any other place, but here in Mozambique it was not taken lightly. The penalty for such a crime was death.

188

I thought about her son Manuel and what would happen to him. He had no father and soon he'd have no mother. It was too much to contemplate, part of that never-ending cycle of death and destruction.

Doña Maria had guessed my thoughts. 'There's nothing you can do,' she said. 'You've got to get out of the country. Don't you dare try anything foolish – too many lives are at stake. If the story is true about Helia then she obviously knew what she was getting into. She knew the risks,' Doña Maria said, her anxiety tempered with sympathy for me. 'Now it's up to you to get the evidence about the children out of the country. In London, my friend Sir Geoffrey Abbot will help you. He'll know who to contact.' She leaned forward and took my hands in hers. 'It's important, Faith. It's the most important thing you can do for your country,' she said.

But it was hard to put Helia out of my mind. We had shared so many wonderful times together. These weren't things one could put aside easily. Fortunately, however, there was a lot to do and much of the rest of the day was spent getting ready for our journey. Juan, who had studied the maps, discussed our situation with Carlos and concluded that there would be ample time to make our rendezvous with the *Santa Monica*.

Later that day he came to find me in the garden. Strangely enough, I had been thinking of David when Juan interrupted. He told me that he wanted to talk to me and drew up a chair. I gazed out at the ocean to the horizon beyond – a distant horizon which would probably soon become our destination.

Juan took my hand. 'I'm sorry about your friend, Helia, but Doña Maria is right. There is nothing any of us can do for her. You have to think about us. You must be focused, Faith, or you won't be of much help to yourself or to anyone else.'

Damn it, I thought. I didn't want to go anywhere. This was my home, the only one I knew. I thought about David and his English breezes and realised that I didn't want to leave. I could feel the sting of hot tears behind my lids.

'You and Rita have had your doubts about me,' he said. I put up a hand in a gesture of denial, but he stopped me. 'It's all right,' he said. 'Under the circumstances I might have done the same. But by now surely you realise that I've done everything possible to help. I would never have collaborated with the PIDE, regardless of their threats.' His grip on my hands tightened. 'You should know me better than that by now.'

I withdrew my hands and slipped on my sunglasses, wondering how on earth one could ever be sure of anything in this country. In Juan's case, we would probably never know, I thought, leaning back in the chair and turning my face to the sun.

'We were so close this morning. It was wonderful. Don't tell me it didn't mean anything to you,' he said. He paused, expecting a response from me, but there was none. 'Well, it meant a great deal to me,' he added.

I shut my eyes, remembering how we had made love earlier. Did all of that not imply trust? How much closer could we have been? But that was then, before I knew about Helia, and before I had to endure the anguish of yet another loss. As I looked at him from behind my sunglasses, sitting across from me, he seemed more like a stranger than a lover.

He lifted the sunglasses off my face. I blinked in the bright light and gazed at him questioningly. He saw my expression and I watched as shadows crept up behind his eyes. Was I wrong about him and was Rita right? Perhaps my own feelings for him had blinded me to the truth. He was right about one thing, though, he had risked his life for us.

The rest of the day and the evening were spent going over our plans and getting things ready for an early departure.

We left around four o'clock the next morning, to get ahead of the military patrols. Carlos drove us the fifteen miles to the convent where Mother Superior had been expecting us. Accompanied by one of the other sisters, she met us at the gate. I was surprised to see how she'd aged – I had always imagined she would stay the same; ageless and tireless.

Carlos dropped us off, planning to return immediately because it was much too dangerous for him to wait around. He delayed only long enough to see us safely into the convent. I watched from the window as he turned the car and with a farewell wave, sped away, the two red tail lights winking at us in the early morning half-light.

Juan and I assisted Rita while Mother Superior led the way with her torch to a secluded outer building which I recognised as the winery.

'Why did you not come back to see us?' Mother Superior asked me.

I felt the old guilt surfacing and was actually relieved when Juan interrupted to remind us that we had to hurry. I was grateful that there was no time to dwell on questions and recriminations.

Mother Superior had prepared a room about the size of a bathroom, which was hidden behind a wall in the winery. I was concerned because it reminded me of the small space behind the wall in Juan's flat where Rita had had such an unfortunate experience. But, in her condition, it was a lot better than subjecting her to an arduous trek.

It seemed that Rita and I had misjudged the nuns. They were helping us at tremendous risk to themselves and the convent. It was one of life's ironies that Rita, who had so little regard for the Church and the nuns, was now dependent on them for her life.

Juan examined her once more, and gave further instructions to the nun charged with her care. I had a few moments and wrote a short message for Mother Superior. I wanted to know whether she'd heard from Angie again.

Mother Superior shook her head sadly. 'She died four years ago. She took her own life. Poor girl, may God rest her soul. She was so confused. So confused.' She paused. 'I thought you'd heard.'

I indicated that I hadn't and Mother Superior made a small gesture of resignation with her shoulder. She paused to reflect before saying: 'It is not for us to pass judgement about others. We can only pray for them.'

When Rita was resting comfortably, we said our goodbyes.

'God bless you, my child,' Mother Superior said to me. 'We'll say a few novenas for you.'

Our contact, Chuva, an old man in a donkey cart, was waiting at the gate. Juan and I were dressed inconspicuously, both of us in long trousers, our hair and part of our faces concealed under caps and darkened with charcoal. We both wore long-sleeved shirts to cover as much of our exposed skin as possible. Our provisions were carried in cloth bundles which we stowed under the straw on the donkey cart. From a distance we looked like two peasants. We could only hope that no one would come close enough to determine otherwise.

I sat on the back of the cart; Juan sat up front alongside Chuva. As we left I felt a pang of anxiety, wondering if I'd ever see Rita and the others again, or even the convent.

Progress was slow. Chuva was careful and very methodical. As a consequence, we plodded along staying well off the beaten track. Occasionally he'd climb down and walk ahead of the donkey, inspecting and prodding the ground with a stick which had a hook attached at the end, to uproot land-mines.

During the day we skirted the small villages and settlements and at night Juan and I sat on the hard ground under that dark sky, brilliant with stars. Under different circumstances it might have been a lover's sky with Juan and I sitting close together, he with a protective arm around me, me with my head resting on his shoulder, while he described some of his dreams and aspirations. But this was a different time and all I felt as he put his arm round me was apprehension for what lay ahead.

We travelled north, following the coastline. Chuva skirted away from the coast where the military camps and *aldeamentos* were located.

In the afternoons we pulled off the road to a safe spot, well concealed from view. I rested while Juan and Chuva went off to trap our supper. The first day it was a rabbit which the old man skinned on the spot. In subsequent days he returned with the occasional unrecognisable carcass. I never enquired about what we were eating; it was enough that we ate to keep up our strength.

Whenever possible I rode on the top of the cart and at the slightest hint of danger, crawled under the straw. It took three days to reach Inhambane, where the secret police were known to shoot recalcitrant captives. We gave the town a wide berth and on the fifth day Chuva told us that he had taken us as far as he could. It was up to us now to get to the rendezvous on our own.

We climbed down off the cart and he gave us final instructions on how to get to the river. He told us that about a mile downstream we were to meet one of the villagers who would help us across. Once across we were to wait on the other side for our next contact.

'Who do we look for?' Juan asked.

'I don't know,' Chuva said. Then, with an abrupt wave, a whistle and a rap of the reins, the animal turned and the old man and his donkey ambled back the way they had come.

On foot the going was painstakingly slow. We were terrified of stepping on a land-mine or unexpectedly running into a patrol. We kept out of sight as best we could, cautiously pushing through the bush and tall grass in our path, never quite knowing what we would encounter. At times the path was so narrow that we could only negotiate it in single file, Juan leading the way.

After picking our way carefully across this unforgiving terrain, watching every step, poking at the ground with a stick the way Chuva had shown us, we managed to get to the river. Half-a-mile downstream the gorge narrowed and the water churned and frothed in treacherous rapids.

We finally reached the river bank, in a state of near-collapse from the heat. Despite our condition we retained enough commonsense to exercise caution, stopping at a discrete point along the cliff to wait and listen for our contact, but the only sound we heard was the roar of the rapids.

There was no one in sight. We were probably the only people for miles around, I thought. Neither of us knew with any certainty whether we were too early, or too late to meet the person who was to ferry us across the river. I was sure that we were too late. We decided to wait anyway, selecting a strategic spot under a tree overlooking the bank.

Although inexperienced, we were fully aware of the dangers facing us; aware of our vulnerability out there in the open. We were clearly sitting ducks, visible from every direction. After about half-an-hour of waiting we thought it best to find a safe spot somewhere closer to the water.

The track to the river was narrow and precarious, and we picked our way down carefully. There was no easy route. We had to get across the river. Across the river was north. North of us lay our passage to safety.

Half-way down we heard voices approaching. In the open, sounds travelled for great distances and we estimated that whoever was coming was still a long way from us. Juan told me to wait, while he clambered back up to see who it was. I watched as he reached the top and peered over the edge of the cliff.

'Soldiers!' Juan hissed. 'Soldiers!' He slid back down to where I was. 'Hurry, let's get out of sight. Hurry!' he urged, grabbing hold of my arm.

We scrambled down the embankment, slithering and sliding on the narrow path, trying to find a foothold on the smooth rocks. I stumbled several times and was pulled to my feet by Juan. We continued down the slope towards the water, propelled by our own momentum. As we reached the river bank, we heard the patrol coming closer.

Our contact was nowhere in sight. 'What are we going to do?' I signed to Juan.

He glanced around anxiously, desperately seeking a way to get across the river.

Suddenly, a voice called: 'This way, this way!' We spotted the man, crouched behind a large boulder, waving frantically. I caught a glimpse of a boat behind another rock. It was small, but it had the all important outboard motor.

The man was beckoning, urging us to hurry. We scurried over the loose rock and gravel to where he was waiting. In my haste, I stepped on a loose rock which gave way and I pitched forward, twisting my ankle.

Juan rushed to my assistance. I waved him on and tried to stand up, but I couldn't and he had to half-drag me over to the cover of the rocks.

'Hang on,' he muttered. 'Hang on. Help us, will you?' he called to the man who by this time had dragged the boat into the water.

A half-mile downstream, like an agitated gut, the rapids swelled and boiled ominously.

While our contact held the boat steady, Juan helped me in. The voices were quite distinct now and he urged us to hurry.

'Soldiers!' he cried, pointing to the top of the ridge where several figures were milling around. 'Hurry! Start the motor.'

But there was no time. The moment we tumbled in, falling to the bottom of the boat, he released it and it lurched forward. There were shots from behind us.

'Start the motor!' he cried from the shore. But the engine was still raised out of the water.

'Hang on, for God's sake,' Juan shouted to me as the boat rolled.

'Row,' the man shouted urgently. 'Row. The rapids!'

Juan grabbed one of the oars. The other was stuck under the bench and I couldn't free it.

'Start the motor!' Juan yelled.

But I didn't know how.

'Grab the other oar!'

I struggled to free it from under the seat. Even as I managed to do so, another danger emerged as we were swept downstream by the current. From behind us shots rang out again and I glanced back to see our contact lying prone on the ground.

Oh, God! We're going to be killed! I thought.

'Start the motor!' Juan cried, crawling on all fours towards the back of the boat which reared and bucked like a horse.

I clambered out of the way, almost losing my balance. Juan managed to lower the engine and with a few frantic jerks of the cord, got it started. The boat shot out into the middle of the river and then lost out against the current which dragged us back.

There was more gunfire. My shoulders involuntarily hunched up around my ears, my head drawn in like a turtle retreating into its shell. The soldiers were at the top of the ridge. One of them had managed to scramble down to the edge of the water. Juan and I glanced around at about the same time and in that moment of distraction, we lost control of the boat. It lunged mid-stream, swirling and spinning like a twig, powerless against the force of the current.

The engine cut out as more shots rang out. At that point the threat of drowning seemed more imminent than any threat from the soldiers. In a desperate bid to control our advance, Juan plunged an oar into the water and using every ounce of his strength, managed to turn the boat towards the bank.

I reached past him and pulled the cord, trying to get the engine going once more. After a few tugs, it started up and for a wild moment we seemed to make progress as the boat bumped along, slowly edging towards the bank. But just as we thought we were safe, the boat spun into a crazy jig. Then for one incredible instant it was suspended above the water, plunged back and once again tossed into the air. With us clinging to it, the boat was smashed to pieces against the rocks. Luckily, Juan and I were thrown clear.

Shaken, but miraculously unhurt, we stumbled on to firm ground. The soldiers gestured from the opposite bank, firing at random, but we were too far away for them to do much harm. We knew, however, that it would only be a matter of time before they came after us.

Juan urged me on. 'There's no time to rest. We've got to get going.'

I shook my head, gasping for breath, unable to put any weight on my foot.

'We have to. The soldiers will be back,' he cried.

195

He examined my ankle. 'It's not broken, but it is a bad sprain. Why don't you wait here?' he said. 'You're not going to be able to walk on it. I'll see if I can find help. Our contact should be around somewhere.'

The possibility of being left alone galvanised me. I would have walked on a broken leg if I'd had to. I tried to get up, but the pain was too intense. It was obviously hopeless to think that I could walk out of there – I'd only be a burden.

'What about them?' I indicated the soldiers on the opposite bank.

'I'll find a safe place for you to hide. They won't expect either of us to still be here.'

'Where will you find help?'

'I don't know. I'm going to try to locate the other contact. Chuva said someone would meet us on this side of the river. Perhaps whoever was waiting thought we had been killed when the boat crashed. We've been swept quite a distance downstream. So I'll go upstream and see what I can find.'

I waited while Juan went off to scout around. He wasn't gone for very long, but it felt like ages as I sat there listening for every little snap or rustle in the undergrowth. To my relief, he returned a while later saying that he had found the ideal hiding place.

We had both been weakened by our ordeal and although he didn't have the strength to carry me, he insisted on doing so. I convinced him, though, that I could manage.

In the end we compromised; with his arm around my waist, he supported me as I limped to safety. The spot was a good one. The thicket all around impenetrable. Not only was it rocky and completely concealed from view, it was also slightly elevated so one could see in all directions.

'If I don't find help we'll both die here,' he told me.

I indicated that I'd be all right.

'If I don't return, wait here until the coast is clear, then follow the river upstream,' he said. When he saw the look of alarm on my face, he said optimistically, 'Don't worry we'll make it.'

His lame attempt to reassure me failed abysmally. I knew what the odds were.

'You'll be safe here anyway. I don't think the soldiers will cross the river. If they do, they'll find my tracks and come after me.'

I had tried to put up a brave front. But the thought of being left in the forest by myself brought all the old terror to the surface. My nightmare had suddenly become reality. I was slowly being nudged towards the edge of that abyss, overtaken by the paralysis of fear.

Before leaving me, Juan made sure that I was concealed from view. I watched him walk west, in the direction of the setting sun, and wondered if I would ever see him again.

The wait seemed interminable. I drew up my knees, hugging them for comfort. There was no sign of Juan returning with help. I continued my vigil, but after a while I began to suspect that he might not be coming back. There was only one solution. I had to see if I could find my way out. He had told me to follow the river upstream. First I had to get to the river. In the distance I could hear the steady roar of the rapids. A sturdy branch served as a walking stick as I hobbled towards the river, drawn only by the sound of the rapids.

The thundering noise grew louder and I assumed I was getting closer to the river. Occasionally I reached out to steady myself on the vines and branches, hanging on with clammy hands, concerned that it was taking me such a long time to get there.

With a sinking feeling I realised that I was lost. I knew that I could not have progressed more than a few hundred feet from where Juan had left me, but I had become quite disoriented and had no idea whether I was heading to, or away from the river, even though I could hear the sound of the rapids quite clearly.

I must have been wandering around in circles for hours. Eventually I found a small spring and sat down on the banks to steady myself and to try to get my bearings. Somehow I had to return to where Juan had left me, so he could find me, just in case he returned. I knew that once the sun went down, darkness came swiftly to this part of the world, and I might never find my way back.

I squatted at the edge of the spring, splashing my face with cold water. I got up, but much too quickly because everything around me suddenly went into a crazy spin. I reached out and tried to grab hold of a tree trunk, but it seemed to slip upward through my hands as if it were being hauled out of the ground. My head struck something hard and then I smelt the dampness of the earth.

I don't know how long I was out, but I was roused by a painful, persistent prodding in my side. I cautiously opened my eyes, only to discover that it was too dark to see anything. The prodding continued. Whatever was causing my discomfort felt like a cold piece of metal. I put my hand out to move it aside and felt a sudden rush of panic as my hand closed around a rifle-barrel.

Alarmed, I struggled to my knees. At the other end of that barrel was a soldier and as my vision slowly began to adapt to the darkness, I distinguished other figures.

Dear God, all that trouble getting here and all for nothing. I started to rise. The blow to the side of my head exploded into a galaxy of stars.

Chapter Nineteen

The blood on the side of my face had congealed into a crust which caused an irritating itch, but since both my hands and feet were bound, there wasn't much I could do about it. Lying there trussed-up like a chicken, I wondered whether I was going to die, when one of the men entered the room. I raised my head and noticed that he was taller than average and quite heavily built. He was staring at me with a peculiar look in his eyes. I returned his gaze, thinking that there was something very familiar about it.

The look in his eyes seemed to trigger a memory. I struggled with it, but it was so deeply buried that I couldn't bring it to the surface. He approached with long, quiet strides, like a panther stalking a prey. I tried to look away, but found I couldn't. I noticed the gun in his belt and struggled to get upright, still trying to remember where I'd seen him before.

'Where are your friends?' he asked.

I shook my head.

'Speak,' he hissed, squatting on the ground by me.

I sifted through my memory, trying to identify him, but it was hopeless. He came up closer and I shut my eyes, shrinking from him, pressing against the wall, but he grabbed me by the shirtfront and jerked me upright.

'Speak,' he commanded harshly. 'Where are your friends?'

I focused on the persistent ache in my ankle. I didn't dare think about my predicament. He drew his hand back and the next instant everything blacked out. It was a peculiar, enveloping blackness and I remember wondering what had happened to the lights. Only when I felt the blood oozing from the corner of my mouth, where I had bitten my tongue, did I realise that I had been struck.

The second time his hand drew back I was prepared and braced myself. The blow landed with throbbing accuracy on my cheek. I could feel the area going numb, and gingerly moved my jaw to determine whether it had been broken. I found I could still move it.

The man released his hold on me and I slowly slid to my haunches. He watched me as he lit a cigarette. I wondered what was going to happen next, my heart pounding so fiercely I thought he must hear it.

Then in a move that surprised me, he leaned forward and slit the ropes binding my wrists and ankles. For one blessed moment I thought my prayers had been answered and I leaned against the wall, massaging life back into my hands. My left eye had swollen shut and I had difficulty seeing through the right one. I had to get away, but I had no idea where I was, except that I was being held in some kind of military fortification.

Taking his time, the man stubbed out his cigarette. He raised an arm and my hands instinctively shielded my face. Instead of striking me, however, he seized both my wrists and brought his face up close to mine. I struggled in vain to free myself and realising that I couldn't fight him, I became rigid and turned my face from him. His face was so close. Those eyes. I knew them from somewhere. He lifted his hand to caress my hair and I saw the tatoo on his arm. I couldn't identify it and although it seemed to strike a chord, I had no idea what it meant.

'Don't be so fussy,' he sneered while I lay as rigid as a board. 'I'm white like you. You want me to give you to one of the black boys?' he asked, pinning me down.

Petrified, I turned my face away. I was numb, almost delirious with exhaustion.

Grabbing a handful of my hair, he yanked my head back. I could feel myself sinking into the cave. Into the darkness inhabited only by creatures from my nightmares. I could feel myself sinking, drifting away. Then at that moment, before I descended completely into the abyss, there was a startlingly loud commotion outside. The man released me and leapt to his feet. I fell back against the wall.

As he reached the door, there was a loud explosion and a burst of intense automatic gunfire. Followed by several smaller explosions. An enormous blast shook the ground and collapsed part of the wall, scattering debris over me. I crouched low, covering my head. The fort was under attack.

Through all the pandemonium, I heard my mother's voice as clearly as though she were right there with me. My father's arms were around me and Lodiya was carrying me through the jungle. I saw the man with the scorpion tattoo. I saw him raise the rifle and I saw my parents fall.

I was whimpering. One moment I was sweating, the next shivering with cold. I could hear the loud clattering from the sky, the sound of gunfire and people screaming. I tried to crawl away. There was another explosion. 'Ma – Mama!' I cried. 'Mama!' I cried again in a child-like voice.

But there was no response. No soft cheek pressed against mine, only the hard wall. I started to cry, the quiet painful sobs wrenched from the depths of my anguish. The shooting went on for several minutes, then as abruptly as it had all started, it ended and an ominous silence fell over the compound.

I felt a hand on my shoulder and when I uncovered my face, I found a woman bending over me, shaking my shoulder as if to rouse me. In that moment everything blacked out.

I discovered later that the woman who had found me, and who had probably saved my life, was Eugenia Chithando, one of the rebel soldiers contacted by Juan. She and her small group had tracked me all the way to the camp. We were fortunate that at the time of the attack most of the garrison of Portuguese soldiers at the fort had gone on a mission. The man with the tattoo was apparently the officer left in charge of the handful who had remained.

It had been sheer luck that the fort had been poorly manned. If Eugenia had attacked a day earlier, she and her cadres would have been annihilated. She assured me, though, that they would not have attacked had the full contingent at the garrison been present.

It took a day's agonising march before we reached the rebel camp. The men found it easier to carry me on a make-shift litter. Once we were safely ensconced, Eugenia described how they had found Juan wandering around near the place where they had made camp for the night. When he had told them his story, she and three of the men had accompanied him to the spot where we had crossed the river three days earlier.

At the river they found the remains of the shattered boat and followed Juan as he retraced his steps to the thicket where he had left me. But there was no sign of me, of course, and eventually they searched around and found the spring and the heavy footprints left by the soldiers. There were several indications that I had been captured.

I was relieved when she told me that in the bushes they had found the pouch containing the evidence about the children, and that it was now safely in Juan's possession and on its way out of the country.

Eugenia told me that they had followed the tracks and had reached the first village only to find that there was nothing left of it. It had been bombed and napalmed by the soldiers. Fortunately, there had been few casualties. She and her men had found the women poking through the debris, dusting off clay pots and the bits and pieces of what had once been their lives.

She and her men had done whatever they could to help before continuing with their search for me. She said that on their way they had met up with a weary unit of guerrillas who informed them that they had spotted an enemy patrol half-a-day's walk to the south. The guerrilla unit was heading north to link up with a larger force. Eugenia had advised Juan to go along with them. She had instructed the men to make sure that Juan got to his rendez-vous in time, stressing the importance of the mission. He was to deliver the pouch to the contact in London in the event that I didn't make it to safety.

They had then split up. Juan had gone north with the first group. The second group consisting of the squad leader and six of the best and most experienced men, was to keep the rendez-vous at the base camp. The third group, comprising of Eugenia and the ten remaining men, went south in search of the enemy camp, suspecting that this was where I was being held.

Late that afternoon after a rest and a debriefing, Eugenia left. We said our goodbyes and I watched her departing with her cadres.

The following morning as I sat out in the sun, waiting to be escorted on the next phase of my journey, I wondered whether I would ever get out alive. I was sick at heart, my face so bruised and swollen, I could barely see through the slits between my lids.

While I sat there feeling sorry for myself, I heard a familiar voice call my name. Astonished, I glanced up. I couldn't make out who it was.

'It's me, Rhonica,' the voice said.

I got to my feet and she greeted me like a long-lost friend, holding me at arms' length, surveying sympathetically the state of my face.

She told me she had arrived during the night and had heard that I was in the camp. There was so much to tell each other. We exchanged news, she speaking calmly while I wrote out my responses on a piece of paper. I informed her about Helia's arrest. From her reaction, I suspected that she already knew. I was also able to assure her that the papers were safely on their way out of the country with Juan.

Before she left for her briefing she advised me to rest because we were expected to leave within a day or so. The good news was that she was going to accompany me for part of the journey to my rendez-vous.

It was strange how my memory was returning in chunks. The grey areas were slowly becoming clearer. Although I had been able to recall certain things as a result of the traumatic experience in the military camp, I knew that it would take a long time for me to recover my voice. I wondered if I had imagined it, or whether I had actually articulated the words, 'Mama, Mama'. In that one terrifying instant in the hut, I had relived the massacre in our village. I was hoping that, with my memory restored, my voice would be too. I had tried to speak after the incident, hoping that a miraculous recovery had been achieved, but there were no new developments.

I should not have been disappointed. The doctor had warned me some time ago that my vocal cords had atrophied. He had told me that even if I were psychologically ready to speak, I would not be able to do so without extensive therapy. I actually looked forward to exploring this possibility with the appropriate medical assistance in London.

I was struck by the irony of this trip to London, especially after having rejected all David's pleas to accompany him.

Rhonica introduced me to her squad. There were sixteen of them in all. Fourteen regulars, Rhonica who was a sergeant, and Matias the young lieutenant who was the squad leader. She told me that they were heading north, first to meet up with a tactical unit in a small village along the coast and then to deliver a supply of ammunition to the base camp up in the area. After that they were expected to combine forces with another group of cadres in order to attack and disrupt military supply lines to the northern provinces.

I had overheard that they were to await the arrival of the *S.S. Hamburg*, which was expected to dock at Porto Amelia on the twenty-sixth. Rhonica warned me that I was not going to make the *Santa Monica*. It was the eighteenth already. She suggested alternative arrangements for me aboard a Cuban fishing trawler on the thirtieth, which would take me to Dar-es-Salaam. When she mentioned the Cuban fishing trawler, it suddenly dawned on me that this was the connection between Rhonica and Helia.

That night when I went to sleep, I carried with me a heavy burden of regret and sadness. It was as though everything and everyone in my life had systematically been destroyed by the conflict. The net had been cast a long time ago and we were all slowly being dragged in by it.

From what I could gather, the weapons smuggled aboard the *S.S. Hamburg* had apparently been broken up into smaller components and were to be secreted amidst supplies headed for the hydro-electric project. The ship was carrying the much-needed supply of arms: Kalashnikov AK 47s, Simonov rifles, 60–80mm mortars and the new 122mm missiles which could be launched from steel ramps along the border to attack far-flung army outposts.

We left a few hours after the men had rested and eaten. Guns were cleaned and readied. Twelve of the men clambered aboard the truck, perching on the ammunition cases in the back. It was to take us as far as the river where we were to cross into government-held territory. The journey was all the more dangerous since it had to be made in daylight in order to avoid the other danger posed by land-mines and military ambushes.

Rhonica, Matias and I were squeezed into the cab with the driver. As soon as we were aboard, he thrust the truck into gear and we lurched off, crashing into the bush over rocks and into ruts. The road was overgrown with vegetation and no wider than a path. In the front the four of us were bumped and jarred, the suspension long since having given up the ghost.

The driver grinned, occasionally chortling with sheer devilment as the three of us levitated and returned to our seats with bone-jarring thumps.

It was tough going and he urged the truck on to perform even greater feats. The men encouraged him as he seduced his vehicle with loving words, casting sly glances at Comrade Rhonica each time she was tossed against him. These she didn't seem to notice.

He was a good driver and he told us that most of his experience had been on jungle roads. It was almost as if the truck was responding to his cajoling as it roared across ruts and through gullies, lurching now and then in token protest when he pushed it too hard. Despite the open windows the air in the cab was stifling. Each breath was hot enough to scorch ones lungs.

It was a slow journey and we had to stop often to move fallen trees and rocks. Each time the truck teetered to a halt everyone piled out, weapons at the ready in case of an ambush.

After consulting with Matias, Rhonica instructed the driver to turn away from the coast, to take the shorter route, despite the fact that we were more likely to encounter patrols there.

We hadn't driven very far from the previous stop when we suddenly screeched to a shuddering halt. Directly ahead of us, a tree had fallen across the track, blocking our path. Everyone immediately suspected a trap and leaped off the truck to reconnoiter the area.

Rhonica told me that they had lost eight men just two weeks before in a trap much like this. My anxiety was evident and she tried to reassure me, telling me that three of the cadres with us were specifically trained to handle land-mines. She dispatched them immediately to check that the area was clear. When the men returned with the all-clear signal, the fallen tree was removed and we continued on our way.

After several miles the track widened and became more like a road than a trail. Progress was slow and Matias seemed a bit annoyed that the short cut had turned out to be so ineffective in saving time.

Eventually we reached the river.

'This is as far as we go,' the driver said. 'From here, you're on your own.' Although there was a lot of grumbling from the men, much of it was good-natured.

'Come on,' the driver called out. 'Get out and face the danger like real men.' He glanced at the two of us beside him and grinned.

The men climbed down, some of them with relief, and tossed their gear on to the ground before they unloaded the truck.

'Watch your step,' the driver called out cheerfully as he turned the truck for the return journey, trading insults with the other men before driving off.

Rhonica assured me that the warning about watching our step was no idle one. The government soldiers had planted mines everywhere.

'You think the soldiers have been back?' one of the men asked.

'Can't be, comrade,' the other replied. 'We cleaned up this road just a few days ago.'

'You clean it up today, they bring back the mines tomorrow,' the lieutenant said.

Rhonica surveyed our surroundings. No doubt she was thinking of the long road ahead and the burden each of them would have to carry. I worried about my ankle and how far I'd be able to walk on it as it was still swollen and painful. But my burden was small in comparison to what Rhonica had to endure. Her pack was no lighter than what was carried by the men. Out of curiosity, I tried to lift it, but I couldn't even get it off the ground. She grinned as one of the men hoisted the pack on to her back. I watched as she checked her gun and slipped her bandoleer over her shoulder, her hand resting lightly on her weapon. Three of the men in the detachment went ahead, prodding the ground with long bamboo poles which had a hook attached to them to upend the mines, which were then salvaged and reused against the government troops.

The rest of us carefully followed in the tracks of the three men, for to deviate might mean instant death or maiming. There were no mishaps and Matias looked pleased with himself when Rhonica complimented him about the good job his men had done sweeping the area.

The local villagers were accustomed to seeing guerrillas and, after a brief exchange with one of them who enquired about the activities of the Portuguese, the peasants went about their business.

Before us lay the river. Locals carrying a variety of goods, from chickens to pigs, waited patiently to cross, scanning the sky for Portuguese planes which often flew in low, strafing the river banks.

It took a while for Matias and Rhonica to complete their negotiations with the men who were to carry the equipment and supplies. They hired about twelve and when the last of the boxes had been hoisted on to the heads of the bearers, the rebels snapped their magazines on to their machine guns and rifles, then with weapons slung over their shoulders, we took off again.

I was able to keep up, using the walking stick one of the men had fashioned for me, but it was slow going. I realised that I was more of a handicap than a help on this trek, but no one complained. They were all very considerate of me and stopped often so that I could rest my ankle. When the going got really rough, the men took turns carrying me on their backs. It was a humiliating experience for me, but necessary so that they could make up lost time.

One of the cadres bringing up the rear hauled a bazooka and was ready at a moment's notice to lob mortar against the enemy. We travelled a considerable distance through a variety of changing landscapes, from a tangle of tall reeds to more jungle which intermittently broke into open grassland before plunging us back into thick, impenetrable bush.

Finally, we reached the open sprawling green of a plateau; below us waterfalls cascaded into a valley. After a short rest we started our descent until the landscape changed back into dry savanna. Soon we were back in the forest so dense that near the ground there was perpetual gloom, broken only here and there by sun-dappled patches. We were nearing a river again. In the distance we could hear the sound of rapids. It was getting dark and we stopped here to make camp for the night.

On the second day, just as we left the cover of the bush around midday, a dull explosion ripped through the air directly ahead of us. The men threw themselves to the ground; the bearers dropped their loads and rushed for cover. The rest of us waited anxiously, listening for the slightest sound that might reveal the enemy location. The tension was almost tangible and, except for the distinctive click of safety catches being drawn on their rifles, there was absolute silence amongst the cadres.

Rhonica sent two men along the flank, communicating by hand signals while she, Matias and Jonas crawled forward through the tall grass. There was another explosion and a high-pitched scream.

Rhonica signalled and four of her cadres rushed forward under firing cover to lob grenades at the forward position. I had flattened myself on the ground, concealed by the tall grass. The soldier with the bazooka came into position and slipped a missile into the tube, directing it at a grove of trees ahead of us. He fired five projectiles, each exploding with a dull thud.

But we were hopelessly outnumbered and Rhonica gave the order to retreat back into the bush. The cadre with the bazooka fired several more rounds to cover the withdrawal while the men zig-zagged through the tall grass. There were several shots and an explosion. One of the men doubled back to help his comrade, who was trapped and was himself caught in mortar fire from the other side. Suddenly there was a loud thud and a painful cry and I knew that someone had been hit. Jonas fired several rounds in the direction from which the mortar fire had come.

Rhonica crept forward to find who had been hit by the mortar fire. It was Akimbo, a young man who had just recently joined the movement. Both his legs had been shattered. Rhonica was shouting for assistance, but the men were engaged. I limped forward. She waved me back, but I carried on, throwing myself to the ground when I reached her, kneeling beside the injured man. She tore the sleeves off her shirt and slitted what remained of his pant legs with her knife, exposing the bloody pulp. We managed to fix a tourniquet around his thighs but he had already lost a great deal of blood.

The shooting had eased. Rhonica slipped an arm around the injured man and hoisted him on to her back. Akimbo was small, but much heavier than she had anticipated. She staggered, almost falling under his weight and then steadied herself. I rushed to help her.

The others were too busy holding the soldiers at bay to notice our struggle with Akimbo as Rhonica tottered along, taking one painful step after another, sweat glistening on her brow, veins in her neck swollen to the size of rope, blood from Akimbo's wounds streaming between her fingers.

His grip around her neck was vice-like. But it seemed she had closed off her mind, not thinking about the choking grip around her neck or the horrific injuries of the man she carried. Each step was an act of sheer will. Then, just as she faltered, two of the men came to her assistance and lifted the barely conscious soldier off her back.

Jonas, who had taken a bullet in the arm, was bleeding, and while I did what I could for Akimbo, giving him a shot of morphine from the meagre medical supplies, Rhonica rested. I regretted not having Juan around. He would have known what to do, I thought, riffling through the first aid kit. Apart from the morphine and some bandages, there was very little else for such emergencies.

I realised that Akimbo was still in shock and was probably not feeling any pain. I knew that there was no hope for him and Rhonica read my thoughts. It was mid-afternoon and it was obviously a matter for much debate whether we could make it with him, or whether it would be easier to get help. The men decided that it would be best to leave him behind so they could rendez-vous with the rest of their group. Rhonica explained that advancing to the camp at the far side of the mountain was out of the question because they were pinned down by enemy fire. Two of the men volunteered to return with the injured Akimbo, but Matias rejected the idea. He knew that Akimbo was not going to make it.

'It would be faster to go around the enemy line to the bush camp on the other side of the mountain,' the man with the bazooka said.

Matias agreed and drew a map in the sand to show the men where they were in relation to the camp.

'If we bring reinforcements from the rear we can flush them out,' Matias said. Rhonica agreed it would be the best thing to do. They took into consideration that I would not be able to travel and based their decision on this as well as their reluctance to abandon their comrade.

'We'll go,' Jonas said, picking two of the men.

'You're going to need all the help you can get,' Rhonica told them. 'All of you go. Faith and I will wait here with Akimbo. The soldiers will believe that we've retreated.'

There was no time for debate.

'It would be better for you to leave him and come with us,' Matias said, taking her aside. 'We'll come back for him.'

'We have our orders,' Rhonica reminded him.

Akimbo's eyes fluttered open.

'There is a cave by the river,' one of the men said. 'I know it well. I don't think they'll find it.'

'Help me with him,' Rhonica said.

They carried Akimbo into the cave and then, leaving us with enough ammunition and a whispered '*Boa Sorte* – good luck', they crept off.

We were in a chamber of sorts. Although it was quite gloomy I could make out the openings of smaller tunnels entering the cave along the ledge five feet above us.

Rhonica and I were resting against the wall with Akimbo lying on a bed of leaves between us. I reached out to check his pulse, but there was none. He was dead. I gazed at Rhonica, her eyes were shut. Her cap had slipped off, reavealing her hair which was braided close to her scalp. There was no point waking her, I thought. There was nothing we could do for him anyway.

I leaned back and as I glanced up at the ledge above us, every hair on my head stood on end. My blood turned to ice as I gazed directly into the barrel of a machine gun. The soldier was lying flat on his stomach, his sights trained directly on me. I saw his face. I thought I could actually sense his finger tightening on the trigger. This was the end. I started to pray, 'Blessed be our father, who art . . .' I could see that his finger was still on the trigger. I waited for the shot. I couldn't have stirred even if I'd wanted to. I knew that if I as much as moved a muscle I'd be dead in an instant and so would Rhonica.

I kept my eyes rivetted on him. My glance locked on his sights, knowing I was powerless to do anything. Rhonica was still asleep. To die like this, I thought despairingly. Poor Rhonica, what an ignominious death for such a brave woman. Such a shame for it to end like this in an abandoned cave where our bodies might never be discovered.

I tensed, preparing for the slap of the bullet. But then the most astonishing thing happened. The soldier placed his finger to his lips, and with a wave of his hand, he backed out of sight, retreating along the tunnel on his stomach. I shut my eyes. I was too weak to move and I lay there for a long time until I heard Rhonica stirring beside me.

Chapter Twenty

I don't know how long we remained there. I had lost all track of time. I remember Rhonica and I left the cave only to bury Akimbo in a shallow hollow in the ground which we had marked out with Rhonica's bayonette and scooped out with our bare hands. Afterwards, I couldn't bring myself to return to the cave, but Rhonica insisted that I stay hidden in case we were spotted out in the open by one of the patrols.

I signed to Rhonica that I couldn't go in there again, not after that incident with the soldier. When she had learnt about the incident, she was equally perplexed as to why we hadn't been killed. I wondered if he had spared our lives because he, like everyone else, had tired of the killing, or perhaps he had felt sorry for us. War did strange things to people.

Much as I hated going into the cave, we had little choice because it was so dangerous to wander around in the open. Ultimately we decided to stay close, huddling together in the mouth of the cave, both of us in a sorry state.

When the men found us we were both suffering the effects of our ordeal. We had gone only a few hundred yards with our rescuers when my knees buckled and I passed out.

I regained consciousness many hours later, lying beside a fire where we had made camp for the night. Confused and disoriented I had no idea where I was and for how long I'd been out. Rhonica told me afterwards that I had slept for almost eight hours, regaining consciousness occasionally only to take a drink of water.

Early the next morning we broke camp and proceeded to our next destination, a small village along the coast. Rhonica seemed very eager to get there. I was slowing their progress and eventually three of the men, despite my protests, took turns carrying me on their backs.

Exhausted, we reached our destination late that afternoon. I had some clear impressions of our surroundings as we entered the village. There was a familiar smell about it, an earthy odour of decaying vegetation and fish, leather and wood-smoke. All along the path into the village we had encountered rebel militiamen lining the way. They seemed to glide in and out of the forest like spirits. Here one moment, gone the next.

These men, some of them barefoot, wearing ragged uniforms and recruited from small villages, were the foundation of the revolution. They were simple people with simple needs who knew the forest like the back of their hands and needed very little to survive. If needs be they existed only on what the forest floor provided, mainly rats and berries.

They endured the constant bombardment by government forces and coped with extreme hardship and poverty. They owned nothing, except what they could roll into a small bundle and carry with them. It was an extraordinary existence, they lived in simple makeshift structures built from material hewed from the bush, their beds pallets of leaves laid on a bare sand floor. Their whole existence seemed to be geared to a way of life which allowed them to pick up and move quickly. The women milled around us as we arrived, babies in one arm and a rifle in the other.

The villagers were Rhonica's people. She told me that they had moved often because they feared reprisals from the Portuguese who knew them to be guerrilla sympathisers. As we entered the village many of them recognised her and called out friendly greetings. Those who didn't, merely stared mutely as she preceded the men through their midst.

But the most unusual sight greeted us as we entered the small clearing in the middle of the settlement. A small crowd had gathered there and from their midst a figure stepped out and waited for Rhonica to acknowledge him. I had never before seen anyone so grotesquely disfigured. Burn-scar tissue covered most of the exposed areas of his body. His head was almost fused to his shoulders, his face a hideous mask.

It took a few moments for me to recover from the shock of seeing him, but by the time Rhonica brought him over to introduce him, I had recovered my composure.

'This is my brother Mario,' she said affectionately. 'The soldiers did this to him. Remember I told you about him?'

I nodded.

She explained that I couldn't speak. He gazed at me impassively through eyes sunken into scar tissue, the rims red and moist like raw, oozing flesh.

My heart went out to him. I had never been so moved by anything in my life. It was as if the sight of Mario had peeled away the last veils of my indifference, of apathy, of fear, of lack of commitment and my blindness to the truth. For the first time I was seeing clearly and for the first time I thought I actually understood what this fight for freedom was all about.

The day after our arrival one of the elders called a meeting of all the villagers to inform them of the possible danger they faced in giving refuge to us and especially to me. The depth of the old man's voice, the way he held his pipe and the way his black eyes probed deep into the souls of his people stirred some ancient memory.

The obscure line between my reality and my dreams dimmed and instead of the gaunt, hollow-eyed man, I saw an old woman calling out to the villagers, urging them to run because Senhor Raul Morais' men had come.

Since my rescue from the soldiers by Eugenia, I'd been having brief flashes of memory, followed by excruciating headaches. When the elder had finished his address, I excused myself and returned to the hut to lie down.

The hut I was using belonged to a woman who had returned to the village after years of absence in the bush, where she had been teaching at a rebel school. The hut contained a shelf and a pallet covered with a blanket. On the shelf, which was supported by two empty cans, were three books. They were all in Portuguese. One was a dictionary, the other a medical encyclopedia, and the third a well-worn copy of the Bible.

I picked up the copy of the Bible and opened it. It was so quiet that I could actually hear the breeze rustling the reeds alongside the hut. It was hot outside, the only relief came from the soft breeze which blew from the ocean. Suddenly and quite inexplicably, I was overwhelemd by a weariness so encompassing that all I wanted was to put my head down and never awaken again.

Succumbing to this exhaustion, I lay down on the pallet and dreamed of David. I dreamed that I was walking beside him. We were in some strange place. He was grey and stooped. We were both slightly breathless from climbing a hill to a house or a hut

213

which overlooked the ocean. I could feel the cool breeze and assumed that we were in England. My dream ended abruptly with someone shaking me awake. I opened my eyes. Rhonica was bending over me. She had come to tell me that they were moving out the next day.

'Faith, I want to speak to you about something important,' she said to me. I struggled up, supporting myself on one elbow, waiting for her to continue.

'Juan has taken the information about the children safely out of the country. We have a message that he has arrived in Dar-es-Salaam. One of our leaders will meet with you when you get there. They want you to talk to the United Nations about what is happening here to the children.'

Surprised, I sat up. I shook my head, totally rejecting such an idea. There was no guarantee that I would get my voice back. How could I possibly speak to such a distinguished group without a voice? How would my story gain attention above the loud clamour of all the other voices concerned with their own stories?

'Please. You must do it. They will listen to you. You will have more credibility because you've gone through this experience,' she said.

I indicated that I had no voice.

'You can sign. We will get an interpreter. You have to do it. You have to speak to them and show them the evidence. Describe to them your own experiences,' she pleaded.

It was a lot for me to think about. I wasn't sure that I could do this or that I wanted to, but I remembered her brother and realised that I had to.

'By the way,' she said. 'The children are fine. They will eventually be smuggled back into the country and reunited with their parents.'

'When?' I signed, indicating my relief.

'We don't know, but it will happen. It's too bad that we had to lose so many of them to rescue the others.'

I didn't say anything for a while and she got up from the ground. 'Juan sent word that Sofia is amongst the children.'

I wept quietly, tears running down my face. Rhonica didn't know how to deal with such an emotional response and stood quite still watching me. Eventually, without a word to me, she walked away and left me to my tears.

We talked again later and I agreed to deliver my case to the

United Nations as soon as arrangements were made by the government in exile in Dar-es-Salaam.

I was sorry that she was leaving the next day, but it was obvious she had a great deal to do. She still had a few days' journey ahead of her before the rendez-vous with the *S.S. Hamburg*. Matias had sent a message to say that he would meet her at a prearranged spot, south of Porto Amelia, with a supply of weapons and a group of veteran fighters.

Jonas, charged with the responsibility of getting me on to the fishing boat which was to arrive within thirty-six hours, would stay behind. We were expecting it to arrive on schedule and Jonas was to row me out to it. Rhonica had taken care of every contingency. I could see that she was a good soldier and would make an exceptional leader.

On the day of her departure, I watched as Rhonica hoisted the gun on to her shoulder and called out instructions to the men. I was sorry to see her go. So many memories had been kindled, thoughts and hopes expressed – mainly hopes for a better world.

'Good luck,' she said.

'*Boa Sorte*,' I wrote on a piece of paper.

'They will be waiting for you in Dar-es-Salaam. Who knows, perhaps I will see you in New York when you get to the United Nations,' Rhonica said.

'Will you be there?' I signed in surprise.

She shrugged. 'Who knows.'

'What will you do in the meantime?' I wrote out on a piece of paper.

'There is much for me to do here. A lot of unfinished business, as you might say.'

'Do you suppose there's hope for Helia?' I asked.

I could see in her eyes that she didn't hold out any hope.

'We expect you back here some day,' she said, ignoring my question because it was too painful to discuss.

'Take care,' I told her.

She smiled. 'Don't worry, everything will work out the way it should.'

'I will see you soon.'

'I hope so,' she said with a chuckle.

Rhonica was no better at goodbyes than I. She held out her hand shyly. I put my arms about her and embraced her, awkwardly separated by the weapons on her shoulder. I had so much to thank her and Eugenia for, including my life.

'*Boa Sorte,*' she called.

I watched her go, standing there until she was swallowed up in the jungle.

Life in the village returned to normal with the departure of Rhonica and the rebel fighters. The women marched down to the stream in single file with their plastic laundry baskets to pound their *khangas* on the rocks. The brightly coloured laundry baskets were an incongruous sight in this remote spot and yet while these women occupied themselves with the domestic routine of village life, somewhere out there a woman would be leading a motley band of rebels against the awesome fire-power of the Portuguese military forces.

That night I sat outside with some of the villagers. The small clay lamps seemed almost inadequate in this immense vault of darkness. David had once told me that there was no sky as totally black as an African sky, where the stars hung so low that one could almost reach out to pluck them from the heavens.

I remembered how I used to lie out in the open at São Lucas, staring up as if the mystery of life locked away in that vast blackness, would be revealed to me. It never was, but I used to imagine all the forces at work there, determining the grand design of our lives.

It was with mixed feelings that I left the village the following evening. I said goodbye to the friends I had made, some of the women accompanying us to the beach. They stood on the ridge with the sun about to set behind them, waving to Jonas and me, as we walked to where one of the young men from the village waited beside the small rowing boat. In the distance I could see the blinking lights from the fishing vessel. They were obviously waiting for us and we had to hurry.

I turned and gave one final wave to the group of women in their colourful *khangas* before climbing into the boat. Jonas helped the young man to push the boat into the water then leapt in, grabbed the oars and shouted '*Adeus!*'

I drew on all my strength, and Jonas watched, grinning encouragingly, as I fought to get the word out.

'*Adeus*', I croaked loudly.

216